W9-BYG-131

*of*

scars

*and*

stardust

# ANDREA HANNAH

*of*

## scars

*and*

## stardust

f|ux
Woodbury, Minnesota

First Edition
First Printing, 2014

Book design by Bob Gaul
Cover design by Ellen Lawson
Cover photo titled *Ni La Neige, bile froid, Explore* by Alexandra Sophie

Flux, an imprint of Llewellyn Worldwide Ltd.

This is a work of fiction. Names, characters, places, and incidents are either the product of the author's imagination or are used fictitiously, and any resemblance to actual persons living or dead, business establishments, events, or locales is entirely coincidental. Cover models used for illustrative purposes only and may not endorse or represent the book's subject.

**Library of Congress Cataloging-in-Publication Data**
Hannah, Andrea.
  Of scars and stardust/Andrea Hannah.—First edition.
    pages cm
  Summary: When Claire Graham returns to Amble, Ohio, to search for her missing younger sister, Ella, she must keep her wolf hallucinations at bay and face the mystery of what really happened two years ago, and whether it is happening again now.
  ISBN 978-0-7387-4082-9
[1. Sisters—Fiction.  2. Missing children—Fiction.  3. Wolves—Fiction.]
  I. Title.
PZ7.H19697Of 2014
[Fic]—dc23

2014020039

Flux
Llewellyn Worldwide Ltd.
2143 Wooddale Drive
Woodbury, MN 55125-2989
www.fluxnow.com

Printed in the United States of America

To all the girls made of stardust.

part one

# *one*

When Rae told me the wolf was watching us in the cornfield again, I laughed. And then I punched her in the arm for being stupid. She used to say that the wolves knew all of our secrets, that with pricked ears they listened to the rumors about Lacey Jordan and the janitor, that the whole pack knew about how Rae had lost her virginity in her mom's spare bedroom two summers ago. Sometimes she said they inched even closer when we smuggled cherry vodka under our fur-lined jackets, the bottles clinking against the buttons on our jeans. The wolves liked cherry-flavored things.

My boots crunched through the icy film covering the cornfield. I followed Rae through the brittle stalks jutting out from the snow as the empty sky smothered us in blue. Her hair poked out from beneath her hat and her breath curdled like sour milk in the cold.

"What are we doing? Seriously," I huffed as I dodged a broken stalk.

Rae laughed, and her pointy nose tipped toward the sky. "Can't you ever just, like, go with the flow, Claire?" She stopped and lifted a puffy green mitten out to her side. "Look at this gorgeous day. Come on, enjoy it! Who knows when you'll see the sun again." She shuffled through the snow, swinging her hands through the broken corn.

"Excuse me, 'when *you'll* see the sun'? Pretty sure you're trapped here too, Rae." But Rae just laughed, still swinging her mittens in lazy figure eights as she kicked up the first remnants of winter behind her.

I followed. Because I always followed.

Rae plopped into a clump of snow just the right size for two skinny girls and chewed on her chapped lips. I sank down next to her, even though I didn't have my snow pants on. Cold seeped through my underwear and made my butt ache.

For a second, I swore I almost saw the wolf, the one that Rae had said tried to pull a pack of cigarettes out of her back pocket one time. But I blinked, and the outline of fur melted into the snow.

Rae's head snapped up and she squinted into the blurry, almost-wolf shadow hidden between the stalks. "I'm totally going to get out of this crappy town," she whispered into my ear, like if she said it too loud, the wolf would howl out her words until they bounced between the sleepy houses. "And I'm going to have an apartment on the fiftieth floor somewhere and my own couch and a chair that's red, just because *I can.*"

I sighed, poking a finger into the snow. "Yeah, me too."

"No. I'm going to get out of here."

I looked up and saw her watching me, eyes narrowed. "I know, Rae. Me too. We're gonna move away together one day."

Rae sucked on her bottom lip. Then she let out a puff of air. "One day is in *three* days."

The day was still around us, so still that Rae's words echoed through the cornfield and the snow and the sky. Except for the snap of a brittle leaf just in front of us and a flash of gray as thick as a secret.

I pulled in a breath between my teeth. Rae wrapped her green mitten around my wrist and squeezed. But if the wolf really was here, listening, it was either already gone or too quiet to be caught.

I turned back to Rae and whispered: "What do you mean, *three* days? You're, like, a year from graduating."

"But Robbie already has," she said.

I scrunched my nose as I poked another finger into the snow. "So?"

"So, Robbie's moving to Chicago. And I'm going with him. We're leaving a couple days before Christmas." She squealed and clapped her mittens together.

"Are you insane?" I stood, brushing the snow from my jeans. "You've known him for, like, a week! And how much have you actually talked to him, since you've just been sucking face with him after your parents go to bed?" I paced between the stalks, my pink hands making circles in the air. "This is just...this is insane, Rae, don't do it."

Rae stood, and instead of looking mad, her eyes were soft and empty. She grabbed my shoulders, and my boots scuffed the snow. "I'm going, Claire. And I need you to promise me something."

I closed my eyes and sucked in the winter air. I was almost afraid to ask. "What, Rae?"

A mitten landed in the snow with a soft thump. I opened my eyes. The blade of a paring knife lay dangerously close to her palm. "What are you—"

Rae flicked the knife and red slithered across her skin. Her eyes flashed as she grabbed my hand. "Now you."

I pulled back but she was too quick; another flick, and then the heat of my own blood pooled in my palm. Rae dropped the knife and held her hand in front of mine.

"Promise me that you won't tell anyone, not even Ella, that you know where I am," she breathed. "Even when they ask."

I stared at her hand, constellations of blood collecting at the creases. "Okay."

"Okay." Rae smiled and pressed her hand to mine. "Blood oath. Non-breakable." We pulled away, and I stuck my hand into the snow to dilute the itchy feeling of dried blood. When I stood up again, Rae wrapped me in a hug. "Now I'm always with you, wherever you go," she whispered. "I know you'll keep your promise."

———

I did keep my promise.

For as long as the wolves let me.

# two

"No, Laura, I'm just as lost as you are about the whole thing," Mom said, stretching the phone cord between her fingers. Her long hair was thrown into a messy knot at her neck. "I'd just tell her if she raids your liquor cabinet one more time, she's going to live with your sister in Alpena."

I sat at the breakfast bar, my flannel pajamas bunched up at my waist. I pulled at the drawstrings. A small, embroidered *R* followed by a crooked *B* stared up at me. "Oh," I said, and Dad folded down the paper and raised an eyebrow.

"Hold on a sec, Laura." Mom wrapped her fingers around the end of the phone. "Do you know something, Claire?" she whispered, her eyes shining.

"About what, Mom?" I asked, even though I already knew. It had to be about Rae. It always was.

"Rae," she whispered. "Laura found a packed suitcase under her bed."

My cheeks felt hot as I ran my thumb over the letters. "Um, no. I don't know anything about that. I just remembered these are Rae's pajamas, that's all. I think she left them last time she spent the night."

Mom nodded and her face sagged. "Why don't you get dressed, okay? Tell Ella to get dressed, too. We'll do your birthday cake before church tonight." She smiled and the bags beneath her eyes tightened. She pressed the phone to her cheek. "No, I thought she might know what's going on with Rae, but she hasn't said anything…"

My stomach churned as I jumped off the stool, still clutching the giant pants so they wouldn't end up around my ankles. Even though Rae was only a year and a half older than me, sometimes it felt more like a decade between us. We'd always talked about leaving Amble, getting in an old beater with a guy who smelled like cigarettes and drove fast enough to make the cornstalks blur on our way out of town. But the idea of *actually* doing it—actually packing up a suitcase and slipping into the night—made me feel a little sick. Not Rae, though.

Dad cleared his throat from the other side of the paper, cutting through my thoughts. "*Do* you know something, Claire? Why Rae has a full suitcase under her bed?" The words were so quiet that I barely heard them over the rustling pages.

My mind tumbled over Rae's plans: snapshots of her getting into a car with a guy who had too much hair and a future that was too unclear to see past the Ohio state border.

*Just tell him.*

I twisted Rae's initials around my fingers. Dad set down the paper and folded his hands over the headlines. "Well?"

The secret burned in my throat like the cheap grape cough syrup that Mom always made me and Ella take if we even so much as sneezed. I swallowed it down.

"I have no idea."

Dad watched me for a long moment before nodding. His eyes flicked back to the paper. "Well, if you remember anything, you know where to find me."

I tried to say something cheery and confident, like "Oh yes, I will most definitely tell you if I hear anything." But a strangled little noise came out instead. I tugged at the pajama drawstrings as I walked down the hall.

"Mom says to get dressed," I said, shoving open Ella's door. She sat in the middle of her room, under her self-made canopy of paper stars and lightning bolts. A riot of rainbow twinkle lights blinked around the window. Remnants of her childhood still clung to the yellowing walls, while posters of bands and boys had started to spread between them like ivy.

"I *am* dressed," she said, smoothing down the stripes on her skirt. She blinked up at me. "What's wrong with this?"

"Ell, it's winter. You'll totally freeze." As I freed her from the too-short skirt, she grabbed at my hand. "Where are those brown pants I gave you?"

She brushed a blond curl from her cheek. "Um, the closet ... *maybe*."

I raised an eyebrow at her before flinging open the closet door. A pile of wrinkly, sparkly clothes smelling kind of like her Cherry Blast body spray tumbled out. I groaned and started picking through the disaster. "Mom is so going to kill you."

Ella threw her hands to her hips. "No, she's not! Have you seen *her* closet? It looks just like mine."

I wrestled with some kind of fuzzy sweater to free the pants, smiling as I turned to throw them at her. Neon yellow and black striped tights crawled up her legs until they collided with a blue tank top that looked like someone had sneezed sequins across it. She looked like a tiny, misguided fashion experiment, like a cutout of one of those outfits that showed up in *Seventeen* and made you wonder if anyone in fashion was sane.

"Please, put these on," I said, laughing. "And throw a sweater on while you're at it."

Ella grabbed the pants, rolling her eyes. I started untangling stray socks and underwear from the closet floor.

"Hey! You need your birthday prize!" she chirped from behind me. A wind chime made of rusty spoons she'd collected from the diner downtown jangled as she opened her desk drawer.

I scrunched my nose. "My birthday prize should be for you to let me destroy that wind chime." I made my fingers into scissors and pretended to cut the strings free from the knob.

Ella laughed, smacking my hand away. "No way. *You* may hate it, but this wind chime is the awesomest. I swear, I get good luck every time it rings." Her hair slid down her neck as she shuffled through the drawer. "So today's my lucky day, not yours." She stuck her tongue out.

My heart skipped a beat. *I could definitely use some luck*, I thought. For a quick second, I considered actually borrowing Ella's wind chime.

"Here it is!" she sang, pulling out a small box wrapped in her own artwork. "Happy fifteenth birthday!"

"Hmm...what is it?" I shook the box wildly next to one ear and then the other. Making Ella wait was always the best part of opening birthday presents. "What could it be—?"

"Open it, open it!" Ella bounced on the desk chair, her pink cheeks glowing.

"Okay, okay." I grinned, tugging the lid off the box. Inside sat a small knitted bird. Threads of periwinkle blue and smoky gray yarn wove through the wings. A fat black bead sat in place for an eye. I picked it up and held it in my palm.

"It's so pretty, Ell," I breathed. I glanced up at her. "Did you *make* this?"

"Uh-huh," she said, nodding. "It's a bookmark, see? The wings can stick out of the book." She grabbed the bird from my hand and tilted it so its wing poked upward. "And it's a bird because I know you want to move away to New York and study clothes and all that stuff. So it's, like, saying you can fly or something."

I took the bird from Ella's hand and ran my fingers over the soft little bumps of yarn.

Ella bit her lip, glancing between me and the bird. "It was Mom's idea."

I smiled and reached to pull her into a giant hug. "Thank you so much," I whispered. "It's the best present in the whole universe."

"Hey girls," Dad said, tapping on the door as he poked his head in. "Mom and I have to run out."

Ella's eyes went wide. "Why? It's Claire's birthday!"

"I know, sweetheart, we're so sorry." Mom pushed past Dad and reached for my hand. "We're going to stop by Laura's and see if we can help her talk some sense into Rae." She opened her mouth to say something but choked back the thought with a cough. Then she said, "She thinks Rae's going to try to leave again." She squeezed my fingers, like her words were sharp enough to puncture my skin. But really they just bounced off of me like butter knives, leaving only an itchy spot where they'd been thrown. Rae *always* said she was going to leave. "We'll still have cake tonight, promise."

I slid my hand from hers. "This isn't the first time she's packed a suitcase, you know," I blurted. "She always comes back anyway."

Rae had tried to run away twice before. Once on her seventh birthday, and once on Halloween last year, still dressed in her evil fairy costume. She always said that holidays were the best days for running away because everyone was too busy to notice until it was too late. But both times Rae had come back on her own, saying it was because she'd forgotten her favorite yellow slippers, or a magazine, or a pack of Diet Coke.

The only difference this time was that Robbie would be driving her. And that between the two of them, they probably had enough money to buy a pack of Diet Coke when they ran out.

"Okay, Telegram, we're gonna go." Dad patted the top of Ella's head and she winced under the weight of his palm or the cheesy nickname; either one. "Claire, look after your sister."

They walked out the door and Ella plopped back under her canopy, making the stars and lightning bolts dance on their strings. I let the air out of my chest.

Relief flooded over me and my stomach tingled with giddiness. On one hand, I knew Rae would be super disappointed if Dad and the rest of the Amble Police Department (all three of them) discovered her plans and made her ditch Robbie and stay home. But on the other hand, if she stayed home, safe and sound, I could keep the secret *and* have Rae around.

The front door clicked shut and Ella popped back up. "Come on." She grabbed my wrist and pulled me into the hall.

"Where do you think you're going?" I asked while Ella combed through the coat closet. A pile of mismatched mittens and totally nasty hats began to grow on the floor.

"*We're* going on a bike ride." Ella turned, her eyes sparkling. "I've got another birthday prize! A surprise prize. Come on." She shoved my coat into my arms, and a small wooden box tumbled to the floor.

"Is this the surprise prize?" I asked, bending down to pick it up. Ella grabbed it out of my hands and popped the lid off before I could even guess what was inside.

She scrunched her nose as she peered at its contents. "Ew, no. This is *not* your surprise prize, Claire." She picked up a dingy knife from the box and wrapped her fingers around the warped wooden handle. Her eyes narrowed as she examined the tip. "Is that—"

"Blood," I said. My stomach churned as I stared at the rust-colored splatters. "I think so."

"Gross," Ella said as she jammed the knife back into the box and chucked it into the closet. "Dad has the weirdest stuff."

I swallowed back the sick feeling in my throat. The sight of blood never failed to make me woozy. "Yeah. Probably a hunting knife." Just a hunting knife. I closed my eyes and forced the vision away. "So what is this surprise you keep talking about?"

"It's not a surprise if I tell you." Ella grinned and crammed a purple hat on her head. "Let's go, or we're going to be late."

———————

Our bike tires whirred as we cut through the dirt road and the cold air. The cornfields on either side of us blurred into a smear of brown and dripped over into the cement sky. The wind made my face sting and my eyes water, and a few tentative snowflakes shuddered free from the clouds. I dug my boots into the pedals.

I glanced back. Our house was a little red speck in the middle of broken stalks. The cornfield snapped and rustled in front of me. Ella jerked her bike in between the stalks and pedaled furiously through the snow.

"Ell—wait." I shoved my bike forward. But the tires just sank.

"Crap," she yelled. Her tires kicked up patches of snow as she inched through the stalks. "Forget this." She hopped off her bike and let it fall to the ground. I swung off my own bike and followed her.

"This way," she huffed. "Right over there."

We trudged through the field. I shivered under my coat as I stepped over the broken stalks that Rae and I had sat between just two days before. The spot smelled muddy and earthy and like spring. No, the whole field smelled like spring. Like the promise of something about to bloom.

"Ell, does it smell like spring to you?"

She stopped and wrinkled her nose. "Nope. It smells like rotting dead things."

I touched the dried leaves and they snapped off in my glove. Maybe I just really wanted it to smell hopeful like spring, instead of dead like winter.

"There, look." Ella pointed to a flickering light in the middle of the field. She bounced and clapped her mittens together. "Come on!"

She pulled me toward her, her fingers around my wrist, my shoulders brushing against the leaves. A head of dark, messy hair poked out from the stalks. A single candle lit up his face.

"Happy birthday!" Grant cried. A cupcake wrapped in silver foil and smothered in chocolate frosting sat in his hand. The flicker from the candle lit up the corners of his grin like a jack-o'-lantern. "For you."

"Thanks," I said. My cheeks felt hot and sweaty. I glanced at Ella, who was positively beaming. "Why'd you do this?"

"You're so dense sometimes, Claire," Grant said, laughing. "Did you forget it's your birthday?" He pulled my glove off by the fingertips and set the cupcake in my palm. "Now make a wish before the wind makes it for you."

I bit my lip. I could wish for anything in the whole world, but all I could think about was the way Grant was grinning and how the freckles on his nose looked just like the Big Dipper, with its handle pointing to his eyebrows. Rae had those same freckles, only hers were sprawled across her nose like a smattering of stars, all disjointed and chaotic. Just like Rae. I swallowed back her secret and the promise I'd made to keep it.

"But what about Rae?" I blurted. I closed my eyes. Every curse word erupted inside of me, at her, for interrupting this moment. But it was too late; Rae had already infiltrated my head. She might as well be standing between Grant and me, pinching the flame on my birthday candle until it died a silent death.

I sighed. "Shouldn't you be back at your house with your mom, freaking out about Rae and all?"

"Please. My sister's not going anywhere," Grant said. "Think about it. If she was really planning on skipping town, would she have left her suitcase sprawled open, poking out from under her bed? Now Mom's going crazy and wants to keep her on lockdown." Grant's eyes flicked to toward the rapidly graying sky. "So seriously, make a wish."

"Come on, Claire, wish for new clothes!" Ella said, giggling. "Then I'll grow into them."

"Okay, I wish for—"

"Shhh," Grant said, pressing a finger to my lips. His skin tasted like frosting and butter. "You can't say it aloud or it won't come true."

I closed my eyes. I thought about Rae and her secrets knotted up inside me. And then I thought of Ella's broad grin and dimpled chin and the promises I whispered to her before bedtime each night: to love her, to make her happy, to always keep her safe.

*I wish I was the best at keeping my promises,* I thought. *Especially this one.*

I blew out the candle before the wind could steal my wish. Ella clapped and Grant laughed. He pulled a box from his pocket. "One more thing."

My heart jumped into my throat. Behind me, a small cry came from Ella; Grant's birthday prize had managed to surprise even her. As I reached for the box, he grabbed my hand and turned it. He ran his thumb over the jagged cut in the middle of my palm. "Where'd that come from?" he asked.

"I don't know. Just a scratch." I slid my hand from his.

He nodded. "Here, I'll hold the cupcake and you take the box."

"No, *I'll* hold the cupcake." Ella smiled, wiggling her fingers.

"You will definitely not be holding the cupcake," Grant said, but a crooked grin spread across his face.

I popped off the lid of the box. A flat leather journal sat at the bottom: a wolf's gray muzzle and sparkling yellow eyes that watched me from between tufts of tissue paper. I sucked in a breath.

"Rae's always talking about how you guys see the wolves out here," Grant said slowly, glancing between my pink cheeks and the box in my hand, "and this one looked cool, with the eyes and everything." When I didn't say anything, he added, "We got it in town, at that new card shop Candice Dunnard opened, you know, on Main? Rae said you'd know what it meant."

Suddenly Ella's warm cheek was next to me, and her hands were pulling the box from mine. She shook out the tissue paper until the wolf journal plopped onto her orange mitten. She blinked down at it before making a decision: "I don't like it." She lifted her eyes and watched the cornfield surrounding us, as if a wolf would appear between the stalks any second.

Grant blinked. "Do you like it?"

Something cold slid across my tongue like an ice cube, and my throat swelled shut. The jewels in place of eyes stared at me like watery yellow moons. I said, "I love it. Thanks."

"Claire, let's go." Ella tugged at my sleeve, glancing at the purple bellies of the clouds above us. She gnawed at her chapped lips and wiped her nose with her mitten. "It's gonna snow."

I was turning to tell Grant goodbye, Ella practically pulling my arm out of my socket, when I caught his eyes watching me: green and rimmed with yellow, just like the tips of the cornstalks in the summer. Then Grant leaned forward and pressed a crumpled-up piece of paper into my palm. His breath brushed the tip of my ear as he whispered, "Did your wish come true yet?"

I shook my head, just enough that his lips bumped into the skin behind my ears in an almost-kiss. I could feel his mouth curve into a smile against my neck. "It will if you come back later tonight."

My heart pounded and sweat webbed between my gloved fingers, and I thought that if there really were wolves, like Rae said, and if they knew all of my secrets, then they knew that my answer was already "Yes" before I whispered it into the cornfield.

# *three*

I clutched Grant's note in my fist as I lay awake. I pressed my face against the wall and listened: a tangle of sing-song words floated through the drywall. Ella was sleep-talking. Which meant she was finally asleep.

Mom said that when she was pregnant with Ella, her belly as big as a watermelon, she went to the Ohio State Fair in Cleveland with my Aunt Sharon. She went to that one because she'd heard that a woman shows up there every year and claims to be the best psychic in the Midwest and that if she gets your fortune all wrong, you get your money back, no questions asked. So Mom asked her about the baby growing inside her. The psychic lady grabbed her hands and told her that Ella's soul was a gift, that she was an angel sent to make us all better, and that we should listen to her words because she wouldn't have very many. Well, Mom might have forgotten all about that prediction, but that lady for sure owed my mom ten bucks. Ella had so many words that she needed to use them up in her sleep.

I threw the covers off my legs and slipped into my boots. I stuffed my flashlight, my house key minus the keychain, and a pack of gum into my pockets and headed for the door. But before I turned the knob, I checked one more time, just in case the words had somehow disintegrated. Rae's invitation, scrawled over a sheet of lined paper, still felt solid in my hands:

> *You're invited*
> *To Claire Graham's (kind of surprise) birthday party!*
> *Field between Lark Lake and Route 24.*
> *BYOB*

And, in smaller print below Rae's invitation:

> *Come tonight (please). And leave Ella at home this time.—G*

I silently pleaded that if there was a God, he would let me go to my own birthday party. And then I swore under my breath as the tired floorboards groaned beneath me. They let out sharp bursts of protest as I shuffled toward the back door, but as I got closer and closer to freedom, they must have figured I was a lost cause and fell silent.

The wind bit at my neck as I stepped out the door, and for a second I thought I heard a whisper coming from the cornfield: *Claire.*

I pressed my lips together and listened.

*Claire.*

The swish of slippers against hardwood behind me. And then the whisper again, louder this time: *Claire! Where are you going?*

I turned and there she was, dressed in polka-dotted pajamas, a ring of messy blond curls framing her face.

"Ell! What are you doing up? Go back to bed!"

"What am *I* doing up? What are *you* doing up? And where do you think you're going without me?" Ella tapped her slipper against the floor with a soft *thud*.

The wind swept down my jacket, pinching at my collarbone beneath my sweater. For a second, I thought about just quietly stepping out the door, leaving Ella in the kitchen with her fuzzy slippers and crust in her eyes. But I couldn't, because as desperately as I wanted to be alone with Grant, Ella was like a stubborn puppy attached to my hip. I sighed. "You can't go, Ell. Not this time."

She stepped toward me, hands on her hips. "Why?"

"Because."

"*Why?*"

I gritted my teeth and let the wind click the door shut behind me. Grant's face hovering over mine, the freckles on his nose pressing against my skin, flashed through my mind. "It's a party for kids in high school, Ell. You can't come this time. I'm sorry."

Something in Ella's eyes flashed, and her fists went limp at her sides. Relief caught in my throat. But as I reached for the doorknob again, she kicked off her slippers so that they slid across the floor and thumped against the oven.

"What are you doing?" I asked. When she didn't answer me, and instead started shuffling toward the living room, I hooked her by the elbow. "*What* are you doing?"

She tugged her arm free and lifted her chin. "I'm almost thirteen, Claire. I'm getting my jacket." And then she stomped toward living room, her bare feet slapping against the floor.

I chewed on my lip as I watched her go, deflated. Once Ella decided she was going to do something, even a tornado couldn't stop her. Literally. Three years ago, I was holed up in the basement with Mom and Dad while the sirens wailed across Amble. Ella had told us she was coming downstairs in a minute; just a second, she needed to check on something, she said. When she didn't come, Dad went to look for her and found her plucking washed-out dandelions in the rain because she "didn't want them to get blown away."

Ella had decided that she was going where I was going as soon as she'd heard my bed creak. And there was nothing I could do about it.

Just then, she burst back into the kitchen, a scarf wrapped halfway around her neck, one boot on her foot and the other in her hand. Her eyes were round and wild and filled up with moonlight as she stared through the window. "Did you hear that?" she whispered.

And then I heard it: a low, melancholic howl ripping through the night.

Ella's bottom lip quivered as she said, "I'm not afraid of them."

I turned and wrapped my arm around her shoulder.

"They sound pretty close." I glanced out the window and pulled my lip into my mouth, my stomach sinking.

Ella's shoulders shook beneath my arm. "How close?" she whispered.

I closed my eyes. How bad of a sister was I if I used Ella's insurmountable fear of Rae's wolf stories to escape into the night? But I couldn't shake Grant's face. I'd almost memorized the way his letters looped around the paper.

*Come tonight (please). And leave Ella at home this time.—G*

"Really close, Ell. By Lark Lake probably," I said, smoothing her hair away from her face.

A guttural sound emerged from the field, and quickly turned into a sharp snarl. A series of biting howls trailed after it.

Ella pressed her head into my shoulder. "You said that Rae was just telling stories. You said they weren't even real, that they were just dogs in Wellington County." Her voice cracked on the word *dogs*. "I know they're just dogs, Claire."

I glanced out the smudged kitchen windows and watched the stalks bend with the wind. Amble's deep farming roots were flecked with whispers of wolves that snapped and snarled, that stained the dirt roads with bloody paw prints, that watched us all with gem-colored eyes. That they were responsible for eight-year-old Sarah Dunnard's disappearance just last month, even though it had never been proven, exactly. Dad and the rest of the police had found pinpricks of her blood, soaked into roots of the cornstalks around her house, but they hadn't found her body.

No one really wanted believe those stories, to admit that the wolves could be real. Still, Amble's exasperated parents used them as a warning if you didn't eat all your peas at dinner—the wolves might be watching, so you better do it. Rae was the only one who actually believed in the wolves, who preached the dangers of cherry pie baking at the church festival and the risk of walking alone past Lark Lake. Until Ella started listening to her.

"They're just dogs, Claire," Ella repeated, her voice cracking over the letters in my name.

I felt my neck grow pink as frustration spread to my cheeks. The clock on the microwave flashed 11:15 p.m. I was fifteen minutes late to my fifteenth birthday party.

I shrugged Ella away and grabbed her shoulders. "Rae was right. They're wolves. I saw one today, in the cornfield earlier." I thought back to the flash of fur I'd seen hidden in the stalks, so similar to a misshapen shadow that it could have been just that.

Ella's eyes grew wide and her lip began to quiver again. "You can't go."

11:16 on the clock. The minutes between Grant and me were slowly ticking away. I pulled myself from Ella and shuffled through the knife drawer. Grabbing a small paring knife, I stuck it in my back pocket. Then I pushed the door open before I could change my mind.

"Look, Ell. I've got a knife, I'll be fine. If I'm not back in a couple hours, you can worry about me. But I'll be fine, Ell. Go back to bed."

And then it was just me and the wind that made the corn crinkle and fold around me and I was running, running, running.

––––––––––

By the time I made it to the clearing in the middle of the cornfield, I'd forgotten all about the wolves. But I couldn't shake the feeling that Ella was somehow still watching me.

"You finally made it!" Rae cried, stumbling through a stalk that refused to stay frozen to the ground. "Whoops." She giggled as she tripped on something that was invisible to me. "I'm a teensy bit drunk."

She wrapped me in a sloppy hug, her breath warm and cherry on my neck. I gently pushed her away and looked at her face. Her green eyes, an exact replica of Grant's, were half-lidded and empty. "Rae, how much have you had to drink already?"

"Just a lil' bit." She grinned, holding up a half-drunk bottle of cherry vodka. Then she shoved it into my hands, its contents splashing into the icy film beneath us. "Rest is yours, Claire-bear." Before I could say thanks, Rae had my hand in hers and was dragging me toward the bonfire gurgling in the center of the clearing.

There were people here—a *lot* of people. Way more than I knew, even though this was supposed to be my party. But by the looks of the lanky guys with beards who were collecting around a tub of liquor bottles and a table littered with shot glasses, and the clique of senior girls who bought their pot from Rae, this seemed more like Rae's going away party than my birthday party.

"I want you to meet Robbie," Rae slurred, pulling me toward the group of guys. But something inside my stomach pinched as she pulled me forward and I dug my heels into the wet ground. Rae turned, her eyes wide with surprise, her lips parted in disbelief. "What're you doin', Claire?"

I frowned. What *was* I doing? I'd always trusted Rae, I'd always followed. Why couldn't I now? I glanced around the party. Groups of girls I barely knew sat huddled around the fire, lips purple and noses red. A couple of kids from my grade orbited around the tubs of beer at the other side of the clearing, but never got close enough to actually take one. And Grant. Grant was nowhere.

I pulled my hand from the crook of her elbow. "Is this really my birthday party, Rae? None of my friends are even here."

"Of course it's your birthday party, Claire! You know all these people 'cept Robbie's friends."

I glanced around again, in case I'd missed something. "No, I don't."

Rae flicked her hand and said, "Sure you do! You know Stacey over there, 'member? We all hung out last summer!"

I glanced at Stacey huddled between two other girls I didn't know by the fire. She did look vaguely familiar. And then I remembered: Stacey had been the first of Rae's friends to get her license, so Rae had invited her over one time to take us to the mall.

"Seriously, Rae? That doesn't count."

Rae bit her lip and glanced back at the group of guys, who were in the middle of some kind of drinking game that involved coins and shot glasses. "Look, Claire, it's your party, okay? I promise," she said without looking back at me. "Now come meet Robbie, please?"

But I still didn't follow. Something thick and cold was stuck in my stomach, pressing me into the snow. "Where's Grant?" I asked.

Rae's head snapped back and her eyes narrowed into hard slits. But before I could think about it, they had melted back to watery green and she was wrapping me in a hug. "Oh Claire, I'm so sorry. Grant couldn't make it. He said it was too cold." She pulled away and kissed my cheek. "Said it would bother his asthma."

The cold in my stomach sloshed violently and I wobbled backward, just for a second. Rae was still watching me, her mouth pressed in a thin line. Then she grabbed my hand and pulled. "Come *on*. Let's meet Robbie." But this time her words came out sharper than they had before. This time, I let her take me with her.

She pulled me toward the group of guys, who'd started pelting their coins at a straggling raccoon instead of their shot glasses. A guy with a nose too big for his face laughed hysterically as the raccoon hissed and rocketed into the stalks.

"Hey Robbie," Rae chirped just as the guys remembered

their liquor on the table. "I want you to meet Claire." She patted me on the head like I was her well-loved rag doll.

A guy turned toward me, his hair matted to his head by what looked like a week's worth of grease and cheap hair gel. He grinned, and only half of his mouth hitched in the corner. "Hey Claire. Nice to finally meet you."

I tried not to scrunch my nose when he spoke, but the combination of some kind of sharp liquor and menthol cigarettes on his breath almost made me gag. I pressed my lips into a tight smile and said, "Nice to meet you."

Robbie grabbed Rae and wrapped his arm around her shoulder so that his hand dangled dangerously close to her chest, and then he kissed the side of her neck. She giggled and whined, pretending she didn't like it, before Robbie turned to me again. "Hey, thanks for letting Rae throw you this party. She just wasn't happy leaving without doing something for your birthday first." His face curved into a half-smile again, and I wondered if the other side of his face just didn't work.

Something itched at the back of my brain just then, a thought that I couldn't quite reach. It was uncomfortable, prickly, and I knew I wouldn't feel good when I eventually found it.

"Hey, you want a drink?" Rae blurted, pointing to the cherry vodka still in my hand. "Take a birthday swig, for me?"

I watched Robbie watching me as I tipped the bottle to my mouth and sipped. It burned down my throat, hot and spicy like a cherry cough drop. But instead of it filling me with heat, I just felt cold instead.

"How'd you even get out of the house tonight, with your

29

mom having you on lockdown?" I asked Rae as I handed her the bottle.

Rae rolled her eyes and huffed dramatically. "Please. My mom's version of 'lockdown' is taking my suitcase." She laughed, and Robbie chimed in like this was somehow hilarious to him, too: "But that's why they make garbage bags, right, babe? To put stuff in." Rae stood on her tiptoes to kiss him, and Robbie grabbed the back of her neck and smashed his mouth to hers.

I grabbed the vodka bottle back out of Rae's hand and pressed the rim to my mouth. Rae and Robbie's faces looked like an abstract painting, all patches of skin and splatters of hair twisted up in each other through the glass. I took a step toward the edge of the clearing, the bottle still lingering on my lips.

Dad once told me and Ella that Amble had the densest cornfields in all of Ohio. He said they were so thick that you could get swallowed up inside them, even in the dead of winter. As I looked out over the tops of the sallow stalks, gasping for life in the bitter night, I felt it: the tingling sensation of being watched.

Hunted.

I took another swig and another step, waiting. If all the stories Rae had ever told us about the wolves were true—that they could smell cherry lip balm from over a mile away, or that periwinkle was their favorite color—then they would come. If they were real, they would come now.

My face was red, I could feel it, and the vodka sloshed in my stomach as I pulled Ella's knitted bird with the beaded eye from my pocket. I held the delicate yarn in my palm like a peace offering. And then I tipped the bottle so that the last of the vodka dripped into the snow.

"Hey! Why're you throwing good liquor away?" someone yelled from behind me. I didn't even turn around; I just kept pouring, watching while the puddles in the snow started to form patterns.

"Hey," the voice said again, from over my shoulder. He clamped his hand around my wrist and ripped the bottle from my hand. "If you want to make puddles, I can piss in the snow for you."

I snapped my head back to look at him. He towered over me, the shoulder of his flannel jacket just grazing the top of my head. And as with almost everyone else here, I had no idea who he was.

He looked down at me through bloodshot eyes and the smirk slowly dripped from his face. "Dude. You're the chief's kid, aren't you? Mike Graham's daughter?" He raised his palms. "Hey. This is, like, the only time I've drank. Ever."

"I don't care," I said, rolling my eyes. I wiggled the empty vodka bottle for good measure.

The guy's whole body relaxed and he pulled a beat-up flask from his pocket. "Whew. So now that I know you're cool, there's something I've always wanted to know." He took a swig from his flask and coughed. "Does your dad tell you the inside scoop on big cases? Do you get to know all the good stuff the *Observer* doesn't report?"

I snorted. "I think you're forgetting where we live. There aren't any big cases in the-middle-of-nowhere, Ohio."

"Nah, not true. Sarah Dunnard. That's been a pretty big deal." He glanced down at me. "You know anything about that one?"

I shrugged. The truth was, everyone in Amble was whispering about Sarah Dunnard's disappearance, but Dad hadn't said anything at all—even though he'd been the one to find the speckles of her blood crawling up the cornstalks. In fact, since he'd been on the case, he'd been acting kind of strange. He'd started spending all his evenings pacing by the kitchen windows and glancing out into our backyard. And one time, I even caught him endlessly stirring his coffee while staring at the kitchen wallpaper, lost in thought. What he was thinking about, I had no idea. He wouldn't let any of us know.

"They haven't found her yet," I said. "That's all I know."

He winced like I'd slapped him with my words. "Probably won't ever," he said. His eyes scanned the stalks that stretched out before us.

"Do you think there's wolves out there?" I asked, nodding toward the stalks. "In there."

The guy continued to stare into the cornfield, his eyes narrowed, like if he squinted hard enough he'd find a wolf waving back at him. He scratched the scruff on his chin that was trying desperately to turn into a beard, and said, "Nah."

I nodded and tipped my chin to look up at him. His face was drenched in light, like tiny fireflies were stuck in the folds of his almost-beard. And the specks of light in the sky wobbled around him, dancing to the beat of the pounding in my head. I stumbled backward, but he snatched my sleeve before I fell.

"Whoa there. It looks like you've had enough of the ol' bottle tonight." He laughed and patted me hard on the shoulder. I sighed, staring at the watery snow beneath my boots. All of a sudden his finger was under my chin and I think he was saying something like, "Why so glum, chum?"

I closed my eyes when I lifted my face up, so that the stars wouldn't wobble behind his head this time. And in that instant, a shock ran through my brain and slammed the itchy thoughts back into focus and set them on fire. And suddenly I knew. My eyes popped open.

"My best friend needed a holiday to run away on. And she didn't want to wait until Christmas." I took a step away from him so his sweaty finger wasn't under my chin anymore. "She needed my birthday. So she made me a party … for her."

"That's not so bad," almost-bearded guy said, taking a swig from his flask. "At least she threw you a party."

I squinted into the cornfield, chewing the skin off my lips. For a second I thought I heard my name in the wind, or maybe it was just the thought of my name. "She said that the wolves are out here, watching us. That they like cherry-flavored things and the color periwinkle. But that's a lie. Everything is a lie." I shoved Ella's bird toward him. "This is periwinkle. And that's cherry." I pointed to the bottle. "There aren't any wolves."

He just shrugged and took another swig. He must have gotten annoyed by me, or figured that I wasn't going to make out with him no matter how drunk I was, because he started scratching his beard like he was thinking again. And then he just walked away, swinging his flask at his side.

I started to turn back toward the fire when I heard the whisper in the wind again: *Claire.*

*Claire.*

*Claire.*

A tiny piece of my heart begged for it to be Grant. I turned slowly toward the shivering stalks and waited, hoped.

*Claire.*

From the darkness, the brittle leaves cracked and groaned. And a short little body, dressed in a puffy ski coat and a wool hat with ears, stepped into the clearing.

Ella had arrived, just like she'd always planned.

# *four*

"Hi Claire," Ella said as she stepped through the stalks. She pulled a jagged corn leaf from her hair. "Ouch! That one was pokey."

I could feel my mouth moving and words jumbling around in my head, *lots* of words that I wanted to say, but nothing came out. Instead my mouth hung open like a hooked fish as Ella cocked her head to the side and said, "What?"

Somewhere in the back of my throat, the words tickled and burned until they bubbled onto my tongue: "What the hell do you think you're doing?"

Just then, almost-bearded guy appeared next to us. He blinked at me, and then at Ella, the skin between his eyebrows wrinkling. "Hey. Hey, why're there two of you?" He wobbled a little, his arms pinwheeling wildly before he centered himself next to a stalk.

Ella trudged up to him until her eyes were level with his

chest. She threw her head up to look at him, and when she did, the little knitted ears on her hat wiggled. She scrunched her nose and stared at him, then said, "Ew, Claire," as if his presence was somehow *my* fault.

I grabbed her arm and pulled her away from him, from the edge of the cornfield, toward the fire. And then I shoved her, just enough so that her eyes grew wide and she had to take a step back.

"Why are you here?" I yelled, even though I didn't mean to.

Now Ella's mouth hung open, and her arms went limp at her side. Finally, she swung a mittened hand up and I imagined she was pointing at me beneath the orange yarn. The corners of her mouth twitched into a smile. "You brought my bird."

I glanced down at my fists. I'd almost forgotten; Ella's periwinkle bird that I'd been using as wolf bait was still smashed into my fist.

Something about the way her eyes lit up when she saw her present in my hand—her innocent bird trapped between my fingers while the world spun around us and the stars bounced on their strings—made me want to punch her and hug her at the same time.

I walked closer to her and she winced. "I'm not going to hit you, Ell," I said, grabbing her mitten. I pressed the little bird into her palm. "Go home. Take this home so I don't do something stupid like lose it." I glanced around at what was left of the party and cringed. "You've gotta go."

Ella blinked at me and held the bird in her palm, like it

was a fragile thing that would crack if she moved too fast. The blood rushed through my ears as I watched her, all mittens and blond hair and pink cheeks. And I realized that I'd never experienced a moment with my sister when she didn't have anything to say. Until this one.

"Ella?" Rae bounded up behind me and stumbled into Ella so hard that for a second, I thought they were both going to tumble into the fire. The silence between us cracked, and Ella was giggling and squealing as she tried to escape from Rae's death grip. Finally, Ella ducked Rae's swinging arms and pulled free.

"Glad you could make it!" Rae screamed, her voice bouncing around the clearing. Before I could open my mouth, she'd wrapped her pink hands around Ella's arm and pulled her away from the fire. Away from me. It only took a second for Ella's knit hat to melt into the chaos of slurred words and clinking bottles.

A heavy hand clamped on my shoulder. "That your sister?" almost-bearded guy asked. I'd forgotten he was still here.

I shrugged my shoulders, trying to squirm free of his sweaty skin. "Yeah." Obviously.

He hesitated, just for a second, but it was long enough for me to know that I wouldn't like whatever was about to come out of his booze-soaked mouth. He tipped his head to the side and squinted through the bonfire smoke. "How old's she?"

I narrowed my eyes. "Why?"

He shrugged. "She's pretty hot, that's all," he said, taking a quick step to the left.

But I didn't smack him, or even yell. Instead I lifted an

37

eyebrow at him and said, "Yeah, she will be. Maybe even by the time she turns thirteen, you creep."

I left him there, mouth hanging open and eyes polluted with fear. We were, after all, the police chief's daughters. I stomped through the cold, the sea of drunk bodies parting with the heat of my anger.

I peered through the fire and found Ella, her infectious giggle carrying through the clearing. She smashed her mittens to her mouth to stifle her laughter as a boy I didn't know leaned over and whispered in her ear.

He was taller but maybe not much older, with a smile that crinkled in the corners and a nose that bent in all the wrong places. A mess of dishwater hair hung over his eyes. His name wafted in front of me like the specks of debris from the fire, but I couldn't quite catch it with my vodka-laced tongue. All I knew is that I'd see him before, probably around school.

Ella's eyes grew wide as the boy's lips moved in hushed words, close to her cheek. She dropped her mittens and whispered something back, but the smile had melted from her lips. She didn't look flattered or flushed or even mildly curious.

She was *intrigued*.

"Ella!" I yelled as I made my way to her. She jolted, and so did the boy beside her, two pairs of eyes round and petrified. I hooked my arm in hers. "It's late. You shouldn't be here."

"She can stay," Rae called from behind the mostly empty tub of glass bottles.

"She was just leaving," I snapped. "She's a little too young for this party, don't you think?" My eyes caught Rae's and the smile sagged from her face. I think even in the haze of cherry vodka and cigarette smoke, we both knew I was challenging her to tell me otherwise.

I pulled my lip between my teeth and waited. Waited for Rae to laugh and dance around my words and tell me that I was being too overprotective, too uptight. Waited for the icy feeling in my stomach to melt away, the one that said Rae hadn't tried hard enough to get Grant to come, for the two of us to burst out laughing about the whole thing.

But Rae's eyes just narrowed; she watched me like I was some kind of exotic zoo animal that she'd never encountered before. I sucked in a breath and waited.

"You know, it's, what—almost one? The wolves come out to hunt between one and three." Rae took a step forward and crossed her arms over her chest. "You *sure* you want her to go back?"

Ella's eyes were so big, and her lips were pressed together so tight, that she looked like one of those bug-eyed goldfish you see in tanks at Chinese restaurants. I chewed on my lip, thinking. I could always go back with her. But the stars were still orbiting the sky, and with the way the cornfield slanted to the left even when I was standing straight, I knew I needed to stay long enough to even be able to find my way back.

And then there was the small spark of hope still flickering inside of me. Maybe it wasn't his asthma—maybe Grant had fallen asleep and Rae didn't wake him up, and he was running around trying to find socks without holes as we spoke. Maybe he was running through the stalks right now, hoping I was still waiting for him.

I grabbed Ella's shoulder and squeezed. "There aren't any wolves in the cornfield, Rae. You're just making it up." I let out a puff of air and gasped at myself in disbelief. I tried to cover up my surprise at my own words by sucking in another quick breath, and then I said, "I poured cherry vodka by the edge of the clearing and I didn't even hear the leaves move in the field. No wolves are coming." I left out the part about offering up Ella's knitted bird as bait.

Rae scoffed and rolled her eyes. "You think they're going to come right up to a clearing? Get real, Claire." She leaned forward so that her cheeks brushed between mine and Ella's jackets and whispered, "They're gonna get you in the field."

"I don't want to go back by myself," Ella said as she pressed a mitten against her mouth. "I can't go back by myself."

"Stop, Rae!" I yelled, wrapping my arm around Ella. "You're scaring her."

But Rae just tipped her head back and laughed. Just then, something that sounded like a warbled howl pierced through the field, at least a hundred yards away.

Ella's body went rigid next to me the same time that Rae's mouth twisted into a satisfied smirk. "See? They're waiting for a late-night, Ella-sized snack." She bent her bony fingers into claws and growled for extra emphasis.

"They're not real, right, Claire?" Ella's lip quivered as she tilted her head into my jacket.

Even though I was still buzzed, I still knew it was stupid, the whole thing. Rae would be gone in less than twelve hours, her *Cosmopolitan* magazines and striped socks all smashed together in a garbage bag in the back of Robbie's car. And I should just let her have her stories about the wolves, because I think a part of her truly believed them. But even though she'd be long gone in a few hours, the way her nonsense stories made Ella's breath quicken with panic and her eyes grow wide—well, that wouldn't go away, no matter how far Rae got from Amble.

I stepped between Rae and Ella and pressed Ella's cheeks between my mittens. "Trust me. You got here okay, didn't you? I need you to go home." I kissed the tip of her nose. "What do I always promise you?"

She blinked up at me. "That you'll keep me safe, forever and ever."

"Right," I said, smiling. "I'll be home in a little bit."

Ella's shoulders softened and she nodded. "Okay. Okay, okay." She sucked in a deep breath. "I'm gonna go home. But I'm *not* going to bed until you get back," she said, jabbing me.

I walked her toward the edge of the clearing, not even turning to face Rae. "Okay, Ell, whatever you want."

"*And* I'm gonna go through your jewelry while you're gone. And maybe your makeup." She tapped a mitten to her mouth. "Yeah, definitely your makeup."

"I guess that gives me a good reason to get back as soon as I can then, huh?" We were at the edge of the clearing now, stepping over the puddles of vodka I'd left in the snow. Ella nodded and smiled, but her lips were tight and her eyes were big and watery. She blinked quickly and said, "See ya later, gator." And then she was gone.

As I listened to her boots tromp through the stalks, the

stars seemed to shudder to a stop on their invisible strings. And I wondered if maybe the stars and the earth weren't moving not because of the vodka in my veins, but because Ella had left, and there was no magic to orbit around anymore. I watched her bob through the cornfield for as long as I could see her, and after that I listened. But all I could hear was the sharp bite of the wind and the promise of a howl in the distance.

# *five*

It wasn't until the sky had turned gray, and the clouds' bellies glowed pink, that I realized my jewelry box was still closed. I gasped, pushing aside my covers as I threw myself out of bed.

Outside my window, winged things buzzed and chirped. Morning sounds.

I stepped onto the cold floor and pulled open the drawers. Necklaces and faded silver rings, still there.

I swallowed the sick feeling curdling in my throat and pulled open my makeup drawer. Eyeliners and lip glosses and nail polish, all carefully placed in their baskets.

My hands reached for the edge of my dresser, still shaking. I closed my eyes. "Think, Claire. Think," I whispered to my haggard reflection in the mirror.

I'd looked for Ella on the way home—I remembered that. There were no broken stalks or sunken snowdrifts that would mean something had happened.

But there were no footprints leading to our doorstep that told me something hadn't, either.

I headed toward Ella's room. My brain pounded *she's fine, she's fine, she's fine* to the rhythm of my heartbeat.

Christmas music floated from the radio in the kitchen and something sizzled in a pan. Mom was humming to "Rockin' Around the Christmas Tree." I sucked in a breath as I tiptoed toward Ella's closed bedroom door. And then I heard it: the shuffle of a paper, probably the sports section, and a low grumble.

I stopped, listening for the paper to stop rustling, for Dad's police chief radar to make his ears prick and his nose sniff for anything amiss. I half-expected him to come running up the stairs, his nose in the air like a hound dog. But instead I heard him say, "Hey Rosie, can you get me a cup of coffee?" and cough.

My hand slid around Ella's doorknob, slick with sweat. I wiped my palm against the jeans I'd been wearing since last night, and twisted.

The sun peeked through her mismatched curtains, and the stars and lightning bolts swayed on their strings above her bed. A pile of sweaters, a basket of headbands, and a worn purple diary sat on Ella's bed.

"Ella?" I whispered. She could still be under there, tucked in with sweaters, fast asleep. Safe. "Ell, you in here?" I pushed off the piles of clothes. An empty rainbow afghan sat in a ball on her bed.

Panicked, I grabbed the diary. Maybe she'd written something, left me a note to tell me where she'd gone. I ran my fingers over the canvas cover and flipped through the pages. All empty, every one of them, except for a few sporadic pencil drawings of lumpy unicorns and hearts dotted with initials I didn't recognize. Of course there would be no entries or notes in here—all of Ella's words came straight from her lips, not from a pencil.

I pressed my hand to my chest to keep my heart from leaping out of it. There were no boots. No puffy ski jacket. No knitted hat with ears thrown on the floor.

No Ella.

I stepped out into the hall and pressed my forehead against the frame. Okay, so she wasn't in her room. She could have hung her coat in the closet. Her boots could be by the front door. She could be wearing her knitted hat with the ears right this second in the kitchen while she picked through the marshmallows in her Lucky Charms.

But she wasn't. I knew she wasn't. Somehow I just knew that Ella wasn't in this house—the sun didn't shine as brightly through the windows and everything seemed dimmer.

So where was she?

"Do you think I should wake the girls?" Mom's voice came from the kitchen. "It's almost nine, and we still haven't given Claire her birthday presents." There was the clinking sound of silverware and a heavy sigh. "I feel terrible, delaying Claire's birthday over Rae. And I don't think we did much to calm Laura down anyway."

I didn't hear Dad's response over the gurgling coffee pot. I was already thumping down the stairs, smacking my bare feet against the wood so they knew I was coming.

"Hark the Herald Angels Sing" wafted from the radio as I walked into the kitchen, and instantly I flashed back to the church pageant a few years ago. Ella had played the angel Gabriel, and she'd insisted on making her own wings, complete with orange feathers. In my mind, I saw her giggling as she knocked baby Jesus out of the manger for the third time with a flick of her outrageous wings.

"Oh, you're up." Mom smiled and prodded the bacon to leave the pan. She didn't know; she couldn't.

"Yeah, I was just about to go into town." I smiled widely. "I have to get some Christmas presents still. Be back later." I turned to leave, still smiling tightly even though she couldn't see my face anymore.

The paper shifted and I just knew he wasn't going to make it any easier today. "Wait a second, Claire." I felt Dad's eyes on the back of my head. "We didn't get to celebrate your birthday yesterday, so we're going to do it this morning. Go wake your sister up."

I whipped around. "Dad, I have to—"

"No, you don't." He neatly folded the paper into halves, not bothering to look at me. "Not right now, anyway. Go wake your sister up."

I sucked in my lip. I *knew* I could find her if I had the chance. I'd check the cornfield first, just to rule it out, but I knew she wouldn't still be in there. She'd be in town, at the bead store, spending her allowance on glass beads with little flowers in them to make last-minute Christmas presents for her friends. I just knew it.

"Okay," I said, and I started slowly back up the stairs. I

needed time to think. How could I explain that Ella was mysteriously missing and that if they just gave me an hour, I'd bring her back home?

The phone rang in the kitchen. Mom's slippers padded across the floor. "Hello?" Silence, except for the last notes of "Hark the Herald Angels Sing." And then, "Oh God, oh God. Okay Laura, let me put Mike on the phone."

The lights flickered around me, and little black stars popped in front of my eyes, and I was going to pass out, I was so going to pass out. They'd found Ella—someone found Ella out in the cornfield. Not in the bead shop downtown. I grabbed the banister and squeezed.

The stool groaned as Dad got up to grab the phone. "What's going on?" he asked.

I heard Mom untangle her fingers from the phone cord. She whispered, "Rae's gone. Laura went to check her room this morning and she wasn't there. Took most of her stuff this time."

I quietly lowered myself to my knees and pressed my head against the floor. Dad was talking to Rae's mom now, asking her questions about the last time she'd seen Rae and all the other things that police have to ask. My heart lowered from my throat to my chest and for the first time since I'd checked my jewelry box, I felt like I could almost breath.

"I have to go," Dad said, and I heard him shifting through the junk drawer for his keys. "We can't officially do something until she's gone for twenty-four hours, but I told Laura I'd check out her room, see if we could get an idea."

Mom sighed and said, "Well, if you're going over there, I

am too. Laura and Grant are going to need somebody." She clicked off the radio. "Poor Laura. Rae doesn't realize what she's doing to her."

I pulled myself from floor and slid into the bathroom just before they walked by. "Claire, we have to run to the Buchanans'. So sorry, sweetheart."

I let out a short breath. "I'm in the bathroom, Mom."

"Okay. We'll be back. Watch Ella, please." The closet door opened and closed, and then the front door opened and closed, and they were gone. And then I could breath.

I shoved my boots onto my bare feet, wrapped one of Ella's polka-dotted scarves around my neck, and flew out the door. Seconds later I was on my bike, tires slipping on the ice, just a couple miles of frozen corn between me and Ella.

————

By the time I rode by Rae's house, I was positive that Ella couldn't be at the bead shop downtown. I'd remembered that she'd spent her allowance when we were in town three days ago, on some periwinkle yarn and new knitting needles. The same yarn that she'd made my bird bookmark from.

And then there was the bird bookmark. I'd given it to her last night to take home, to keep safe. I knew she'd never lose it, because it wasn't hers to lose. She didn't lose things that were important to other people, especially me.

It was nowhere in the house.

Which meant that Ella had never come home.

Somehow, I wasn't completely panicked yet. Because

to me, Ella was magic, bright and bubbly magic, and that kind of magic just didn't get taken away. It just didn't.

As I came up to Rae's house, I saw Dad's clunky police car tucked into the driveway. Grant's silver bike was sprawled across the front porch. I let my feet hang off the pedals and the bike slide to a stop, just out of sight of the front window.

I could tell them.

I could tell them that Rae had left with some guy named Robbie who had a half-moon smile and heavy-lidded eyes. And that she'd packed all of her things in garbage bags and was probably somewhere out of Ohio by now.

I could tell them that Ella was with me at the party last night, even though I'd told her not to come. And that now she was missing.

No. She wasn't missing.

I would find her. She'd be sitting in the field, knitting flowered hats or trying to decide if she should take home the half-frozen raccoon she'd found in between the stalks and feed it chicken soup. I'd take her home, and make her drink the cheap cough syrup that Mom always gave us, and put her to bed. And I'd make her leave the raccoon.

I would find her, and everything would be okay.

My stomach hitched as I caught a glimpse of Grant in the window. His hair was poking up all over his head, and his cheeks looked raw and windswept. I couldn't see his freckles from here, but I knew they were tumbling across his nose as he rubbed it.

A part of me almost threw down my bike and stomped up the steps and asked him why he'd given me that note if he wasn't planning on coming to my party anyway, and didn't he know that was really rude? But I didn't have time for that. I'd deal with that later.

I dipped my head below the stalks as I rode past the front window. No one turned, no one noticed. I stood on the pedals and pumped through the snow, the wind whipping through Ella's scarf around my neck.

I rode for another mile, watching the cornstalks for any sign of life. When I got closer to the clearing, my heart started to pound again and my hands grew slick with sweat.

I almost rode past the spot, but it was the scent that made me brake so hard that my bike wobbled and slid on its side into the snowdrift. I stood and sucked in the air through my nose.

Cherry Blast body spray.

My heart roared in my ears like a wild, out-of-control ocean. I brushed the snow off my jeans and took three steps into the field.

She lay in a ring of snow, her arms stretched out at her sides. Her eyes were open, gray and dull and mirroring the grumbling clouds above us. Blood, so much blood, sliced across her mouth in angry lines and splattered across her puffy white ski jacket. Shaking, I reached down and opened her little mittened fist. My periwinkle bird stared up at me with an accusing beaded eye.

Your mind does funny things when it goes into shock. I didn't scream, or yell, or even cry.

I started singing.

The words to "Hark the Herald Angels Sing" flooded my brain, and I sang them to her.

Because right then, she looked like an angel with orange-tipped wings, dancing in the church Christmas play.

A beautiful, bloody snow angel looking toward the sky.

part two

# *six*

"I need a light." I slid a cigarette from Danny's box and trapped it between my fingers. He tugged a box of matches from his coat pocket and tossed it to me. I lit a match and puffed. "You know, it's a lot easier to just carry a lighter."

A second match snapped as it flickered to life. He stared at the flame while it licked at his fingertips. "But matches are more fun."

I nodded. "True." Smoke mingled with the cold as it curled from my lips. The bell rang behind us.

Danny raised an eyebrow, his cigarette dangling from his mouth. I looked up at the sprawling stained-glass window that marked the entrance to the Poller Academy. A dozen angelic faces cradling textbooks beamed down at me. "Not today," I said, shaking my head.

Danny's face broke into a crooked grin as he stubbed

out his cigarette. He grabbed my hand. "Excellent. I've gotta make a run anyway."

I followed him through the alley, back toward East Houston. The hum of New York traffic popped in my ears. I pulled my hand from his. "I haven't been to Chemistry in, like, a week."

Danny tugged at the sleeves of his varsity jacket, covering his exposed wrists. "Come on, Claire. It's cold." He pulled me across the street.

I followed.

We wove through streets sprinkled in tiny lights and fat Santas. Rows of windows were lit up with gold and silver. Towers of shiny presents and fake snow threatened to swallow me as my heels clicked against the pavement. I tucked my head into my jacket and watched the sidewalk.

"What time is it?" Danny glanced over at me. Then he snapped "Never mind" and rolled up his sleeve to check his watch. "I forgot. You can't look at Christmas shit or your brain melts."

I swallowed back the sick feeling bubbling up in my throat and kept walking. The last notes of "We Wish You a Merry Christmas" floated from a storefront across the street. It sounded how a million razor blades felt.

"Stay here," Danny said. I heard the crunch of a paper bag as he shuffled through his jacket. "Be right back."

I stood on the corner, shivering under my scarf. "We Wish You a Merry Christmas" had turned into "The Little Drummer Boy," and I hated that song even more. I always hated the last Christmas song more than the one before it. I turned toward the shop window.

A white eyelet dress blinked down at me. A halo of light soaked it in gold as the delicate fabric hugged the mannequin. I pressed my palm to the glass.

I tried to force it down, as I did the sickness in my throat, but her name clawed its way to the surface just like it always did.

*Ella.*

I bit my lip. Twelve-year-old Ella twirled in the buttery cornstalks, the hem of her sundress swishing against her bare legs. From somewhere far away, Mom called us in for dinner. "In a minute!" Ella yelled, pressing her pink hands to her mouth to stifle a giggle. I closed my eyes, but she was still there.

I thought about buying the dress, wrapping it in silver and gold and sending it to her for Christmas. But I knew I never would. It would sit in a box under my bed, collecting dust with all of the other things I'd bought and never sent. All the things I wouldn't know if a girl with a sewn-up face would even want anymore.

I watched the air from the vent lift the hem of the fabric, my palm still pressed against the window. Besides, I wouldn't even know what size to get.

"Hey." Danny slid in next to me, hooking his fingers around my belt loop. He pulled out a small plastic bottle from inside his jacket. "Got a little booze. You in?"

I glanced back up at the dress. "Yeah, I'm in."

The two most important things I took with me when I left Amble, Ohio, two years ago were Ella's periwinkle bird and enough guilt to suffocate me. I left almost everything else behind.

The days following the incident were a blur. I know there was an unzipped suitcase that Mom shoved full of clothes I never liked, and hushed phone calls made by Dad. There was the beep, beep, beep of Ella's hospital monitors and the tangle of gauze, dotted with blood, wrapped tightly around her face. There were whispers of stitches and speech therapy and hysteria and a brand new start in New York. And there were screams. I'm pretty sure they were mine.

Mom's watery eyes floated into consciousness. "You have to go, Claire," her voice echoed. In my mind, she smoothed back the hair hanging over my eyes. "You're not coping."

"But I have to find the wolves," I'd told her, clutching a piece of paper in my fist.

Her mouth twisted into a frown. "No, honey, you don't." She paused, chewing on her lips as if she were chewing on her thoughts. "If anything, you have to get away from them."

I swallowed the puke at the back of my throat and opened my eyes. The same slip of paper lay across my chest now, its edges yellow and curling. The muted walls wobbled around me.

I tossed the paper to the side and rolled off my bed. My fingers slid through dust and darkness under it until they reached an empty liquor bottle. I shoved it into the corner with a *clink*. And then I grabbed the box.

It was an old Macy's box from a sweater Aunt Sharon had gotten me two years ago. It was the first thing she'd bought me after my parents shipped me off to New York. I ran my fingers over the red star, thinking it didn't really matter where the sweater had come from if it never fit anyway.

I opened the lid and peeled back the tissue paper. A bunch of shiny, useless things looked up at me. I picked up a beaded flower ring that I'd bought at a shop in SoHo. I tried to slip it on my finger, but it was too small. The tissue paper crinkled as it landed back in the box.

My hand brushed the cool metal of a compact nestled between a headband and a googly-eyed giraffe keychain. I scooped it into my palm and clicked it open.

"Holy hell," I breathed. I leaned in. My dark, sunken eyes stared back at me. I pulled at the clumps of mascara stuck to my lashes. I blinked, and the skin under my eyes fluttered. "You look like shit," I said, snapping the compact shut.

I threw myself back onto my bed and unfolded the slip of paper. Ella had pressed it into my palm just before I was forced to pack my bags and get out of Amble. I don't know why I did this, really; I always used Ella's loopy handwriting as punishment, especially after a night raiding Danny's parents' liquor cabinet. My eyes scanned the only sentence on the page. I made myself read it. Twice.

I ran my finger over the words. Every loop, each heart-dotted letter: it all made my stomach twist. But with what, I wasn't sure. Every time I looked at Ella's note, it killed me to think that her words were confined to paper and pink glitter pen, so much so that I thought more than once about taking Danny's matches to it. But bubbling under those letters was something else—desperation, maybe? This note was the only thing that told me the wolves were real.

Which meant I was exactly one slip of paper and four words away from insanity.

# *seven*

Aunt Sharon looked startlingly like Mom, especially when she was angry. They both had this thing where they pinched the bridge of their nose and kind of rocked in a chair, like if they kept moving, whatever had rattled them wouldn't be able to catch on.

But the thing was, in the two years I'd lived with her, I'd seen her do the whole rocking thing way more than I ever saw Mom do it back in Amble.

"Just go to school, Claire." She let go of her nose. Her skin was pink and raw between her eyebrows. "That's all I ask. That's all your parents ask. Just graduate. One more year."

I blinked up at her from over my cereal bowl. "I do go to school."

Aunt Sharon got up from the couch and shuffled through a stack of week-old mail. She pulled out a letter on cream-colored stationery with the Poller Academy seal bent up in the corner and tossed it at me. "You go to school when you feel like it."

This was very, very true.

"Claire, listen." She sighed, and her eyes got all soft and watery and I knew the worst of it was over. She put both hands on my shoulders just like I use to do to Ella when I really wanted her to listen to me. "You're so smart. And so creative! What happened to making dresses, going to design school at NYU? Don't you still want those things?" Her eyes scanned my face, and the wrinkles around them tightened. "What happened to that girl who used to *want* things?"

I stared into my cereal bowl and pushed around my Cheerios. I still did want things. They just weren't the same things anymore.

"I'm going to school today." I grabbed my bowl and shoved it under the faucet, hoping the running water would drown out her withering sighs. But it didn't matter if I couldn't hear her; I could feel her watching. I turned around and pressed a smile to my face. "I swear, I'm going. I want to drop by that fabric store on 37th after school, anyway."

This seemed to make her happy enough to believe me. A smile spread across her face and her shoulders relaxed. "Good girl. Do you need some money?" She reached for her purse and I didn't say no. The truth was, I never really needed money; Danny always bought our liquor and anything else he could get his hands on. But Aunt Sharon had more than enough money from her gallery art to pay for our apartment off the Hudson, not to mention half of my tuition to Poller. So what was the point in saying no?

"Thanks," I said as she handed me a fifty-dollar bill. "I can get a lot of fabric with this." I forced the muscles in my mouth to hitch up and show some teeth. I'd figured out that this was the kind of smile everyone liked, the one with teeth. It was the one Mom and Dad liked to see in the pictures Aunt Sharon emailed them, to show them that I was happy and safe and sane. I imagined Mom patting Dad on the back and saying, "See, she looks so happy. It was for the best to send her there, Mike." But really, if they looked a little closer, they'd see that smiles are just muscles and that they can easily be faked. It's what's behind the eyes that's real.

I started down the hallway toward the closet to grab my backpack, even though the only things inside of it were a pack of gum and a pen that had exploded inside the front pocket a week ago. I was halfway out the door when Aunt Sharon said, "Hey Claire?"

I poked my head back inside. "Yeah?"

"What kind of fabric are you going to get? I really need a new dress." She was smiling behind her sketchbook, but I knew better. She was still leery, still hoping that I'd prove her wrong and come back with an armful of fabric and an actual smile on my face.

"I'm thinking eyelet," I said, and I didn't even bother to fake smile. Then I stepped out the door and into Manhattan without looking back.

---

Sometimes I had to remind myself that Ella was not actually dead. That she was alive on the planet, breathing the same oxygen I was. And sometimes I thought that maybe she'd actually sucked in the exact same gasp of air I'd recycled a week or a month or a year before, and that maybe we still shared that one little breath. But I mostly just thought things like that after I'd had too much to drink.

I usually reminded myself that Ella wasn't dead on the subway ride from school to Midtown. The ride was thirteen minutes long, which turned out to be the perfect amount of time to think about someone, miss the way they used to be, and go tumbling down when you remembered that they could never be that way again.

And that it was all your fault.

I pinched my earlobe, trying to force down the anxiety building in my chest. My shrink had told me about that one—about squeezing your earlobes when "non-productive feelings" bubbled up. It was supposed to calm them.

It didn't work.

*Why did I let her go into the cornfield that night?*

*Why didn't I realize sooner that she hadn't sifted through my jewelry box?*

I bit my lip to try to force down the sadness clotting up my throat. Ella's purple eyelids fluttered open in my mind, her eyes empty and lost. She hadn't remembered the days following the incident either.

I was just starting to click into full-fledged panic mode when Willow nudged me and said, "What's your problem, Stare-Claire?"

Willow was always coming up with nicknames for me that rhyme. Stare-Claire was her favorite, though, especially when I was zoning out on the subway.

I nudged her back. "I don't have a problem. What's yours?"

"My problem is that it's—oh, approximately 1:33 p.m. on a Wednesday, there's an entire bag of free pot just waiting to be smoked, and we're still three minutes away."

I picked at a hangnail on my thumb until it started to bleed. "It's 1:33 p.m. on a Wednesday, and we should be in French right now."

"Touché, Mer-Claire. See? French like crazy." Willow laughed, and her lip ring wiggled in her mouth. "*Mer* means 'sea' in French, in case you missed too much class to pick that one up."

I rolled my eyes and watched out the dank windows as 54th's underground terminal chugged to a stop. The doors hissed and Willow practically smashed an old lady in the temple to beat her out the door.

I let Willow work her way through the crowd and skip up the stairs two at a time, not bothering to try and keep up. I wasn't stupid; she wasn't my friend because she just couldn't stay away from my optimism and sunshiny personality. She was my friend because Danny always had extra pot after a deal.

And I didn't even care.

It had gotten easy, the not caring thing. It was almost too easy to skip school and ditch all my dreams of the cutting counter at the fabric store. At least I still had the fifty dollars.

By the time I reached the top of the steps, Willow was

bouncing on the balls of her purple Converse shoes and flapping her hands. "Let's go, let's go, let's go."

"Chill," I said as I walked past her. "He's usually right here, up on this corner." I weaved through the bustling streets, leading Willow to her ultimate destination.

"There he is. Hey Danny!" Willow yelled, straight into the lens of a bald guy's video camera. "Hey, we're right here!"

Danny turned and gave us a half-smile before cocking his head toward a massive building across the street. "My parents are working. We'll go to my place."

He bolted across the street, his red hair glinting under the watery sun like a lit matchstick. When a taxi almost smashed into him, he just calmly held up the bag full of pot in his fist and thrust it toward the driver like some kind of brown paper stop sign. He was definitely a true New Yorker.

Willow was the same way. One time the traffic lining Times Square was so thick that it blanketed the streets in rubber and metal, tired business men on their way home from work. Willow just bounced between the cars, humming the *Harry Potter* theme song to herself, even when the traffic lights flicked to green.

I preferred to wait at crosswalks until the blinking man told me it was safe to go. And even then I still scrabbled across the street like a jittery little rodent scurrying from under a trash can lid.

I let out a breath as we stepped onto the sidewalk and a delivery truck bumbled behind us. Danny led us up the marble steps of his apartment building, past the doorman, and into a gilded elevator that had sparrows painted on its ceiling.

Every time I saw the sparrows, I imagined Ella saying, "Why are there birds in the elevator? Birds don't go in elevators, duh." And then suggesting rainbows or thunderclouds or fuzzy bear cubs or something else just as likely to *not* ever end up in an elevator.

Willow grabbed the bag out of Danny's hand the second he unlocked the door. "I've been waiting for this all day," she squealed. "Where's a lighter?"

I curled into the corner of a leather chair that was sidled up to a window almost as big as the wall. Willow and Danny sat in chairs on either side of me, passing the joint back and forth. They didn't even bother to ask me anymore. Danny had spent the better part of the fall semester trying to convince me that pot was ten million times better than alcohol, and that it was the best for making out and eating Cheetos and taking naps in a chair. And you didn't even feel sick in the morning. But it smelled like the family of skunks that had nested behind Dad's shed back in Amble, and it made them both look like they were one IQ point away from drooling on the carpet.

They finished that joint and started working on the next, and by the time they were done with that one, my eyes were taking longer to open after every blink. And instead of seeing darkness when I closed my eyes, I saw splotches of color, like bubbles filled with reds and yellows that popped when they reached my eyelashes.

"You feelin' it, Claire?" All of a sudden, Danny was standing over me, blowing smoke directly into my face. "You are now," he laughed. And the edges around his ears started to blur and wobble.

I shrugged. The whole thing should have made me mad, but it seemed like a lot of effort. And I didn't know what "feelin' it" felt like, but if it meant that the lights flickered on and off like dying stars and the walls didn't stand straight anymore, then I guessed I was.

Willow's eyes scanned my face, big and round like a cat's. "Stare-Claire is *totally* feelin' it." I blinked, and her eyes were gone and there was only the window.

Something flickered in the shadows of the kitchen.

Something so dark it was almost black.

And something big. Really, really big.

It was back.

I think if it could have, my heart would have crawled up into my head and pounded in my ears. But it was too tired, too high. It was reclining on the Lazy-Boy, eating leftover Cheetos. So it stayed.

But the wheels slowly churning in my mind told me to freak out anyway. It's just that my mouth wouldn't really move to scream like it should. I imagined a pile of drool pooling on the carpet, and I burst into a giggle instead. All of a sudden I was standing up and still kind of half-giggling, and my tongue felt thick and heavy in my mouth.

"Where're you goin'?" Danny asked. He was lying down with his mouth hanging open, and patterns and colors from the TV splashed across his teeth.

"Bathroom," I mumbled. And then I used the crooked walls to lead me there.

As soon as I stepped through the door, I couldn't unglue my eyes from this big silver dish, shaped like a seashell, which was tucked into the corner of the countertop. The string of bulbs that hung over the sink were reflected over and over again in the smooth crevices of the dish, like strings of tiny pearls laid out to dry. It was filled with a tangle of jewelry—necklaces and hooped earrings and rings that all glittered with fat stones.

And I giggled again as I poked my finger through Danny's mom's jewelry. Because it was kind of funny that pot made you notice every little thing and alcohol made you notice nothing at all.

Then my fingers were on two round yellow stones the color of melted butter. I held them in my hand, the posts sticking into my palm.

They stared at me.

They stared at me like big, jeweled wolf eyes.

Glued into the cover of a journal that came from the new stationery shop on Main.

And then they swiveled on their posts and blinked into my palm, blinked into the pink scar that still slithered across my skin. And I swore they were whispering, whispering so loud they were almost yelling: *You didn't keep Rae's promise. You didn't keep her secret. Now you have your own.*

My secret. I'd hugged it so tightly to my chest for so long that my heart had been almost crushed under its weight. But now, here, I was alone in this ridiculously ornate bathroom, and my secret wanted to be spoken. Just once. I could do it. No one would hear me.

I looked at my reflection in the mirror and tried to ignore the purple bags under my eyes. "The wolves are here, in this city," I whispered. And then I slapped my palm over my mouth, even though it was true. The wolves *were* in the city—the same ones that had sliced up Ella's face and most likely plucked Sarah Dunnard from her backyard like a spindly little weed.

Everyone said it wasn't possible, that the wolves couldn't be in Manhattan. But it also didn't seem possible that "rabid raccoons," as the *Amble Observer* had reported, were responsible for Ella's stitches. Whenever I asked Aunt Sharon, or even my shrink, why Dad had told the paper it was a raccoon even after the doctors said Ella's cuts were too "clean" to be caused by an animal, no one gave me an answer. There was no other evidence. No weapon. And when they asked Ella about the attack, she claimed the last thing she remembered that night was hugging me goodbye in the clearing.

But then she gave me the note, her secret and mine whispered onto lined paper. And then came the shadows, the tufts of gray flitting across alleys. They'd followed me. And they weren't going to leave me alone any time soon.

My hand curled into a fist and I imagined the note pressed against the yellow stones. My mind ticked back to the morning they found Ella in the cornfield. I swore I could still smell the moldy rugs at the police station, the way the interrogator they brought in from Toledo stared at me until I cracked open and spilled out everything I knew about Rae's plans.

I threw the jewels back into the seashell dish with a

clink and ran down the hall. My feet felt heavy and my eyes felt heavy and the scar in my palm burned like a fresh bite.

I ran through the living room and Willow and Danny's eyes followed, but they stayed silent and stoned. I threw open the door to the balcony and stepped into the dusty Manhattan skyline. I sucked in the city air, but it was the meal equivalent to popcorn: it never filled me up. It wasn't crisp and untouched like the air that pressed between the cornstalks.

I closed my eyes, but even from behind my eyelids, I knew they were still there.

The howls that bounced between skyscrapers.

Pricked ears peeking around the windowsills.

And the yellow eyes that always, always watched. That had watched every single day since I'd found Ella.

All of a sudden, there was a warm hand—a human hand—on my back and Danny was saying, "What's your problem?"

I opened an eye and looked at him. He stared back with a question mark in his eyes. He didn't see them. He didn't hear them. His arm slid around my shoulder so that his fingers grazed my chest. And then he was pressing his chapped lips against my neck and all I could think about was how it could be possible that he didn't hear the howls bellowing over the traffic.

I slid out from under his arm and said, "Do you hear that? You have to hear that, right?"

But he just kept staring, mouth still hanging open, eyes still half-lidded. For a second he looked like he might be listening, but he just pinched his lips together. "You're crazy."

Then his hand was on my wrist and he was pulling me inside. "Come on, let's go to my room."

"No." I jerked my wrist free. I was scared enough now that my heart jolted to life, and it pounded furiously in my chest. I grabbed my purse off the couch and headed for the door. "I have to go home, like right now."

Danny trailed behind me, and I thought he might offer to walk me home since I was shaking so bad. But he just leaned against the door and said, "Call me when you stop being such a freak." And then he slammed it in my face.

---

When I stepped into the sparrow-lined ceiling of the elevator, it looked different than it had an hour ago. The patches of clouds peeking out from behind wings looked dim and thirsty, like they'd just dumped out all of their rain and still wanted more. And the hot lights above made patterns of rainbows in the mirrors, and I couldn't help but think that if Ella were here, she would have been right: maybe thunderclouds and rainbows do belong on elevator ceilings.

Manhattan still looked the same: crisp and symmetrical and full of gray. Even the sky looked like it was full of cement. But somehow that was different, too: not because of what it was made of, but because of what I knew was hidden inside.

When I first moved to New York, I'd thought that concrete was safe. Way safer than open sky and cornfields. I'd thought that Ella's note only applied to Amble. But the wolves had found me here anyway: in paintings draped in Aunt

Sharon's gallery, stretched across book covers and T-shirts in tiny shops in SoHo, in my dreams. I couldn't get rid of the scratchy feeling in my stomach that told me they remembered me, that they hadn't forgotten. That Ella's almost-death was because I'd laughed at them and poked at them and told Rae they weren't real. They would let me forget about them for a little while—a week, maybe two—and then they'd send me the whisper of a shadow or the scream of a nightmare. They were watching me, warning me all the way from Amble, telling me to never come back or they'd take care of me.

My shrink called this a "phobia."

He said I had an irrational fear of something that couldn't exist. He'd pretty much spent the past two years trying to convince me that wolves who liked cherry-flavored things and periwinkle cloth didn't exist. He occasionally still pulled out the wolf migration maps and dog-eared *National Geographic*s to use as "proof" whenever my words skirted around what I'd seen in the city. I'd gotten used to smiling and agreeing that I'm crazy.

But I'm not.

Ella's note was proof of that.

A car horn blasted in my ear and I jumped to the other end of the crosswalk just before I got soaked by the drainage water pooling near the curb. I shook my head and cleared the fog. I was ten feet from the steps to the subway, and I'd managed to cross a busy street without even flinching.

And I still had the thirteen-minute ride home to think about Ella.

All I thought about on the ride was that Ella was a lot of things, but she wasn't a liar.

At least she wasn't a liar back then. I didn't know what she was now.

The subway hissed to a stop and suddenly everything snapped back to normal. The buildings weren't hunched over and the Christmas lights in the windows didn't flicker. It was like there'd been a storm that had bent the city to its will, and then it disappeared so that the traffic lights and the skyscrapers could heal. The storm left from behind my eyes, too, and everything inside was clear again.

I watched my boots as they clicked on the sidewalk. These heels were dangerous, and definitely needed supervision to avoid an awkward collision with the pavement. The grooves blurred as they swept under me, and I could tell by the broken, uneven panels that I was just a few feet from home.

I was about to step over a jagged crack down the middle of a slab of sidewalk when something dark and smeared caught my eye.

I stopped and stared at it for a long time before my brain registered what I was looking at.

A paw print.

A really big, bloody paw print staining the cement.

My hand shook as I reached down to touch the sidewalk. I brushed my finger over the print. A dash of red colored my skin.

I stood up and quickly glanced around, hoping that somebody, anybody, was around. But as if by magic, the street was empty. The first time I'd ever seen a deserted street in New

York. While I'd almost come to expect threatening howls and stalking shadows over the past two years, this was something else entirely.

There was nothing left to do but run.

I held my arms in front of me for balance as my heels echoed frantically around the empty street. I watched them fly under me on every other sidewalk panel: more paw prints.

I hadn't prayed since the last night I'd sat by Ella's bedside at the hospital, before I had to leave. But as the paw prints burned a trail in front of me, I said this prayer:

*Dear God,*

*If you still listen to me, I need you to make these paw prints go to the building across the street, or do a U-turn and head back toward the subway, or, better yet, disappear.*

I stopped in front of my apartment building, closed my eyes, and held my breath for as long as I could.

I opened my eyes.

And a trail of prints, still slick with blood, crawled into the cracked front door of my apartment building.

# *eight*

Rae had always said that the wolves started out as regular, boring wolves that stalked rabbits and crept across the Midwest in packs. But when they crossed the Michigan border into Ohio, something changed. The woods melted away to flat plains and jagged cornfields, and the wolves got hungry. Rae said they killed a girl in Elton, a toddler who'd slipped into a cornfield while her parents drank too many margaritas on their back deck. She had a cherry sucker in her mouth. The wolves never went back to being regular wolves as they traveled across the country, Rae said. Not after they got a taste of blood and skin and cherries.

Then, after the toddler, there was Sarah Dunnard, taken right from the cornfield edging her backyard. And then there was Ella.

And maybe next it would be me.

Ever since I'd left Amble and the wolves had started

to appear in New York, I'd been careful not to keep anything cherry-flavored on me. So I threaded my shaking fingers through my pockets, searching for a missed cough drop or lip balm. I gasped as I suddenly remembered Danny's cherry-laced lips, pressed against the skin beneath my chin.

I closed my eyes. They couldn't possibly have smelled that tiny burst of cherry through the sewers and smog of the city.

When I opened my eyes, there were two more paw prints on the steps leading to the elevator. And then a mess of blood pooled in the cracks between the tiles.

There was another one as soon as I stepped off the elevator, onto the twelfth floor.

And one smack in the middle of the flowered doormat, splattered against the lilies like an awkward, sticky rose.

I held my breath as I dug in my purse for my keys. My mind pinwheeled, searching for anything to make this not real.

"The door isn't open," I breathed as I shoved the key into the lock. "Claire, if there were wolves here, the door wouldn't be closed, okay? Stop being stupid."

I shoved open the door and slammed it closed behind me.

The hallway was drenched in shadows so thick I felt like I was choking on them. I snapped on the light and they disappeared, just like the paw prints did when I'd pushed them out into the evening.

Aunt Sharon still wasn't home.

She'd had an opening at the gallery tonight, which meant she'd be home hours later, tipsy on champagne and the strap of her dress drooping below her shoulder. I thought about calling Danny and inviting him over, just so I wouldn't have to be alone. But then I remembered the way he'd curled his nose up at me, like he'd just smelled something rotten, right before he slammed the door in my face. I couldn't do it.

But it didn't matter anyway. As I glanced around the flowered rugs (Aunt Sharon had a thing for flowers, probably because there weren't any in New York), I saw that there wasn't a single print. Even on the empty rectangle where a rug usually sat, the floor shone clean under the hall light.

My shoulders relaxed, and I think I took my first real breath since I'd left Danny's apartment.

I shoved my boots into the rack in the closet and slid across the floor in my socks like I was nine and back in Amble again. Ella and I used to have dance parties in our socks every Sunday morning before church. I'd surf across the hardwood in pink striped socks, and Ella would follow in slippers dotted with purple narwhals.

I laughed as I stepped into my room, remembering. Ella went through a phase when she was about eight where everything needed to have a narwhal on it. She'd begged Mom for narwhal slippers for Christmas, and when Mom obviously couldn't find them (because, really, who wants narwhal slippers), she special-ordered narwhal fabric online to make Ella slippers. When Ella figured out that narwhals were actually real, and not a cross between a unicorn and a beluga whale, you would have thought someone told her the sun wasn't going to come out again.

I flicked on my light and headed to my dresser. I dug

through the top drawer, which was full of tiny trinkets and old keys that used to belong to something important but I couldn't remember what.

There it was, crammed in the back corner: a small, worn shoebox filled with pieces of who Ella used to be. I opened it and dug through the beaded jewelry and lavender stationery until I found the crumpled photo I was looking for. Ella was positively beaming in her full-body narwhal costume, a glittery paper horn poking the ceiling fan above her. I let my eyes glance down at her throat, her mouth. Her pink lips that used to stretch across her teeth, the dimples in her cheeks that didn't exist anymore. The little depression on her neck that was ripped out.

The last time I saw Ella, before Mom and Dad shoved me out of Amble, she'd looked like a stitched-up doll of herself, jagged lines criss-crossing her lips. I never got to see the stitches come out and her twisted little mouth move again. I never got to hear her words again.

So I let myself look at who she was before, just for a second. I pressed my fingertip to her smile and smiled for her. Even with her lips hidden and shadowed, she was still magic.

I bent down to get my sweatpants when something caught my eye. I dropped onto my knees and poked my head under the bed.

Ella's periwinkle bird stared back at me, unblinking.

I cupped it in my hand like a fragile thing that might break if I breathed too hard. The tips of its wings were frayed, and little strings dangled around its body like party streamers.

And there was blood.

At least, I thought it was blood. I was pretty sure. A dark spot had soaked through the yarn, right through the chest. I pulled the bird between my fingers and the spot stretched wider, revealing a burgundy center that still looked fresh.

I threw it down and scrambled to my feet.

Something like a half-scream ripped through me.

I started to run out of my bedroom, a scream still stuck in my throat, but paused in the hallway. Images flicked through my head: the bloody bird staring up at me, followed by Ella's bloody face. My insides churned and black spots danced in front of my eyes, but I turned back into the room. I held my breath as I opened my dresser drawer and pulled out the shoebox. The note was still there, tucked carefully beneath the other pieces of Ella. I took it out and threw myself onto my bed.

I would have bolted, run through the streets of Manhattan screaming, but there was nowhere to go. Nowhere was safe from the wolves, not even my city or my room or my own head. I curled into a ball on the mattress, clutching Ella's note in my hand, praying the words would seep into my bloodstream and pump into my brain and remind me that this was real, that they were real. That I wasn't crazy.

I pressed my forehead into my knees and cried until my jeans were splotchy and cold, waiting for the words to sink in.

# *nine*

I would have stayed there, clutching that note, all week if Aunt Sharon hadn't stumbled into my bedroom.

She came home around dawn, giggly and hopped up on wine and pâté. I heard her humming around the kitchen for a while, searching for a bottle opener. After about three minutes of digging through drawers, the light from my room must have caught her eye, because she found me still curled up against the mattress, shaking.

"It could have been a raccoon," she said, rubbing my back. "Or anything, really. There are all sorts of animals running around those alleys."

Of course. I'd heard this before, back in Amble. The rabid raccoon as an excuse for Ella's attack. Apparently people liked to blame the unexplainable on raccoons.

I scooped up Ella's bird from the floor and poked my finger at the spot of blood on its heart. "Yeah, maybe."

Aunt Sharon stared at me for a second longer than was comfortable for either of us. She gave me that look most people give me when they find out about my story. Which is why no one in New York knew it except for her, and only because she had to.

"Oh honey, come here." She pulled me into a tight hug and I could smell the bitterness of red wine still on her breath. "I don't know what kind of paw prints you saw, but they don't belong to a wolf. You don't need to be scared."

"Okay." I stared at the scuffed tips of her heels as she kissed my forehead.

She let me go and rubbed my shoulder, still watching me with those sad eyes. "It's probably a good thing you have an appointment with Dr. Barges later today."

I groaned. I'd forgotten it was Thursday, and Thursdays were the days I went to my shrink's delicate glass office and spoke in words sharp enough to shatter it. Even after two years together, Dr. Barges had never quite grown on me.

I had to do something quick. The idea of spending another hour of my time staring at the back of Dr. Barges's clipboard made me shudder. "But it's my birthday!" I said. "Can't I go a different day, maybe sometime next week?"

Aunt Sharon stopped in the doorway and I knew she was thinking of how to force me into it. "I'll tell you what. I'll walk you down to his office and do some shopping while you're there. Then we can meet up at that fabric shop you like and have a big fancy dinner for your birthday, okay?" She smiled sweetly. "Sound like a good plan?"

Yeah, a great plan—for *her*. I couldn't find any loopholes. Totally trapped. "Fine," I mumbled, staring at the floor.

"Don't worry, Claire. I have big plans for your birthday." She winked. "Now why don't you try to get some sleep, honey. Okay?"

I waited until her bedroom door clicked shut before I nestled back down and pulled the blanket over my eyes. I didn't think I'd be able to sleep, but the corals and pinks of the sky and the puffy clouds that looked like they were lit from within comforted me. Because at least when everything was washed with daylight, I could see better. I could see them, if I could ever catch them.

———————

I figured Dr. Barges would sign me up for a crazy home if he could make a case for it.

At first it used to bother me that someone who was supposed to know the difference between crazy people and sane people thought I was a freak. But then I learned how to say just enough to keep him up at night wondering if I just had an overactive imagination or if I would sneak into his apartment in the middle of the night and cut his face off with a steak knife.

I liked to keep it this way.

When I entered his office, he was eating a tuna sandwich at his desk. I plopped into the chair in the farthest corner of the room. The whole place stunk.

"So, tell me about these paw prints," he said, wiping his mouth with his hand.

I swiveled the chair so that it faced the Manhattan skyline. "They were all over the sidewalk and the steps to the apartment. They were bloody." I closed my eyes.

"Mmm." I could almost see him nodding his head while he picked at the lettuce in his teeth. "That's very interesting. How did you feel when you saw them?"

I rolled my eyes. "Awesome."

I expected him to give me some crap about how I would never be able to get to the root of my "phobia" if I couldn't be serious with my emotions; the usual. I tilted my head back so that my face caught a watery ray of sun and waited. He shuffled his sandwich wrapper and sighed. Papers rustled, his desk chair groaned, and I knew without opening my eyes that he was standing behind me with my file between his fingertips.

"I think it would be a good idea to take a look at these again," he said, dropping the manila folder into my lap.

I flipped it open, even though I'd already seen what was tucked in here a million times: a map white-washed at the creases, a couple of photocopied articles smothered in yellow highlighter. This is what I liked to call my "mock file." This is what Dr. Barges tried to pass off as my patient history when I knew there had to be another file here somewhere, one that spelled out my crazy on three-ply copies.

I looked at them again while he watched me. The map was something that must have been pulled out of an ancient library book. To me, it looked like nothing more than paper filled with red arrows and dotted with faded trees. To Dr. Barges, it looked like the truth.

"Follow this arrow," he said, and his finger appeared on the map. It swooped through Canada and into the shaded splotches of Minnesota, Wisconsin, Michigan, and the northern tip of Ohio. "There is positively no wolf population in New York. So we have to come to the conclusion that the wolves you feel are following you simply cannot exist."

I nodded obediently. I used to fight back when Dr. Barges brought out the map. But then I figured out it was safer this way, with the pretending.

He shuffled the contents of the folder until an article stared up at me from my lap. "Why don't you re-read this again, just as a refresher." I bent my head over the page and watched the letters snap together, although they didn't make words in my head. They didn't need to; I already knew what they said.

"What does it say?" he asked softly.

Acid bubbled up in my stomach, along with guilt. I couldn't help but think that this is how Rae must have felt, back in Amble, when she preached everything she knew about the wolves, warning everyone to trash their cherry lip balm and periwinkle socks (although she refused to take her own advice and still hauled cherry vodka into the cornfields). No one ever listened to her. Just like Dr. Barges never listened to me, and insisted I recite passages from books *he'd* picked as proof.

"It says that wolves almost never attack humans unless

provoked." I swiveled my chair around so I didn't have to look at him.

That's exactly what the police thought, too. They said that if Ella's attack had been caused by wolves, or raccoons, or whatever, she must have teased them. But they hadn't seen the look on her face as she trudged out of the clearing that night. I don't even think she knew I'd seen it. Her eyes were polluted with fear, and her bottom lip trembled just before she pulled it between her teeth. There was no way Ella was going to stop on the way home to taunt some animal. She wanted to get through the cornfield and under her twinkle lights as fast as she could; that I knew for sure.

"Exactly," said Dr. Barges. "So, we have the map that tells us the wolves cannot exist here, and the articles that tell us it's not in a wolf's nature to attack humans. Think about those things and imagine another alternative to those paw prints you saw. What else could have created them?"

The acid rolled over into my throat, into my mouth, and it felt like poison eating away at my tongue. I stood up and my "file" fluttered to the carpet. "I don't know. Whatever you want me to believe. Dogs, okay? It was probably big dogs running around Manhattan. Or a raccoon." I tugged my purse over my shoulder. "I need to go meet my aunt."

Dr. Barges tilted his head and watched me for a second as he rubbed the skin on his neck. "You know, Claire, have you thought about taking a trip back home? Perhaps to visit your sister?"

I blinked into the sun, waiting for his words to melt into

my brain and make sense. But they just rolled around and stumbled all over each other. "Go visit my sister?" I repeated dumbly.

"Yes, go visit your sister. Back in Ohio. It's been a long time since you've been home to see your family."

I barely registered his words. Ella's pink cheeks and orange mittens bloomed in my thoughts. What would she say to me if I showed up at her door? More importantly, what *could* she say to me, and what would her words sound like coming from a semi-new face? The thought made me desperately sad and hopeful at the same time.

I chewed on my lip and stared out at the skyline. Little dots of snow clung along edges of the windows. It reminded me of how the first snowflakes used to line the weathervane outside our house, making the arrow blink white against the sky.

"Claire?"

"I don't want to go home," I said, turning to look at him.

Dr. Barges leaned back and rubbed the loose skin around his neck. He cleared his throat and said, "And why not?"

*Because there are wolves there that are waiting for me. Ella's note said they're waiting.*

In my mind, I was holding the crumpled slip of paper in my hand. Ella's loopy writing, the crooked letters that smiled up at me—those never changed, even though the sounds they made were trapped behind her stitches. Her perfect little hands had pressed the paper into my palm just before the nurse came to tell me visiting hours were over that day. Just before Mom pressed a train ticket to Grand Central Station into my other palm.

*They're watching you, Claire.*

# *ten*

My heart flip-flopped. Even after the riot of police and IV bags and morphine and bloody snow, Ella had still believed me. She knew that it was the wolves that did this, that they were real. She knew that they were waiting for me, too.

That's what I wanted to say, what I almost threw up like word vomit all over Dr. Barge's stupid plaid tie. But I'd learned a long time ago to pretend that the wolves weren't real, so I instead I said, "I just don't want to go home."

Dr. Barges cleared his throat again, which was seriously getting annoying. He did that whenever he wasn't sure how to take me and he needed extra time to think. Then he let out a soft puff of air. "Fears and phobias don't just go away on their own, Claire. You can't hide from them forever."

"I'm not hiding from anything," I said, standing. "I live in New York now. There's nothing I can get in Amble that I can't get here."

He took a sip from his water bottle and swished it around his mouth. I rolled my eyes again and turned toward the window. I swear, a conversation with Dr. Barges took ten times longer than it had to, with all of his stupid coughing and drinking and neck-rubbing.

Finally he swallowed and set his elbows on the table. "You and I both know this isn't about what you can purchase in New York City. I'm afraid that until you decide to face your phobia of the wolves, right at their origin, you'll feel haunted by your past forever." He stood and looped his fingers around his belt buckle. "Sometimes the unknown is far scarier than what's really there, when you're ready to look."

I glanced at the clock ticking on his desk. "Looks like I've taken up my fifty minutes." I shoved on my coat and grabbed Ella's old polka-dot scarf, wrapping it loosely around my neck. "See you next week."

I was almost out the door when I heard him cough again, and I knew it was coming. "Hey Claire," he said, and I slowed but didn't turn around. "Just think about it, okay?"

"Will do," I said, and I was out the door.

———

Not long after I arrived in New York, I realized that Amble was made of just as much concrete as Manhattan, maybe even more. Even though its cornfields and dirt roads swayed with the wind and softened with the rain, everyone who lived there was hardened with cement on the inside. You went to church every Sunday even if you didn't believe in God. You blamed disappearances and stitched-up faces on rabid raccoons. You believed, or you didn't. Most of the time you didn't.

Which was why people like Rae ended up running away as many times as it took to break free; they weren't crammed with enough cement, they weren't quite heavy enough to stay put. They still believed in stars and wolves and that magic or something like it existed. And if they'd stayed, Amble would have punished them for it.

It was for this reason that Dr. Barges's little lesson in logic melted off me as soon as I stepped onto the street. Because the thing about evidence is, you can find it anywhere. For every stupid migration map, there was one of Rae's stories. For every scientific journal article, there was the flash of gray in the cornfields, the snap of a stalk, or Sarah Dunnard's blood staining the cornstalks by Lark Lake after her disappearance. And then there was Ella's note:

*They're watching you, Claire.*

I glanced between the buildings as I turned onto 37th. I called Danny's cell phone four times before I reached the fabric store. And then I sent him my fifteenth text. He never answered.

I'd hoped that after his brain started working again and his eyes defogged, he'd text and tell me that he was sorry. And then he'd tell me to come over because his parents weren't home and he had a birthday present for me. But he must have remembered his words: *Call me when you stop being such a freak.* And he must have thought that twenty-four hours wasn't long enough to cure the freak out of me, because he didn't even bother with a "happy birthday" text back.

A blast of something cinnamon slapped me in the face as I stepped into the shop. I instantly caught Aunt Sharon's bleached hair bobbing through the reams of green and blue chiffon.

"Hey," I breathed, trying to force the cold air out of my lungs. "What are you looking at?"

"Hi, honey! How was your session with Dr. Barges?" She wrapped me up in a tight hug, like if she didn't smash me to her peacoat I would run away before she could catch me.

I pulled the ends of her hair from my face and said, "It was fine. He's not worried about me."

She let me go and tucked a strand of hair behind my ear. No matter what I told her, she always had that sad look in her eyes. I think I could have told her I'd won the New York State lottery and was giving her half of it, and she'd *still* look like that.

"Really, I'm fine," I said, smiling. The motion felt weird around my teeth. "Starving."

Aunt Sharon's face broke into a real smile, the kind that people use freely until something almost destroys them. Then they reserve those smiles for something fantastic enough to make the muscles in their mouth twitch. "It's too early for dinner, so why don't we hit up this shop first. Dinner's at Lombardi's at seven."

I scrunched my nose. "That's, like, two hours from now."

Aunt Sharon shrugged. "It was the only time open. We'll get you one of those pretzels to tide you over!" She wrapped her arm my shoulder. "Come on, let's go look at the eyelet. That's what you were hoping to get yesterday, right?"

"Yep." I felt the heat creeping into my neck and ears. I'd told Aunt Sharon that I didn't come home with a ream of eyelet last night because the shop was out of the color I wanted. I always felt bad when I lied, but somehow I kept doing it anyway; lies just dribbled out of my mouth because they felt like it.

A tinny sound wafted from Aunt Sharon's oversized purse, and she swore under her breath as she raked through the dozens of crumpled receipts to find her phone. "Damn it, where is that—hello?" she answered, her voice breathless. She stepped away from me and the cramped aisles to take the call.

When she disappeared around the corner, I moved toward the back of the store. This was where the eyelet stayed hidden, mostly because it was used for table cloths and fancy napkins that you don't have to throw away. But sometimes it was used for delicate dresses for girls with pink cheeks.

Tears pricked the corners of my eyes as I stared at a row of it. I wrapped a tuft of white eyelet in my fingers and pressed my thumb into the delicate holes. In my mind, I saw myself stitching a hem and snipping triangles in the fabric until they resembled sleeves.

I threw down my handful of fabric and turned away.

*Why am I always so hellbent on torturing myself?*

Why did I want to make a dress for a girl who probably wouldn't even take it from me?

As if on cue, "Hark the Herald Angels Sing" floated down on my shoulders like soft snow. I leaned my head back, the eyelet pressed into my hair, and laughed. While there was very little I remembered from the days following the incident, one image constantly flicked across my eyelids: Ella, a bloody snow angel in the cornfield, staring up at the sky, like if something hadn't clipped her wings she would have returned home.

And then: singing, soft and shaky. For a long time I hadn't realized it was me, my voice floating in the space between life and darkness.

And then: a feeling like my own blood was draining from my body, pooling with Ella's in the clumps of snow. But now I know that it was hope, not blood, leaking from me. I never did get it back.

And then: a hand on my shoulder, hurried syllables, a pair of eyes the color of a cloudy morning.

And then: screaming.

I wasn't crazy. I just loved Ella. And I was ready to do anything to keep my promise, to keep her safe from the things she feared the most.

She gave me that note for a reason.

"Claire?" Aunt Sharon turned the corner and caught me with my eyes closed against the eyelet. When I looked at her, her eyes were watery and the lines around her mouth were still tight.

I blinked. "What is it?" I whispered, but the sinking feeling in my chest told me I already knew

"I just..." she started, pinching the bridge of her nose. The details around her were starting to come into focus. For the first time, I saw her fingers shake as they clutched her cell phone. And the way she'd shoved her wallet back into her purse, like she wouldn't have time to use it.

"What's wrong?" I asked. I started chewing on my lip, because something prickly at the back of my brain was already whispering her name, and my heartbeat began to throb in my ears.

Aunt Sharon closed her eyes and breathed, like what she was about to say was so heavy she had to take a second to pull together the strength to say it. I waited, but I already knew. Sisters just know.

"Claire, I don't know how you're going to take this, so I think it's best if we just take a cab back home and talk." She reached for my hand. "I don't have all the details yet, but it's about Ella."

# *eleven*

I hadn't thought about Rae Buchanan in more than five second spurts since I'd left Amble, but she was all I thought about as Aunt Sharon's muffled voice droned through her bedroom door.

One time, when Rae and I were eleven and ten, and Ella was seven, we went out into the cornfield to have a tea party. Ella had wanted to have one so badly she'd jumped on my bed every morning for a week, begging me to pack up the plastic tea set with her and take it into the field. But she said it wasn't really a party unless there were at least three people there—three *girls*—and so I convinced Rae to come too.

As we set up the plastic cups and stale banana muffins, Rae told me for the first time that she was leaving Amble as soon as she could. I remember ice dripping into my stomach when she told me, and the feeling of cold running under my skin. But it wasn't because Rae said she was leaving; it was the way Ella looked when she said it. Her eyes grew as round as moons, but she wasn't scared. There was something else prickling up inside of her—*interest*. She didn't tell Rae she shouldn't go, or that she was stupid for leaving, like I did. I remembered her just asking a lot of questions: *Why would you leave? How are you going to leave? When?*

Rae was my best friend, but I knew I could learn to live without her. I think there was a part of me that expected all along that Rae would eventually leave me. She always reminded me of a caged animal—pacing, staring out between the bars with wide eyes. Waiting until someone left the door ajar, even for a second.

Ella, however, I thought would stay.

And at first, it seemed like she would. She was the golden child of Amble, the dimple-faced girl filled with laughter and light. Ella always got her choice of part in church plays (which was usually some oddball, obscure part like the angel or townsperson #2 in *Joseph and the Amazing Technicolor Dreamcoat*). She played soccer and decorated her ceiling with stars and lightning bolts, and secretly painted *Ella lives here* on a bench in town with orange nail polish. She had it all in Amble. Why would she ever leave?

So when Aunt Sharon eventually came out of her room, her face raw and swollen, I couldn't help but think that whatever had happened to Ella wasn't because she'd wanted it to.

"Claire, sit down." Aunt Sharon patted the couch next to her. "I need to tell you some bad news."

I sat and I waited.

"It's about Ella."

I nodded, trying to swallow down the impatience bubbling in my chest. We'd been over this.

Aunt Sharon took a deep breath and said, "She's missing."

I waited.

And I felt nothing.

But it wasn't the same kind of nothing I'd felt when I found Ella half-dead in the cornfield two years ago. It wasn't the kind of nothing that consumed me so that I could stare at bloody rip across her face and still be able to sing her Christmas carols.

This nothing felt empty.

I assumed that part of the emptiness was because I already knew that something terrible had happened to her. But I figured the rest of it was because I'd expected it all along, since the day I left Amble.

I'd taunted the wolves my whole life, yelled into the stalks that they weren't real. I'd teased them that night, splashing the snow with cherry vodka and dangling periwinkle yarn into the star-splattered sky.

The wolves were still after me. They wouldn't stop hunting until they killed me.

*They're watching you, Claire.*

They'd waited as long as they could, watching for my hair to get tangled in corn leaves so they could tear out my throat when I wasn't paying attention. They'd followed me in the shadows of the city and painted the streets red with their bloody paws. But when I left Amble, I'd never come back.

So they took her as ransom.

They wanted me back in Amble.

"Claire!" A finger snapped in front of my face. "Claire, are you going to pass out?" Aunt Sharon started to press the buttons on her cell phone, probably to call an ambulance or something overdramatic like that.

"I'm fine, I'm fine." I pulled the phone out of her hand. "I'm not going to pass out, I swear."

Aunt Sharon's shoulders slumped and she pressed her hands into her face. "That poor, poor girl. After everything that happened before, now this." She choked back a sob. "What are Mike and Rosie going to do? What are we going to do?"

"I don't know," I said, and I stood up. But that wasn't the truth. "I'm going to my room." That *was* the truth. I stepped over Aunt Sharon's purse and headed toward the hallway.

Before I turned the knob, I'd made up my mind.

I had no choice.

It was me or Ella, and I'd already let them hurt Ella once. Now it was my turn.

# twelve

It's a funny thing, when you decide it's okay to die. When Mom and Dad sent me to New York, they'd thought I'd wanted to die then, that they'd find me hanging from my doorframe strung up by Ella's blinking rainbow lights. But they were wrong.

I wanted to find the wolves.

I wanted them to know I didn't care if they still watched me.

I wanted to watch her learn to talk again, watch her half-eaten lips learn to make sounds again.

I didn't want to die then.

And I still didn't. But that itchy feeling prickling at the back of my mind always told me that I'd have to face them one day. The wolves were waiting, and they didn't care if I wanted to live.

The train was only five miles from my exit, about a half

an hour outside of Amble. I hadn't stopped chewing my lip since Philadelphia, and now I had a bloody crater pooling there.

Hysteria bubbled up in me and I started to giggle. Even when I pressed my hand over my mouth, I couldn't muffle the manic laughter coming out of my throat. The guy next to me shifted his *Time* magazine so there was a wall of glossy pictures between us.

The two most important things I took with me when I left Amble—Ella's periwinkle bird and a mountain of guilt—I took with me when I went back.

I couldn't stop laughing about that.

The train lurched to a stop, metal screeching against steel until the seat beneath me stopped rumbling.

Outside the sign said, *Welcome to Elton, Ohio.*

I was home. Or, close to somewhere that used to be home.

I sucked on my lip and stared out the window.

There they were, my parents.

A part of me hadn't expected them to show, especially not Dad. Why would they? We'd barely spoken over the past two years, except for the obligatory birthday phone call (which didn't happen that year because of Ella's disappearance) and an occasional silly card in the mail from Mom, signed with just X's and O's along the bottom.

And yet they were here, standing in the snow with red ears and windswept hair, looking extremely three-dimensional.

I grabbed my backpack and stepped off the train, holding my breath the whole way down the steps.

"Claire," Mom breathed. She stared at me with the same round eyes she'd passed on to Ella. Her mouth hung limp against her face, and I couldn't tell if she was happy to see me or if she was going to turn on her heel and walk back to the car without another word.

"Good to see you, Claire," Dad interrupted. He stepped in between Mom and me like I was some kind of rabid animal that would rip her heart out and patted me awkwardly on the shoulder. "Glad you could come stay with us for a while."

I pressed a smile to my face, the one with the teeth that they liked. But inside, Dad's words made me cringed: *Glad you could come stay with us for a while?* What was I, one of Dad's second cousins from Alabama? I was his *other* daughter, the one he sent away when he couldn't bear to look at her anymore. I almost reminded him of that, right there in the middle of the train station five seconds after our first physical contact in two years. But I caught the look on nestled between the lines in Mom's face, and I couldn't.

She looked ... *happy.*

Like she might actually want to touch me.

She gently pushed Dad's arm out of the way and wrapped her arms around me, her fingers twisting through the waves in my hair. I closed my eyes and let myself relax into her coat. She still smelled the same: like lavender face soap and freshly baked biscuits, even when she hadn't been cooking. "I'm so glad to see you," she breathed into my hair. "We've missed you so much."

I blinked quickly and pulled myself away from her. I couldn't cry, not about this. This was a good thing, a nice thing; why waste tears on something that was supposed to make you feel good?

But everything that made me feel good also made me ache inside, like a muscle I hadn't used for way too long. I didn't think I knew what it was like to be happy anymore without hurting at the same time.

"It's cold out here," Dad said. He had a tight smile on his face that must have mirrored mine, and I wondered how long it had been since he'd really smiled too. He patted Mom's shoulder. "Let's go back to the house."

Even the way he said "the house" made my stomach hitch. It wasn't *our* house, not a house for all of us. It was their house, and I was just a visitor in for the holidays. I'd even packed my own pillow and blanket because I wasn't sure if my bed was still there anymore.

I followed them through the swirling snow and into the parking lot. I blinked away the white congealing in the corners of my eyes as I searched for the old Taurus. But we made a quick right at the only Taurus in the lot and headed for a smoky blue Explorer.

"You got a new car," I said as I pulled myself inside and slid across the leather seats.

Dad's eyes caught mine in the mirror. "We needed a more reliable vehicle for the winter, to get Ella to her speech therapy appointments and such." His eyes flicked away from mine and I caught Mom shooting him a death-stare.

Her face softened as she turned in her seat. "That Taurus

was on its last legs anyway, sweetie." She smiled. "Don't worry about it."

"I'm not," I said, staring out the window. "I'm just tired."

"Why don't you go ahead and relax? You've had such a long trip." She turned around, and I caught her chewing on her lip in the side mirror.

I didn't think I'd be able to sleep, not in this car with these people who said they were my parents but felt more like aliens posing as them. But the hum of the engine and the heat creeping through the car pushed me into sleep, into dreams that I wasn't ready to have just yet.

At home, I sat in my bedroom for a long, long time.

Longer than they probably thought was normal, considering I said I'd be down for dinner in ten minutes.

But I couldn't get over how everything looked exactly the same, but so different at the same time.

Like the walls. I remembered putting up the wallpaper behind my bed a month before I left. It took Mom and me half a day just to do one wall because glue bubbles kept creeping up under the seams. After I left, I'd missed that wallpaper because I used to trace the flower petals along the headboard until I fell asleep. But now it just looked stupid, babyish.

Then there was everything else that seemed so much smaller.

There was a tiny pinprick of light that was still eye level with my bed. Ella had found an industrial-sized nail at a building site in town and brought it home. We'd used a hammer and a pair of needle-nosed pliers to force a tiny hole the wall. I used to stare into the hole and watch Ella whenever she was sleep talking, and I think she watched me at other times. Because she always seemed to bring up stuff that she shouldn't really know. As I stared into that hole now, all I could see was a tiny speck of a yellow wall. I swore it was bigger before.

After an hour of shifting through dresser drawers and staring at the ceiling, I knew it was time. I couldn't avoid them forever, at least not if I planned to find Ella.

The whole kitchen smelled the way the stove smelled after the burner had been left on too long, kind of like leftover food and burnt metal. Mom and Dad sat at the breakfast bar, whispering, while the sound of the churning coffee pot muffled their words.

"Claire!" Mom stood, and her coffee splattered across the counter. "I wasn't expecting you."

I glanced around the cleared countertops and the chugging dishwasher. "Did you guys already eat dinner?"

"We weren't sure you were ready to come down yet," Dad said into his mug.

"But I made a plate for you," Mom added quickly, a tight smile wrapped around her teeth. A tight, fake smile.

I nodded and slid onto the empty stool across the breakfast bar from them. Mom bustled around the kitchen, opening drawers and making the microwave beep until a plate of steaming lasagna sat in front of me.

She tapped her nails on the counter as she scooted onto the stool next to Dad. She pressed her mouth into a thin line. They both watched as I picked up a fork and pushed the cheese around my plate.

"You still like lasagna, right?" Dad asked, his eyebrow hitching. "Your mother made it just for you."

I shoved a glob of cheese in my mouth. "I'm a vegetarian," I said through open-mouthed bites.

"Oh," Mom said, her eyes flicking to the plate. "Oh."

I set down the fork and folded my arms across my chest. "I'm not really hungry. But thanks anyway."

Mom started to move toward my plate, probably to have an excuse to get away from me, and Dad shifted in his seat and traced an invisible pattern on the granite with his finger.

The clock ticked in the corner. How long had I been down here, enduring this special form of torture? I tilted my head past the fridge to watch the seconds shed their skin as the clock hands jerked forward. Four minutes. Four freaking minutes.

My eyes trailed over the details of the kitchen. It was almost like being in a time warp; nothing had really changed. There was the same chip in the counter where Ella had slammed the rim of a stubborn pickle jar, the same butter-yellow wallpaper, only now a little more faded. Even the same family photo—taken just two weeks before I left—hanging in its tarnished frame. The whole house was the same, except for the family inside it.

I narrowed my eyes at the wallpaper beneath the clock. "When did that happen?"

The spoon Mom was washing clanged as it hit the edge of the sink. "When did what happen?" she said. Her voice was tight, like her throat was forcing the words to retreat back into her thoughts.

I stared at the back of her head as she continued to furiously scrub the spoon. Dad still sat at the counter, tracing his finger around the rim of his mug. My stomach hitched. Something wasn't right. I watched as they both fumbled with porcelain and silverware, but neither of them dared to even look at the charred wallpaper, the imprint of a flame licking the edges of the kitchen floor. Something had clearly caught on fire.

"When did *that* happen?" I asked again. I pushed my stool out from under the counter and went to stand next to the spot, just for good measure. Just so they couldn't ignore it—me—any longer.

Dad sighed. "I don't know when exactly, Claire. It was months ago. It's not as big of a deal as you're making it out to be." He plastered a no-teeth smile to his lips. "Just some vandals. It started on the outside of the house and it burned up a little of the drywall, wallpaper. That's all."

"Then why didn't you fix it?" I asked as I knelt down beneath the clock. I pressed my fingers into the wall, and was surprised when they sank into the spot. It felt almost like stepping into half-melted snow, all mushy and unstable. When I pushed farther, a sliver of the wallpaper split at the seam, and I could see just how far the damage stretched.

"Oh," Mom said, waving her hand dismissively from the sink, "I just need to pick out some new wallpaper, that's all. You know how indecisive I am about that sort of thing."

I pressed my lips together as I ran my thumb over the wallpaper. In all the years I'd lived in Amble, no one had dared to approach our house with so much as a roll of toilet paper, let alone a match. These weren't vandals; they were arsonists. Someone must have been furious enough, and bold enough, to snap a match to life next to the police chief's house.

I wondered if it was because of me.

Because of the reputation I'd left behind, like a bad taste in Amble's squeaky-clean mouth. I was the one who'd let her twelve-year-old sister walk home by herself because I was too drunk on alcohol and possibility to go with her. I was irresponsible, and when I'd been forced to leave town, I was irrational and delusional. I was the cavity, rotting away the foundation that Amble was built on: *strange things like this just don't happen here.*

They're just stories. You don't blame disappearances and stitches and blood-speckled cornstalks on stories.

Did they punish my family for my stories?

I snapped my head around to look at Dad. "Don't you have some kind of hidden camera you have access to at the station? Couldn't you have used that, or something, to catch them?" I narrowed my eyes at him. "You're not really the type to let people get away with something like this."

"Claire," Mom said softly. She slipped onto a stool across from Dad and placed a pink, soapy hand on top of his.

Dad glanced up at her and patted her hand. "It's okay." He turned toward me and sighed. "I don't have access to that type of equipment anymore, at least not without asking for consent."

"Consent?" I scrunched my nose. "Who would you possibly need to get consent from?"

Dad swallowed and stared at his hands for what seemed

like forever. Finally, he said, "From Seth. I'm not the chief anymore. It's been over a year." He turned his back to me and headed for the coffee pot, signaling that this was all he was going to say about it.

My heart slid into my stomach. I watched his shoulders slump on his way across the kitchen. He looked like he was carrying a million invisible pounds. And really, he was. Only the weight wasn't his to carry.

It was mine.

I could only imagine what they'd said about me, about him, when I left. I wondered if it was why he wasn't chief. Did Amble demote him for spawning me? Or did he choose it? To take care of Ella after the attack?

Dad dropped his spoon into the sink and started toward the staircase with his mug. Mom began to bustle around the kitchen, flicking off light switches. Panic began to thread its way through me; my opportunity was slipping away. For now, it didn't matter why Dad wasn't the chief anymore. I'd figure that out later. The important thing was that he'd been chief when they found Ella that day, two years ago. I had to muster up the guts to ask, or else this entire trip back to Amble would be nothing more than a waste of time and train ticket.

"You both know why I'm here," I said, taking a deep breath. "I need you to tell me what you know about Ella's disappearance."

When they didn't say anything, I started toward the hallway, my stomach clenching with hunger. Just as I stepped around her, Mom said, "Claire, wait. Just wait." She closed her eyes and pressed her hand to her chest, and for a second

I thought she'd stopped to pray. But her eyes fluttered open and she said, "Sit down. We'll talk."

I sat. Mom took another heavy breath and Dad began to trudge back to the kitchen, staring into his mug the whole time, like if he looked hard enough he'd find a one-way ticket back to New York in my name. I waited. This wasn't going to be a conversation that I started; I needed *them* to tell me. I needed them to want to tell me.

After a long minute, Mom reached across the counter and took my hand in hers. "Claire," she said, "I want you to understand something. Nothing dragged your sister away." She blinked quickly, staring at a spot on the wall behind me. "Nothing with four legs, anyway."

I tugged my hand free and wiped it on my jeans. "You can say the word, Mom. I won't go all psycho on you and blow up the house."

Dad looked up from his mug for the first time since I'd slid onto the stool. He locked his eyes on mine, a tactic he'd taught Ella and me a long time ago; the police always burned a hole in you with their eyes when they were trying to scare you.

"Wolves," he said, his voice cracking on the word. "There are no wolves, Claire."

I stared back at him and lifted my chin. I wanted him to know that I wasn't afraid of him, of what he thought about me and my "imaginary" wolves.

Dad stood up like a grizzly bear lumbering to its feet, pressing his knuckles into the countertop until they were as white as the bone beneath his skin. He lifted an eyebrow.

"Really? You think wolves dragged your sister away? Animals don't go around kidnapping people, and that's a fact." He spit out the word "fact" almost like he couldn't get it off his tongue fast enough.

I sucked in my lip. He was right. At least, under normal circumstances, wolves and bears and hungry-looking dogs didn't execute kidnappings. But these weren't regular wolves, and these certainly weren't regular circumstances.

Still, I broke my gaze from his, conceding. Even I knew how crazy it sounded to argue for the existence of cherry-loving wolves. And if I was going to figure this out, I needed to be as boring and bland as Aunt Sharon's cooking attempts.

"So, then, tell me what you do know," I said.

Dad grasped the edge of the counter and gritted his teeth. "One day she was here, and the next day she was gone. No note, nothing. The department is still searching for her, but it's damn near impossible to find a missing person if I can't give them a motive. And I don't think I can." Dad sighed heavily. "I thought ... she was adjusting, after the incident. I thought she was happy again."

I clutched at my heart. *She was happy.*

*Again.*

But how long after the accident had she been *unhappy*?

"She *was* happy here," Mom insisted, reaching to grab Dad's fingers. They both seemed to melt into their stools like lumps of snow thawing in April.

Something in my heart pinged and I couldn't help but feel sorry for them, even though they'd sent me away. Because they already had one daughter they thought was crazy, and now their prettier, saner daughter was missing. But I also knew that talking to them was only going to get me so far.

I needed to know the truth about what had happened to Ella.

If I wanted to find her, I was going to have to do it alone.

I told them I was tired and kissed them good night. And then I went to my room to start planning.

# *thirteen*

Where do you begin looking for a girl made of scars and stardust?

This was the question I asked myself as I wrapped a scarf from the hall closet around my neck the next morning.

When I opened the door, it looked like all of the clouds that looped over Ohio had been body-slammed into the earth, where they'd shattered like glass. Everything was coated in a fine layer of filmy white, and tufts of fog wafted between the broken cornstalks.

I stepped out in the new layer of snow and immediately walked to the back of the house. Since the damage caused by the fire had bled into the bowels of the interior, I knew it had been more than just a surface stain. But exactly how much damage was done, and how much my parents had covered up, I didn't know. I needed to know.

I ran my hand over the aluminum siding. Still the color

of an overripe tomato, like it had always been. But when I reached the corner of the house that contained the kitchen, the paint felt gritty. Fresh.

I pressed both hands over the area, trying to gauge how much of the house had been eaten away by the fire. I stretched my arms over my head. The new paint kept going, higher than my fingertips could reach. My mouth suddenly felt like it had been stuffed with cotton balls. What had they been doing that day, the day Amble decided to light up the police chief's house? Had Ella been right here, in the kitchen, knitting periwinkle birds and eating peanut butter and banana sandwiches when she smelled smoke?

My fingers finally found the edge of the new paint, wrapped around the other side of the house. They also found the whisper of a word there, a dash of spray paint that had wiggled its way through the fresh paint like a memory that refused to stay quiet.

I touched the edge of the letter. It could be any letter with a curve, really. There wasn't enough of the paint showing to tell.

That inch of spray paint gnawed at me. There was a secret hidden under there, one that mattered to me even though I didn't exactly know why. I glanced around the side of the house. Dad's old, beat-up shed still loomed over the edge of the cornfield. I smiled to myself; Mom had been nagging Dad to chop that thing down and use it as firewood for years. But Dad insisted it stay, said he couldn't bear to demolish his tiny space shoved full of rusted rifles and car parts and dented buckets of oil and paint.

*Paint.*

The thought bloomed in my mind and I rushed toward the shed, kicking up snow behind me. If there was paint in the shed, there was probably some kind of paint thinner or tool I could use to chip away the secret on the siding. I tugged at the door, and but it didn't budge. It was only then I noticed a small padlock looped between the handles.

I scrunched my nose. Dad never used to lock the shed.

I glanced back at the house. Uncovering this particular secret would have to wait.

The wind lashed at my face, warning me to get moving before it dumped another layer of snow over the dirt roads and trapped me inside the house. I had no idea where to begin, so I started walking toward town, mostly because I had nowhere else to go.

One of the perks of living in New York City is that you don't need a driver's license. One of the perks of living in a place like Amble is that you do need one, so you can take yourself places you told your parents you wouldn't go.

Now I was taking myself as far as the two-mile walk into town, which is exactly where I told Mom and Dad I was going.

I was totally going to need a license if I intended to do some investigating.

I let myself brush through the stalks with gloved fingers as I trekked down the dirt path leading to Grandon Road. I thought I would panic when the Explorer turned down the path and sliced between the fields on either side. But I didn't.

Because dead corn was just dead corn in the daylight.

It was night that you had to watch out for.

I turned onto Grandon, my fingers still breaking off the brittle leaves. They floated behind me like lost balloons bobbing in the wind.

I imagined a gray wolf with wiry fur staring at me from between the stalks. This time, though, I didn't feel afraid. I *wanted* them to come; I needed them. If they had Ella, I needed them here so I could make them give her back.

No wolves came, and my heart sank.

I squinted through the stalks, waiting. Nothing. I'd come all the way from New York to find them after they'd hunted me there, and now there wasn't a single wolf waiting in Amble.

They weren't going to make this easy.

Just about when I thought my fingers were going to fall off and rattle around inside my gloves like marbles in a bag, the sign for Main Street poked through the white-washed sky. I sighed in relief and jogged the rest of the way there, even in my good boots.

The street was mostly empty, just a long strip of cracked pavement and sagging Christmas wreaths. Just like with a lot of things here, I'd always thought it was bigger.

I passed a cluster of shops that hadn't been here before: a diner with red plastic booths and a neon sign that blinked *World's Best Cherry Pie*; the stationery shop that had opened just before I left, the one where Grant had bought my yellow-eyed wolf diary; a bead shop with a purple awning.

I pressed my nose against the glass and looked inside the bead shop. Rows and rows of delicate silvers and brilliant oranges lined the walls on one side, and blue and greens and reds lined the other. Ella used to love this place. This was probably where I needed to start, somewhere filled with color and shiny things that would catch her eye like a kitten chasing sparkly wrapping paper.

I started to open the door when, as if on cue, the door of the diner across the street opened with a jingle and a flood of warm, sugary cherries blasted me in the face. It smelled exactly like Ella's Cherry Blast body spray. My stomach hitched with hunger and nausea at the same time. I hadn't eaten since those two bites of lasagna last night, and I was starving. But even so, I would not eat the World's Best Cherry Pie.

I shut the door before the shop owner could greet me and ran across the empty road without looking twice. So, so much easier than crossing 45th in Manhattan.

The cherry smell smacked me across the face again when I opened the door, and my stomach churned.

The diner was mostly empty, except for a guy about my age with cropped dark hair sitting at the bar area. I wanted to sit anywhere else but next to him, even in the booth next to the bathroom. Not because I had an aversion to guys or anything, but because I wasn't sure I wanted to talk to anyone in Amble just yet.

"Right here, hon," said a waitress with ratty hair, cocking her head at the counter. "We're only seating at the bar for lunch today."

I pulled myself onto the stool and reached for a menu. The cover felt slippery. It was like trying to hold on to a soapy glass. I scrunched up my nose as I flipped through the pages.

"What're you having today?" the waitress asked. Her ratty hair was the chemical color of strawberry soda.

"Um," I said, flipping through the menu.

"Our pie's on special. Best in the state." She tapped her nails against the counter.

Just thinking of the cherry pie made me shudder. "I'll just have a cheese omelette." The creases in the menu crinkled when I snapped it shut. "Thanks."

"Sure thing," she said, heading to the back counter to grab a still-gurgling pot of coffee. She filled the empty mug next to me, the one that belonged to the guy squinting into his newspaper. "There you go, Grant. Refill's on the house." She winked, but he just mumbled "Thanks, Kate" from between the lines of the local news section.

My eyes flicked down to the table and the tingly feeling of a fierce blush blossomed in my cheeks.

*Grant.*

No. There were other Grants in Amble. There was Grant Carpenter, who was in Ella's grade. He had hair the color of straw and a one eye that twitched when you talked to him.

And that was it.

I looked at him out of the corner of my eye. It could definitely be *the* Grant. It probably was. He looked the same as I remembered him, for the most part, except for the way he moved. I watched as he licked his lips before pressing them to the rim of his coffee mug, and how he swallowed it down, black, without even flinching. He tilted his head as his eyes scanned something in the paper, and he tapped the tip of his pencil in the middle of the headlines, like the rhythm would make him think better. And then he turned in my direction, just enough, and I saw them: the freckles patterned across his nose like a mini Big Dipper.

Without looking at me, he opened up his paper so that it sprawled onto my section of the counter, yawned, and said, "It's impolite to stare, you know?"

I froze like a rabbit caught in a snare, my eyes wide and shoulders rigid. I stared at the counter in front of me.

I'd thought he would say something like *Claire? Claire Graham? Is that you? Oh my God, you look so great! Hey, I'm really sorry about not going to your birthday party that one year, I was a jerk.* But instead he flipped up the edges of the paper so that the crossword puzzles splattered between us.

*He must not recognize me, that must be it.* Because if he did, I knew he'd put down the paper and hug me and maybe buy me coffee.

"Here you go." The waitress had appeared in front of me and slapped a jiggly cheese omelette down. "Need anything else?"

I shook my head and she drifted away, humming "Frosty the Snowman" even though Christmas was over.

I twisted the egg around my fork. He didn't know it was me. But did that mean I should tell him?

All of a sudden, he flashed in my mind the last day I saw him. He was outlined by the picture window, his face and neck pink and his hair tousled from the wind and corn leaves. He looked so much younger in my head, more like himself.

I set down the fork with a clink. "Do you know who I am?" I asked, almost whispering.

He put down the paper and rubbed his nose, making his star-freckles fold in on themselves. "I know who you are, Claire."

A shiver dripped down my spine, and even though the diner was packed with stuffy, stale air, I suddenly felt cold. "Oh," I said, but it came out more like a squeak. I cleared my throat. "Oh. I, um, I didn't know." I shoved eggs into my mouth, mostly because I didn't know what else to do with it. Obviously using it for speaking was a terrible idea.

I could feel his eyes on me while I shoveled more food in my mouth. He folded his hands over his paper. "I heard you were coming back into town for a little while. I knew it was you as soon as you walked in."

I swallowed and looked him—really looked at him—because I could now. His eyes were still that melty green color, like the first pale shoots poking through the snow in spring. And there was the Big Dipper, and the way his mouth always looked like it turned up even when he didn't mean to smile. But there were tiny fracture lines under his eyes now, and he looked like he was heavier somehow even though he hadn't gained any weight. Kind of like some invisible sadness pressed him into the earth while the rest of the world floated around him.

I wondered if I looked like that, too.

He sucked down the last dregs of his coffee and said, "So what are you doing back in Amble, city girl?"

"Just visiting," I said. "You know, it's been a while."

Grant didn't say anything for a long time. He picked at a nail and cleared his throat a few times, and I remembered that

that's what he used to do when he was thinking. I used to call him "S&S" when we were kids: Slow and Steady. Grant never did anything or said anything without thinking about it at the speed of a tortoise crossing Route 24. I waited, because that's the understanding Grant and I still had, even after all these miles and all this melancholy.

Finally he turned to me, his eyes flashing. "Did your dad tell you I'm in the deputy police force program at the station?" he asked. I shook my head. "Yeah. They needed an extra person down at the station after..." He studied me for a second, and the look on my face must have told him he could finish his sentence. He cleared his throat. "After your dad took over a lot of the paperwork stuff instead of being chief. You know—filing, phone calls, that sort of thing. He still goes out sometimes and writes a speeding ticket. Anyway, I think I want to be an officer, go to school for it."

I blinked away the thought of my dad being a glorified secretary. "I thought you wanted to be an architect, build stuff in Chicago?" I asked.

Grant waved his hand dismissively. "Nah, not anymore. You know, police work is really interesting. You learn a lot about people, sometimes even things they don't realize about themselves." He stopped to clear his throat. "Your dad's teaching me some things about motive. Did you know that every crime or disappearance or whatever has a motive? People don't just do things because it's sunny that day or they're in a bad mood because their credit card got declined or something."

I nodded. "Yeah, I've heard that before."

"You, Claire Graham, did not come to Amble to hang out with your parents or because you were bored in New York." Grant raised his hand and the waitress nodded. "You came to Amble to find your sister."

The waitress came over and waited while Grant smoothed out the crumpled dollar bills from his pocket. Something about the way she stood there, hunched over Grant but watching me out of the corner of her eye, made my skin crawl. When she left again, he looked at me and said, "You came because you thought we wouldn't be able to find her without you."

I did what Grant did and waved my hand, but the waitress just stared back at me like I'd asked her for the check in Chinese. Grant mumbled something and then flipped his hand up again, and she nodded and went to the cash register. I must have forgotten how to speak Amble while I was gone.

"I've got this," Grant said as he pulled another stack of scrunched-up bills from his pocket. He must have noticed me watching him laboriously smooth them out over the edge of the counter, because he added, "My wallet got torn up in the washing machine," with a tiny smile pressed into the corners of his mouth. It was the first time he smiled since I'd walked into the diner, and it made him seem a little lighter.

"Thanks," I said as we started toward the door. "You didn't have to do that."

He shrugged and pulled a knit hat over his head, shadowing his eyes. "Yeah, no problem."

"You're Mike Graham's daughter, right? Claire?" We

both turned around to see the waitress still standing at the counter, clutching Grant's crumpled bills in her fist.

I glanced at Grant, but he was staring at something on the sleeve of his jacket. "Yeah, why?" I asked.

Her eyes narrowed but her lips twisted into a smile, a definite no-teeth smile. It made her whole face scrunch up, like she'd smelled something rotten. "Oh, no reason. Just thought I recognized you from ... *somewhere*."

I felt a light touch on my shoulder—Grant's fingertips guiding me away from the counter. She still watched us as I let Grant move me toward the street. "You two be careful out there, okay?" she called after us.

The bells jingled as we stepped into the cold. "What was that all about?" I asked, turning toward Grant.

His hand brushed my elbow before falling limp at his side. He shook his head, staring out at the empty street behind me. "You know how Amble is. Everyone feels like everyone else's business is theirs." He started to shift his body toward the opposite direction of where I needed to go. "Don't worry about it."

I wanted to stay with him, to attach to him like a barnacle on the bottom of a crusty old ship and sail with him wherever he went. Because being around Grant was a little like being around Ella; he was still like liquid sunshine that I could drink by the gallon and never get full of. He always made me feel better, even if he pretended he didn't know me or didn't want to talk to me. Something about him was magic too. Like Ella.

Grant shoved his hands in his pocket and said, "Well, I guess I better get going. I've gotta get to work."

"Oh. Okay. Well, it was really great seeing you, after, you know, years." I started to walk away, back toward the cornfields looming in the snow. Back to the cold.

"Hey Claire," he called. I turned around and saw him still standing in front of the diner, shuffling on his feet. "I've got two questions for you."

I walked back to him, wrapping the scarf tighter around my neck to force out the seeping cold. "Shoot."

"First question: if you're looking for Ella, you're doing it in the wrong place."

"That's not a question."

He lifted a finger and said, "I've been reading through a lot of old case files lately, studying, and the answer always seems to be closer than you'd think. You need to look in the place where this whole thing started, where the most bits and pieces of her are. So, my question is, why aren't you looking in her room, through her stuff, right now?"

I sucked in my lip and looked up into his eyes, which seemed gray under the shadow of his hat. And then I said something I didn't realize was true until I said it to Grant: "Because I'm scared to."

But he didn't even flinch when I said that. He just nodded slowly and cleared his throat. I waited, because he'd told me to without words. Then he said, "I know a little bit about searching for someone."

"From working at the police station?"

He didn't answer, and for a second I thought the wind had swallowed up my words. But then his eyes flicked back to mine and when he looked at me, all heavy and sad again,

I knew he'd heard me. "No," he said softly, "from being Rae Buchanan's brother."

I closed my eyes and swallowed, and younger Grant flashed behind my eyelids, his bike sprawled across the porch steps, wheels still spinning. The panicked look on his face in the window.

I opened my eyes and he was still watching me, his head cocked to the side like he was reading the headlines of his newspaper. "What's the second question?"

Grant broke into a smile, a real one, I could tell. "Can I give you a lift home?"

"That would be great." And without my even trying, my face broke into a grin too, the kind with teeth and everything. A real, live grin.

# *fourteen*

I stood outside of Ella's door and tried to breathe.

But forcing breath into my lungs pinched, like they were already filled up and sagging with lead, and my whole body was too heavy for even one more breath of air.

When Grant drove me home yesterday, I'd tried to listen to everything he said about working in the police station, how he could go through any files he wanted, how he'd found out that Catie Spencer had gotten arrested for a DUI right out of high school. But mostly I just heard the timbre of his voice, the way it rolled over the vowels like honey smothering biscuits. And his scent made the whole car fill up with soap and wet earth. He smelled clean and dirty at the same time.

But I did remember one thing he said to me.

When we pulled into the driveway, Grant turned to me and shifted his seat belt. "When you go into her room, look back the furthest you can," he said.

"What do you mean?"

"I just mean that you might find clues from when you knew her when she was little, and other ones from when she was older. And then you can kind of stitch them together. That's how most investigations work. The successful ones, at least." He turned again and stared out the windshield. "It's strange, but I think most people know what's going to happen to their lives, right from the beginning."

I thought about what Grant had said as I touched Ella's doorknob.

Had I known what was going to happen to my life, right from the beginning?

In a way, I guess I always had. I'd always told Ella that I was going to move to New York one day, that I'd have to leave her but I'd come back to visit sometimes.

I'd kept my promise. I'd come back. She was the one who didn't stay.

I clutched the knob and reminded myself why I was here.

I was here to find Ella.

I had to start in her room.

I sucked in a breath and pushed the door open.

When I opened my eyes, my heart slowed and my body relaxed. I don't know what I'd expected to find, but it definitely wasn't anything like this.

Paper stars and lightning bolts pinwheeled on their wires above me, just like they used to every time I'd barged through Ella's door. Rainbow twinkle lights still slithered around the window, and Ella's gnarled afghan still sat in a ball in the middle of her bed. It was like I'd stepped through a time warp and was magically fifteen again, like I hadn't drunk vodka on the corners of Manhattan, like I spent my free time drawing in my sketchbook in the cornfield.

But there were things that were different, too.

Between the prints and drawings of dresses I'd given Ella, a bunch of new pictures had cropped up on the walls. Some of them were replicas of what I'd drawn, except with quivering lines and dress models with crooked smiles. Drawing was never Ella's thing.

There were other things, too. There was a map of Amble tacked to her corkboard, its edges yellow and fraying. And next to that was a photo of Ella and a boy with shaggy blond hair that curled around his ears, and eyelids that drooped over his eyes like he was sleepy. He was looking at the camera out of the corner of his eye while he kissed her temple. Ella still had the same twinkle in her eye that I remembered, but her smile was different. It wasn't a real smile with teeth. What was left of her lips pressed together in a line, with the corners turned up just a hitch. A shiny pink scar tore across her face and crawled down her neck. My stomach lurched.

Something pinged at the back of my brain and I remembered: Ella's infectious giggle and mittens pressed against her lips and a boy—*this* boy—whispering in her ear the night of the party. The night she was attacked.

I ran my finger over Ella's scarred mouth. What words did she say to him about that night? What words *could* she say to him?

I opened my palm and stared at the scar that cut across my own skin. We'd both got our scars from someone else:

mine from Rae's selfishness, and hers from my mistake. It always seems to work out like that, anyway; all the scars we get are because someone hurt us enough to give them to us.

Across from Ella's bed was another corkboard, one that I recognized from my old room. This one had a picture of a few stone-colored buildings, with block letters that read *Welcome to Madison, Wisconsin!* And around the postcard, Ella had pinned a dozen knitted birds just like the one she'd given me. They were all different colors—some chocolate, and some a splattering of reds and purples, and another that was black. But none of them were periwinkle.

I turned and looked around the room. It reeked of Ella, down to the half-painted wall behind her headboard, because she'd probably changed her mind halfway through. But none of it felt any more special than it had two years ago. Everything seemed zipped up tight, like Ella's knitted birds and faded photos would never tell me where she was.

I left and the door clicked shut behind me.

Grant had said to start from the beginning, but it was hard to know where the beginning was when everything orbited around you in circles.

I moved down the hallway and hopped over the loose floorboard that always creaked. The last thing I wanted was for Dad to think I was creeping around Ella's room looking for evidence of wolves. It'd be just one more reason for him to make a case to Mom to buy me a one-way ticket back to New York.

I lay down on my bed and stared up at the faded ceiling.

How was I supposed to find a girl who hadn't left any clues behind? No other notes, no messages.

There was a part of me that wondered whether Ella would have told me about her trouble with the wolves even if she could. After all, I was in New York and hadn't been invited back to visit. But if the wolves were still watching her, hunting her, Ella would have wanted to tell someone. Or at least, someone who believed her. But Rae was missing and I was absent, and she was stuck here, alone and scared for her life.

I sat up in bed and moved my hands over my eyes. "I'm so sorry, Ell," I choked. "I'm listening now."

I waited. But, of course, nothing happened. Ella was too far from Amble to hear me anymore. I smashed the heels of my palms into my eyes to force back the tears collecting there.

When I opened my eyes, I was looking at my old jewelry box.

Something tingled in my chest, and Ella's face flashed in my mind. I saw her standing in front of me, breath hot and curdling in the cold, her eyes filled with moonlight. *I'm gonna go through your jewelry*, she'd said. *And your makeup. Yeah, definitely your makeup.*

But didn't I check my jewelry box and makeup kit the next morning? I remembered seeing all of my necklaces carefully in a row, and all of my rings propped up in their holders and just knowing, right then, that Ella had never come home.

I pulled open the drawers anyway and looked. There was all of my old jewelry, well, most of it anyway. I recognized the dusty hole where my pearl ring used to live. That one had always been Ella's favorite, and I wouldn't be surprised if I found it under a rug or tucked in a drawer in her bedroom. Or maybe even on her finger now, wherever she was. I knew it was there the morning after the incident.

I pulled out the drawers again and dug through the rows of beads and silver, but I didn't find anything there. I sighed, defeated. I stuffed the tangle of necklaces back into the bottom drawer and tried to shove it closed. The jewelry box shifted, and something purple and old poked out from beneath it. I grabbed it.

A purple, canvas diary, with dirt smudges around the edges, stared at me.

I blew on my hands. It felt like I was holding a handful of ice, and my hands wouldn't stop shaking. I curled my fingers up to my lips.

It was a notebook. Ella's notebook.

And it was in *my* room, under *my* jewelry box.

There was only one reason why Ella would have put it here. She'd wanted *me* to find it.

And no one else.

I took a deep breath and pulled my hands away from my face. My heart roared in my ears as I picked up the book and flipped it open.

Ella's loopy handwriting scrawled across the page. It read,

*These are The Diaries of Ella Graham: Part Two.*

# *fifteen*

*The Diaries of Ella Graham* weren't what I was expecting.

I thought there would be a smattering of lopsided unicorn sketches and snippets of stories about how Ella had vandalized another park bench with orange nail polish. I was expecting pages filled with heart-dotted letters and stories filled with light.

But there were none of those things.

I flipped through the diary, ran my fingers over the indents her glitter pen had left behind. I scanned through the pages quickly, searching for one word in particular:

*Wolves.*

I didn't find it. I dipped into Ella's life after my exit from Amble, entry by entry.

The first one I read was a story about how Ella had managed to find an escape route from speech therapy at Amble's crappy excuse for a hospital. That part made me laugh; it was so Ella. She'd mapped out a stairwell on the second floor that was usually empty and wrote about how easy it was to slip past the security station. Apparently, she'd felt like her words were clear enough now that she didn't need therapy, but Mom and Dad disagreed. So Ella started smiling and waving cheerfully when they dropped her off and then spent her afternoons in the bead shop downtown instead.

I flipped to a random page in the middle, dated seven months ago:

> *He walked me home from therapy today. He met me out-side of the outpatient center after, and he kissed me. He didn't even flinch when he kissed the scars on my mouth. I never forget that, no matter how many times he kisses me. How lucky I am that someone will kiss me at all.*

My eyes drifted to the heavy-lidded boy on the corkboard and my heart twisted. How many other boys had winced at the idea of kissing Ella before this boy agreed to?

Shortly after that entry came more about the boy—and I imagined pink blooming on Ella's cheeks as she wrote about him. I turned the page to another one, from just a couple of months ago.

> *They're going to come for me, I know it. They're going to take me. I know he'll save me before it's too late.*

I groaned, pressing my fingers to my temples. Guilt seeped through the cracks in my heart until I was sure I felt it shatter in my chest.

I should have stayed in Amble, I should have fought Mom and Dad to stay by Ella's side. But I didn't; I couldn't. My brain and my heart and everything in me wasn't functioning. Leaving felt like a relief, in a way.

I swallowed and started to flip through the rest of the entries, all of which were from the past year. From what I could tell, most of them were about this boy, about his quiet patience and his kind eyes. I kept scanning through the pages, watching the months flick by.

Finally I reached a page titled *November*—just last month—and there were no more entries. A fat square of paper slid from the diary, into my lap.

I unfolded it, my pulse quickening. But it was just a map, white-washed in the creases and stamped with the words *Amble Public Library* in the corner. I scrunched my nose. It was a map of Michigan, one Ella could have easily gotten from Dad's atlas in the study. So why rip one off from the library?

A tiny pinprick of red near the top of the mitten-shaped state answered my question. I bent the map toward the light. Frantic red ink stains encircled the town of Alpena.

"What's in Alpena?" I said, and the sound of my own voice made me jump. I blinked, taking in the dusty light streaming through my windows. How long had I been here reading?

I shook out the diary, just in case there were any other secrets or stolen maps hiding in the creases. To my surprise, a loose sheet of paper, torn at the edges, wafted to the floor. I scooped it up and read:

*I know what happened to Sarah Dunnard.*
*The same thing is going to happen to me if I*
*don't get out of here.*

And then, in hurried letters:

*He's going to kill me.*

# *sixteen*

"'Ello?" Grant's voice answered, still thick with sleep.

"Grant," I breathed into the phone. My hands shook so violently that the screen jiggled against my cheek.

Something in my voice must have alerted him to the panic rumbling inside me, because I heard his mattress shift and he said, "Tell me what you found."

"A map," I started. "And her diary." Grant breathed on the other end of the conversation and I could tell he was in think-mode. I didn't wait for him to respond. "It's a map of Michigan, and she says something about how they're coming for her." I didn't say anything else.

"Who?" Grant asked, and all the hope inside me sank. There was a tiny part of me that had hoped he'd know, or at least suspect. That the wolves of Amble had left a trail of bloody paw prints for other people to find while I was gone.

"I don't know," I answered. "But the map has some town called Alpena circled. Have you heard of that place before?"

There was a long pause, and then throat-clearing. Finally, Grant said, "Yeah. I've heard of it. It's nothing special."

I sighed into the receiver. "I think I need more information. Can you help me?"

Another pause. And then: "Of course. What do you need from me?"

I forced the words out of my mouth before I lost the guts to say them. "I need access to the police records of Ella's attack."

----------

I didn't tell Grant that I was sure Ella had slipped her diary under my jewelry box because she knew I'd come back for her, that she needed me to find her. She hadn't given up on me, despite all the miles and minutes between us. Maybe she even remembered my promise to always keep her safe.

I also didn't tell him that the reason I needed to see the police records was because I was searching for the hint of wolves between the pages.

As the engine of his truck rumbled beneath us, I glanced over at Grant in the seat next to me. Some things about him were so different now, but some things were exactly the same. As soon as I'd told him what I wanted, he'd just sat on the other end of the phone and breathed into the receiver for a minute. And then he'd said, "I'll be there in twenty minutes," without even telling me that what I was about to do was illegal, or better yet, that I was crazy.

"So it just said, 'They're going to come for me'?" Grant asked, looping his fingers around the steering wheel.

I nodded and shoved my hands into my lap. Even with mittens on, my fingers still felt thick and purple beneath the wool. It was one of those days in Amble that never seemed to warm up, not even by one degree, even when the sun looked all warm and buttery in the sky.

Grant cleared his throat, just a low grumble like the engine of his truck, and stared through the windshield. I waited, as I always waited while Grant strung together the words he needed to say what was on his mind. Finally, he stole a quick glance at me and said, "Do you have any idea at all who she's talking about?"

I chewed on my lip. I could've told him that I thought it was the wolves, come to pluck Ella from Amble the same way they'd stolen Sarah Dunnard. I could've told him about the note Ella gave me before I left for New York. But I didn't say anything about wolves with jagged teeth and yellow eyes.

I knew how crazy that would sound, talking about Rae's stories and Amble's folk tales like they were real.

And I didn't tell Grant about the "He's going to kill me" part either. Not yet. Grant was logical, analytical. He would hear the word "he" and dismiss any possibility of it being something less than human Ella was afraid of. Grant would say "he" sounded like a person, and he'd probably be right— I mean, there *was* the boy, and his kisses were sprinkled throughout Ella's diary like a fine snow.

I sighed heavily. I just needed more evidence—something

concrete that could convince Grant of the wolves' existence—before I told him everything.

When I looked up, Grant was staring at me, eyebrow raised.

I blinked back at him. "What?"

"I asked you if her diaries said anything else important. Anything that you remember."

I shifted my eyes to the smudges of brown cornfields whizzing by the window. "Just a story about how she escaped out the hospital's side door whenever she didn't feel like showing up for speech therapy." I cleared my throat. "Pretty typical."

Grant nodded silently, although I was pretty sure he didn't believe me.

The truck engine churned as he pulled into the parking lot of the police station. My stomach clenched into a tight fist. There was only one other car in the parking lot, and it belonged to Amble's new police chief and Dad's old deputy, Seth Fineman.

"There it is," I whispered, staring at the timid gray brick of the police station. I must have looked like I was about to freak out and jump out of the truck screaming, because Grant reached over and wrapped his hand around my wrist. I gasped; not because I didn't want it there, but because I was surprised. Even through his gloves, his hand felt warm and tingly, like that peppermint Chapstick you buy at the drug store that makes your lips sting in a good way.

"We can get to all the records easy," he said. "The computers I need are at the other end of the building. We don't even need to go through the front door." He squeezed my wrist and I thought his hand might leave a warm, puckered mark on my skin. "It'll only take a couple of minutes, then we'll be out. I swear."

I nodded and stepped out of the truck, into the swirling snow that bit at my ears. Grant pressed his hand against my back as he led me around to the back entrance of the dumpy building. He pulled out a string of keys, all of them clunky and tarnished and important-looking, and pawed through them until he pulled one free and shoved it in the lock.

As he started to open the door, I whispered, "So you're important enough to have keys to, like, everything?"

Grant shrugged, shoving the keyring back into his coat pocket. "Remember how I said I was in the deputy training program?" I nodded. "Yeah, well, I'm the *only* one in the deputy training program." A small smile crept across his face. "Turns out not a lot of people want to work for the Amble Police Department."

There was a rush of heat as we entered the building, but I still felt a blast of blistering cold in my chest. I hadn't been to the police station since the day of the incident. Somehow I'd managed to block out the sagging gray ceilings and walls, but I could never forget the smell: the place smelled like a combination of mildew and soggy cups of coffee. In fact, everything inside smelled like wet snow, and even the walls were covered in tiny droplets of condensation.

As the smell hit me, I bit my lips shut and plugged my nose. I did that the first time, too, when they'd brought me here. That part I remembered. I'd been screaming and crying, so hard that I could taste the previous night's leftover mascara running into my mouth. All I'd wanted was to stay with Ella, so badly. I begged my dad and the other cops. I told them about the wolves, and about the bonfire and the birthday party and how I'd left cherry vodka sizzling in the snow. I told them about Rae, even though I'd promised her I wouldn't, because my promise to keep Ella safe was always the most important one. They still never found the wolves. Instead, they used what I'd told them about the party to search for Rae. They never found her either, as far as I knew.

Before all the questions, one of the other Amble cops had snapped handcuffs ten sizes too big around my wrists and prodded me into the back of a car. Dad just stood there, kicking a lump of ice from the back tire and frowning. And that was when he was chief. He could have stopped them, but he didn't. Now he was basically a human filing cabinet and Grant's babysitter with a badge.

They'd brought me here, and as soon as I smelled the walls and the carpet and the rotting desks in the front room, I gagged and held my breath. That's all I smelled for the next thirteen hours while that guy from Toledo questioned me.

*Did you see any animal prints at the scene?*

*Was anyone with you when you found your sister?*

*Did she try to communicate with you at all?*

*Yes.* Yes. Ella communicated with me with her half-lidded eyes and her bloody face, with her thoughts and her heart, because she was my sister. But how could I even begin to explain that?

"Earth to Claire," Grant whispered as he wiggled his

fingers in front of my face. I shook my head, and Grant's face and crooked grin came back into focus. "Welcome back." He pushed open a door that looked like it could lead into a closet and gestured for me to follow him inside.

I stepped into the only room I'd never been in before, probably because I'd never known this *was* a room. Its walls were wet and gray, just like in the rest of the station, but the room was completely circular, like someone had cut away all the corners with a pair of scissors. One small, dingy window cast shadows across the two whirring computers in the middle of the space.

Grant shut the door behind us and pulled the extra stool from the corner next to him. I sat and watched as the computer yawned to life.

"It's not much," Grant said, typing in some kind of password. "But it'll get the job done. Where do you want me to start looking?"

I tapped my fingers against my jeans, thinking. Where I really wanted to start looking was at Sarah Dunnard's records. I needed to know the connection between her case and Ella's, and why Ella would say that the same thing that happened to Sarah was going to happen to her.

I wanted to be able to thread together the clues from both cases, and show Grant paw prints that were missed, or how both girls were wearing periwinkle and smelling like cherries—*something*, anything. But I couldn't tell him to look up Sarah when I'd ask to see Ella's records. Besides, I knew I was lucky he was even letting me in here in the first place.

He was watching me, fingers positioned on the keyboard.

"How about we just start with 'Ella Graham,' okay?" He clicked an icon on the screen and started typing before I could respond.

The computer whirred to life and a stream of what looked like articles flooded the screen. I leaned in, my shoulder brushing Grant's, but neither of us shifted away.

There were at least a dozen articles from the *Amble Observer* about the incident, but that wasn't what I was here for. Where were the actual records—the facts, the notes, the case files? I stole a glance at Grant, but he looked just as confused as I did.

"That's weird," he finally said, scrunching his nose. "Look. There aren't any evidence records in here. The only things in her file are newspaper articles."

My stomach knotted. It just didn't make sense. Why wasn't there anything in the police database about me, or Ella, or any kind of hard evidence about what happened that night? Something was missing.

The floorboards in the hallway groaned and I gasped. Grant's mouth dropped open but he said nothing.

"Grant, is that you in there?" Seth's voice boomed just outside the door. "What're you doing?"

Grant stared at me, pure panic etched into the lines around his eyes. I leaned into him and whispered, "Tell him you're here, quick."

When my lips brushed the skin beneath his ear, his eyes fluttered and his brain started working again. "Yeah, I'm here. Just doing some extra work on that graffiti case at the elementary school." He hopped off his stool so quickly that it shuddered. "Just about to come out and grab a cup of coffee, actually."

I squeezed into the sliver of space behind the door as Grant threw it open and stepped into the hall to greet Seth. My heart throbbed in my ears and the cool dampness of the wall pressed into my skull.

"Oh. I'm glad you're here then," Seth said. "I've got a lead on that. I was going to tell you about it the next time you came in." I heard Seth pat Grant on the back. "Let's get you some coffee and I'll show you what I've got."

"Great. Right behind you," Grant said. To anyone else on the planet, he'd have sounded as normal, calm, and thoughtful as always. But I could hear the hint of panic still lingering at the edges of his syllables. I wanted to tip my head out of the shadows and whisper to him that I'd be okay, but he quickly shut the door before I had the chance.

I let out a breath. And then I hurried back to the computers, practically throwing myself onto the stool. I knew I only had a few minutes at best before Grant would try to escape Seth and come back. And I knew he'd still try to help me find information about Ella's case, even if we had to sneak back in again. Right now, I needed to find out everything I could about Sarah Dunnard.

I erased Ella's name from the search bar and began typing as quietly as I could. When I hit enter, this time it was Sarah's name that swam across the screen. Once again, various newspaper articles flooded the screen, but no facts, no evidence. I clicked on the first article at the top anyway.

*Eight-year-old Sarah Dunnard was reported missing last
Friday after she disappeared from her backyard Thursday
evening. Amble police chief Mike Graham was the first
on the scene and is currently leading an investigation to
find the child. There are no leads at this time.*

I clicked through a few more articles that followed the
case as it developed. The next one reported spots of blood
at the base of the cornstalks by the clearing near Lark Lake,
right next to the Dunnards' house. Another described prints
of some kind, which had been distorted by a heavy snowfall
and were unidentifiable.

I opened an article near the bottom of the list. This one
was the most current, dated a few months after I'd left for
New York.

*Amble police chief Mike Graham resigned from the Sarah
Dunnard missing persons case this afternoon and then
promptly announced his subsequent resignation as chief.
When asked to clarify his position, Graham simply stated
that in light of new evidence in the case, he did not feel
adequately unbiased to proceed with the investigation.*

*"I think it's crap," Candice Dunnard, mother of Sarah,
stated to the Observer. "We trusted him to keep us safe
and to find Sarah, and he failed."*

*Several anonymous sources believe Graham's resignation
has to do with the eerie similarities between the Dunnard
case and the case of his own daughter, Ella. Just two months*

*ago, his youngest daughter was discovered critically injured and unconscious. The cause was never determined, and no weapon was found at the scene in order to convict a suspect.*

My mind reeled, and I saw smudged prints and delicate drops of blood that looked like tiny rubies littering the snow. And cold days and cornstalks. Little snow angel girls with rosy cheeks and empty eyes. There were so many similarities between Ella and Sarah and what had happened to them.

But there was one huge difference. While Sarah Dunnard's disappearance happened only a month before Ella's attack, Sarah's incident was a missing persons case—which polluted Amble's residents with fear while the police searched for her. Dad had only given up and resigned after they'd found some kind of new evidence. Ella was different; she'd never disappeared after her attack.

Well, until now.

I needed to read all the articles about Ella's incident. There was something we were missing—that everyone was missing. There had to be something more. As I started to type Ella's name into the blinking search box again, I heard footsteps thumping down the hall.

"I'm just going to check the record of that one kid—the one with the mohawk." Seth's voice seeped through the walls. I jumped up from the stool, clicking at the screen furiously until the database closed.

I didn't have time to hide before the door flew open and Seth stood in front of me, a Styrofoam cup in his hand and a bewildered look on his face.

"Um—"

"GRANT," Seth boomed, and Grant instantly appeared at his side, his shoulders slumped in defeat. He looked at me with an expression that said *Sorry, I did everything I could.*

I put my palms out in front of me and said, "I was just waiting for Grant. He was giving a ride home and said he needed to stop here." I plastered an awkward, no-teeth smile to my face. "I didn't touch anything."

Seth narrowed his eyes at the blank computer screen and then at me. He took a step forward, his bulky frame causing a shadow to drape over me. "You're lying. You look just like your father when he's trying to lie. All twitchy."

I tried to keep my body very still as I lifted my chin to look him in the eye. "My father doesn't lie."

To my surprise, Seth's mouth twisted into a smirk. "No, I suppose he doesn't. Mike just doesn't ever tell all of the truth." His eyes narrowed. "Even about the facts."

All of a sudden, Grant was by my side, his fingers wrapped around my wrist. "I think I got what I needed, Seth. We're leaving now." He pulled me forward, through the door and around Seth's belly.

"Grant?" Seth called after us, just before we reached the back door.

Grant turned around and squeezed my wrist like he had in the truck. "Yeah?"

Seth looked at me, even though he was supposed to be talking to Grant, and said, "Don't ever bring her back here again or I'm going to have to fire you." And then he walked down the hall in the other direction, his boots shuffling against the faded carpet.

# seventeen

"Where have you been?" Dad sat at the breakfast bar, dressed in his cop uniform minus the chief's badge. He sipped on his mug like he was bored just asking the question.

I didn't say anything; I just tossed my purse onto the counter and pulled out an oatmeal-colored mug from the cabinet.

Dad didn't prod me to respond, and I didn't rush to answer. We'd always had a mutual agreement like that, where we allowed the other to think. In fact, out of everyone in the family, Dad and I were the most alike—contemplative, yet gutsy when we had to be. Even all the minutes and miles hadn't changed that.

And now I was contemplating how much to tell him about what I'd read at the station. How much to ask about Sarah Dunnard, about Ella.

"I was with Grant," I said slowly. "Looking up some old files in the police database on Ella's attack."

Dad's mug hit the counter with a clink. "What do you mean, 'looking up some old files'? How's that supposed to help anything?" The words tumbled out of his mouth in a rush.

"Dad, I'm looking for Ella," I said. "You know this. You know that's why I'm here."

He bent over his mug, running his finger around the rim. "Did you find anything?" he asked, staring into his coffee.

"No," I answered. I could hear the defeat in my own voice. "We didn't have that much time to look."

He sighed. "Claire, I know there's a part of you that still believes in this stuff about the wolves. But when will it be time to let it go and start thinking about other possibilities?" He paused for a second and stared at nothing in particular. "There have to be other possibilities," he said quietly.

I felt my eyelashes flutter on my skin, and for some reason, the corners of my eyes felt hot and itchy. I hadn't almost-cried since the night Aunt Sharon told me Ella was missing. But being this close to Ella and still so far away from her hurt more than the hundreds of miles that had stretched between Ohio and New York.

Dad stood up and moved in front of me, shadowing my escape to the staircase. He put both hands on my shoulders and I flinched. "There was no evidence of forced entry. Certain things were missing from Ella's room: a toothbrush, some books, pictures." He rubbed my shoulders and sighed. "People who aren't planning on leaving don't take those things with them, honey."

I thought of Rae, then, and how she'd packed all of her underwear and shoes in a garbage bag before she left. And how I'd seen her toothbrush sticking out of the purse slung around her shoulder.

The articles, the paint on the house, the secrets—they all clawed at my tongue. I wanted to spit them out at Dad. I wanted to make him tell me everything—about what had happened with Sarah, about the wolves. About Ella. But it all just curdled in the back of my throat. I couldn't do it, not until I figured out the rest of the truth myself. Mostly because I knew he wouldn't give it to me, anyway.

I pulled away from him. "Yeah. You're probably right." And then I headed up the stairs.

I knew he was watching me the whole way up, and I knew he wanted to tell me something, anything, that would change the way I felt about the wolves. But the truth was there was nothing to say about it anymore.

If what Dad had said about Ella was true—that she had packed up her things—then why had she left her diary behind? Of course she would have taken her diary. There was a part of her that knew she was going to be taken—she'd said it herself in her entries. The only explanation I could come up with was that she wanted me to know about it— about what took her.

Or about who.

I had to find her, whether Ella had her toothbrush in her purse or not.

The problem was, I was stuck. I couldn't get back into the station without Grant's help, and after Seth caught us, I wasn't sure Grant would risk taking me back there again. I paced my room, thinking.

An idea bubbled to the surface and I stopped in a ray of watery light pouring through my window. Even if I couldn't find anything on Ella right now, I could still search for information on the wolves. There was the map Ella had left in her diary. Maybe she wanted me to search for wolves in that town she'd circled.

I was reaching for my phone to call Grant when a long shadow diluted the sunlight splattered across my floor. I glanced out my window.

Dad was trudging through the freshly fallen snow, back toward his shed. When he reached it, he paused in front of the door and then turned to look behind him, not once but twice. Then he reached down and plucked an old, chipped garden gnome from the snow. Something silver flashed in the sunlight as he tipped the gnome upside down.

A key.

He shoved the key into the padlock. I thought he'd open the shed door, but he didn't. Instead, he just locked it up again, and fiddled with the lock. Then he tried to open the door, shaking the handle until the whole shed wobbled. When he decided the padlock was doing its job, he replaced the key and the gnome and started toward the house.

My eyebrows knitted together as I watched him, flushed and full of secrets. I gazed out at the backyard.

Or maybe it was the shed that was full of secrets.

# eighteen

Grant stared at the computer screen for a long minute, scratching his head. "I think my eyes are going blurry. This thing is basically ancient." He rubbed his face. "Whose idea was it to come do research in the library again?"

My lips hitched into a smile. "It's your fault you don't know the topography of Michigan." I took a breath. "Or anything about wolves."

When I'd called Grant about wanting to investigate the Alpena area more, he'd gotten strangely quiet. I mean, Grant was usually quiet, but in a thoughtful way. Not in a freaked out way. I didn't know what it was about that map, or that town, but he froze up whenever I mentioned it. I realized that the only way I could get him to help me figure out what was there was to tell him the truth.

And so, I told him part of it. I asked him for a lift to the library, and on the car ride over I told him about the note Ella had pressed into my hand at the hospital, about the wolves and the warning. Grant didn't say much in response, but he didn't tell me I was crazy either. I guessed that was a start.

I pointed to the map on the computer screen. "Here. Up here, almost at the top of the state. This is where the packs originated."

Grant leaned over me and squinted at the screen. He smelled like some kind of ocean breeze shampoo and peppermint. "Where does it say that?" he asked, wrinkling his forehead.

I glanced around the dank little library. In the corner, a girl with long dark hair and way too much eye makeup watched us. I dipped my head below the monitor and whispered, "Are you done with your million-and-one questions? A hundred different websites have confirmed it." I tapped the screen just north of Alpena. "This is where the wolves came from."

Grant nodded slowly, his eyes glazed over. "Yeah."

I snapped my finger in front of his nose and he twitched back to life. "It says it right here," I said, pointing. "'In 2008, the DNR reintroduced wolves to the northern lower peninsula, where they successfully bred. All lower peninsula wolf packs originated from this region.'"

My eyes scanned the fuzzy map on the screen. Michigan, Minnesota, Wisconsin, and the northern tip of Ohio were flecked with blue: wolf migration patterns. I reached for the mouse to click out of the website. But just before I tapped, a pinprick of blue flashed over the right side of the screen. I leaned in so close that the dust lining the edge of screen tickled my nose.

"Grant, look. Do you see this?" I whispered. "That's totally blue there, right?"

Grant's eyes darted to the screen, almost like he was afraid to look at it. But when he saw the fleck of blue positioned over New York City, his eyebrows drew together and he blinked at the screen. "Yeah," he said slowly. "Yeah, right there. Looks like one little speck of wolves found their way to New York. Probably just one pack."

I smiled to myself. "I *knew* there had to be wolves there. And Dr. Barges told me there couldn't be any."

"Who?" Grant was staring at me, his face inches from mine.

I felt the start of a blush blooming on my cheeks. "Oh, um. No one."

Grant swiveled his chair away from the computer. Something about the way his shoulders slumped and how he kept picking at his fingernails made me wonder if he secretly thought I was out of my mind, even though I knew he'd seen that blue fleck on New York City. But the way he wasn't clearing his throat told me he didn't really have anything to say to me.

"Hey Grant," came a voice over top of the monitor. I peeked up and saw the girl with the long hair and the caked-on mascara that made her eyelashes look like fat caterpillars. She glanced at me and gave me a tight smile, the kind without teeth. "What are you doing here?"

Just then, it came flashing back to me, like a wad of algae or a lost flip flop or something pulled from the bottom of

Lark Lake that made the sand pucker. *Lacey Jordan*. We'd gone to school together a hundred years ago.

Grant's ears grew pink and his knuckles turned white around the mouse. "Just looking some things up," he said.

Lacey nodded before he even finished talking and immediately snapped her eyes onto me. She pressed her lips into smile again and said, "Claire Graham, right? Do you remember me?"

I returned the courtesy smile and said, "Kind of. Well, we were just on our way out." I stood, clicking out of the browser. The last thing I wanted to do today was pretend to have a nice talk with Lacey Jordan.

It seemed to offend Lacey that I wasn't fawning all over her like all the guys in school did—mostly because they knew how she'd given it up to a senior in the cornfield one night—because her smile quickly disappeared. "So, I thought you weren't ever supposed to come back to Amble, isn't that right?"

I blinked at her for a minute and then turned to Grant, who was still fiddling with his stupid fingernail at the desk. "What do you mean, I'm not supposed to come back to Amble?" I asked. Unfortunately, it sounded more confident in my head.

Lacey shifted her massive, ugly purse and flipped her hair over her shoulder. "Oh, just some silly rumor that you're, like, not even allowed to set foot here because of what happened to your sister." She cocked her head to the side. "So what are you doing here?"

I felt like I'd swallowed an ice cube and it was slowly, slowly sliding down my throat, coating everything inside me in cold. My mind churned like bath water sloshing out of the tub: the way Dad had pulled me out of Ella's hospital room right when she was starting to recognize me again; the one-way ticket, wrapped in an orange holder, stuck quietly into my purse. How I was never invited back to Amble to visit.

"Lacey, stop." Grant was standing now, but I didn't remember him standing up. He pressed his palm in between my shoulder blades, and the coldness inside me started to melt. "Come on. Do you think they would have let her leave if she was guilty?" His hand slid up my shoulder so that his fingertips brushed against my neck. "Those are just rumors." But he didn't sound so sure when he said it.

My head snapped up to look at him, and I tried to swallow down the panic rushing into my chest. "What do you mean—*guilty?*"

But Grant didn't answer. Instead, his grip around my shoulder tightened and he shot Lacey a death-look.

Lacey stared at Grant's hand on my shoulder for a long time before her eyes flicked back to my face. "Mmm. Rumors. Just like those rumors about how your dad screwed up the evidence when he was out looking for Sarah Dunnard and couldn't wrap up the case. Some people even say he hid evidence on purpose, that he went all psycho out there. But those rumors turned out to be true, didn't they? Runs in the family, I suppose." She batted her fat eyelashes at me before turning to Grant. "I have to get to the salon before it closes, so I'd better run. Will I see you at my New Year's Eve party tomorrow? My mom's out of town." She smiled again, and this time she actually looked pretty, younger. Even though I hated her.

Grant shrugged, but he didn't move his hand from my shoulder. "We'll see."

Lacey pulled a pair of leather gloves from her purse. She looked me up and down and said, "Better watch it, Grant—you know how Amble doesn't like crazy." And then she sauntered through the library, waving back at us with a quick flick of her hand.

I watched her go, but the only thing I felt was the warmth of Grant's hand on my neck, and the way it felt heavy and light at the same time as it slid down my arm. He wrapped his fingers around my wrist and squeezed.

"Don't worry about it," he said.

I pulled away from him, the corners of my eyes prickling with heat. "What's going on, Grant?" Those were the only words I could choke out without completely losing it. I just had to hope he knew what I meant.

Grant tipped his head back and sighed. "Claire, I think we need to talk."

I took a step back from him, hoping he couldn't see my hands shaking. "We couldn't have 'talked' when you drove me home from the diner? When we went to the police station? *When I called you this afternoon?*" I took another shaky step back. "You've had a lot of time to tell me what the hell is going on with—with my dad, with Ella, with *me*. And you didn't." The last words cracked on my lips on their way out, and I knew I couldn't talk to him anymore.

I weaved through the stacks of books and ancient computer desks toward the front of the library, past the million pairs of eyes following after me.

What did they see when they looked at me?

*Guilty.*

*Crazy.*

I threw open the door and stepped out into a day the color of quiet, with thoughts that screamed violently in my head.

# *nineteen*

I stomped through the streets of Amble, smashing the snow under my boots with satisfaction. I didn't want to talk to Grant; I couldn't. Not yet.

I was halfway to my house when a heard the chugging of an engine creep up behind me. I kept going, eyes forward even when I heard it slowing down.

"Claire," Grant said, his voice windswept and breathless. "Please. At least let me take you home."

I shook my head and kept walking.

"I'm so sorry I didn't tell you," he continued, practically yelling out the passenger window. "I should have."

Something snapped just then, and all of my guilt and shame and sadness roared out of me. In a split second I was next to the truck, staring at Grant, clutching the edge of the open window. I wanted to scream at him, punch him, at least tell him what an asshole he was for keeping all this a secret from me. But the only word that would come out was, "Why?"

Grant's face melted as he reached over to push open the door. "Get in. I'll tell you everything I know."

I sucked in a breath and pulled myself into the truck's cab. I wanted the truth. I knew I did. But the possibility of what Grant had to say to me right now felt like a brick wall, one built on top of my rib cage, crushing oxygen from my lungs.

I stared at him. "Go on."

He rubbed the skin between his eyebrows and swallowed. "The police found you in the cornfield, next to Ella. I guess...you were pretty shaken up."

Shaken up was an understatement. I remembered my heartbeat rattling in my chest; blood—hot and red—slicing across the snow; flashes of diluted blue and red lights reflected on my skin. Humming. Screaming.

"Your dad was too, obviously. And in any case like this, where there's a person in the immediate vicinity of a victim, there has to be a formal investigation. Your dad...he couldn't do it. So he called in the team from Toledo." Grant reached out to touch me, but I pulled my hand away before his fingers grazed mine. "They named you a suspect as soon as they came into town."

And in a snap of an instant, I was back at the station, across from some detective I'd never seen until that day. His questions flooded my mind:

*Where were you before you found her in the field?*
*Why were you looking for her over a mile from your home?*
*How did you know she was at that location?*

"Oh my God. Oh my God." I pinched the bridge of my nose. I was totally going to pass out. I heard Grant shift in his seat and then his hand was on my back, keeping me steady. It the only thing keeping me from tumbling out of orbit. "But how—" I started.

"How did you not get charged with anything?" Grant said. "I'm sure there's a reason."

"There has to be a reason," I repeated, rubbing my eyes. Suddenly, the weight of this day had left me exhausted. "Cops don't just let criminals go scot-free."

"I suppose—if I had to guess—I'd say it had something to do with the fact that there wasn't a weapon or anything like that at the scene. How could they charge you?"

*How could they charge you?* Grant's words rang in the space between my ears. The fact that they even suspected me at all made my stomach ache.

"Some of the residents weren't pleased, though. They kind of thought it was an open-and-shut case after you were found at the scene." Grant paused to swallow, and I could practically see him contemplating his next words. "And then when they heard about you singing and talking about wolves…well, it made them even angrier that you didn't admit you were guilty and just plead insanity."

*Guilty.*

*Crazy.*

"Why didn't you tell me this?" I whispered. I pressed my palms to my face to hide the heat creeping into my cheeks. All this time, I'd been asking Grant to help me find Ella, when he already knew about her case and what everyone thought of me. I'm sure I looked crazy to him.

Grant shifted again, and this time he wrapped his arm over my shoulder and squeezed. "I didn't want you to think that of yourself," he whispered into my hair. "I know you wouldn't hurt Ella. I saw how much you loved her."

I gently pulled away so I could look at him. "I have to find Ella. I have to figure out what happened to her. Everyone needs to see that I didn't hurt her. She has to tell them." I pulled the fat square from my pocket and smoothed it out. I tapped the frantic red ink stains near the top of Michigan. "I have to know what's up here."

*I have to know if the wolves took her there. If she knew that's where they'd take her.*

Grant tipped his head back and closed his eyes. After a minute he said, "There's one thing I know of in Alpena that might've attracted Ella there, if she went on her own."

"What?"

Grant sighed. "That's where Rae lives now."

# *twenty*

The whole thing was easier to plan than I'd thought it would be. After Grant told me that Rae had moved up to Alpena when she and Robbie broke up and her mom didn't want her back in Amble, I knew my next step was to go there. The wolves were there, and the person who told the best stories about them was too.

We agreed that if we were going to go, we'd have to go soon, while there were enough distractions. I told my parents that Grant had invited me to go with him to a New Year's Eve party, but I didn't say whose. I didn't really have to; everyone in Amble knew that Lacey Jordan always threw the craziest parties in the clearing behind her house. There were always tubs of liquor that Lacey's older brother brought home from his college frat house, and everyone and anyone looking for a drink seemed to find their way to the clearing like a moth to a flame. Sometimes even adults. In fact,

I think the only person in town who hadn't been to one of Lacey's parties was her mother. Mrs. Jordan worked forty-five minutes outside of Amble, and often had to stay at her job during the week to finish up paperwork. By the time she got home the next morning, every last liquor bottle and pile of puke was always gone. Good thing, too—Mrs. Jordan was not one of those people I'd like to see pissed off.

As it turned out, Rae was right all along: holidays really are the best time to plan an escape. I would have to thank her for that tip when I saw her. Mom and Dad usually hosted their own New Year's Eve party every year—it was one of those things that distracted them for days prior as they argued over how much liquor was appropriate to use when spiking punch.

So that's what I'd been expecting when I made my plans with Grant, but there was no gaudy punch bowl or greasy cocktail weenies this year. There was no party, and I couldn't help but wonder if it had everything to do with Dad's resignation and the bitterness of the town that still stained our aluminum siding. But it didn't matter anyway; they'd planned a quiet dinner alone, and acted almost relieved that I'd have something to do with myself.

They didn't even seem to care when Grant's truck rumbled into the driveway at four o'clock, daylight still spilling through the kitchen windows. Mom hugged me with one arm while she zipped up her dress with the other and Dad said "Have fun" while searching for his favorite tie.

"Hey," Grant said, and somehow it meant more than "hey." His eyes were round and iridescent, like green marbles lit up under the sun. His cheeks and nose were flushed, and for the first time since I'd seen him, his mouth stretched into a broad grin. "You ready?"

"Yep," I said, and I felt the corners of my own mouth hitch into a smile.

Everything about Grant was contagious, especially the calm he radiated from every inch of his body. Most people seem itchy in their own body, like they can't wait to get home and unzip their skin. But Grant was always content with wherever he was, even if it was in a truck for a four-and-a-half hour drive up to Alpena to hunt for wolves he wasn't sure existed, and to see a sister that didn't really either.

I watched him as we drove, the ice collecting in dangerous ringlets on the trees as we got farther north. His shoulders slumped in his seat and he laid his head back as he drove. If I wanted to, I could probably have leaned over and looked up his nose. It seemed like an odd position to be in, driving on an ice-splattered highway while looking like you're ready for a nap instead.

Two hours into the trip, just as I felt my head bobbing against the window, my phone buzzed in my lap.

"Phone," Grant murmured, his voice was heavy, almost like it had woken him up too.

I touched the screen and saw Danny's name grinning up at me.

*When r u comin back?*

I stared at the cursor, blinking, waiting. I'd sent Danny a text the day I left for Amble; I'd practically begged him to meet me at the train station to kiss me goodbye. But he never responded, just like he hadn't on my birthday. And now he wanted to know when I was coming back? Why now?

A week ago, I would have told him I was coming back as soon as I could, that I missed him and couldn't wait to see him again, that I was sorry for being a freak that day, it wouldn't happen again. But now I didn't feel like it.

I clicked the phone off and threw it into my purse.

Grant rubbed his eyes and asked, "Was that your mom?"

"No," I said. "It was no one."

He nodded and leaned forward to flick on the radio, which sounded crackly and dry through the speakers. That was another awesome thing about Grant that I'd forgotten these past couple of years: he waited for you to tell him things instead of forcing them out of you. And if you never told him, that was okay too.

It was like we were in a time warp, because I swore we'd been talking about who was texting me just a second ago. But then I lifted my head from the window and saw stars flecking the inky sky. Grant yawned next to me and reached over to pat my knee.

I stared at his hand on my jeans. "I fell asleep."

He smiled. "Yeah, for a little."

I pulled the map from his lap and squinted into the dark. "How much farther?"

Grant shrugged, but it was getting so dark now that I could just barely make out the lines of his shoulders. "Just a little farther." The truck slid on a patch of ice as it rounded a corner onto an almost invisible road. He straightened the wheel and let out a breath. "It's getting icy."

I tried to look out into the night, but I couldn't see past the headlights. Fat clumps of snow splattered against the windshield with such force that the road beyond them was almost completely blocked out. The tires still churned beneath us, slow and unstable. At one point, the entire back end of the truck started to slide off the road. I grabbed for the dashboard.

"It's right up here," Grant breathed. "Right up here."

I don't know why I did it; I didn't even think about it. I wrapped my fingers around his. And then I squeezed, just like he always did to my wrist when I was nervous or afraid or anything else hurt. My heart didn't jump in my chest; my palms didn't start to sweat. I just looked out the windshield and imagined how much more dangerous it was out there than it was in here with him.

"You know why I have to find them, right?" I said into the dark.

He didn't say anything for a long time. The tires whirred and slid beneath us, and I thought he might be concentrating on that instead. But then he squeezed my hand and said, "I know."

I looked at him; his eyes were lit up like cat's eyes under the moon. "I'm not crazy."

He squeezed my hand again. "I know."

The truck's headlights bounced as Grant hit a pothole and I got a flash of tall house with gray siding at the end of the road. I leaned forward and put my free hand on the dashboard. "Is that your aunt's house?"

And then the tires got quiet, and even the ice stopped

splintering into delicate spiderwebs beneath us. Grant flicked the headlights off, still staring through the windshield.

"That's Rae's car," he said, pointing. "That red one in the driveway."

I squinted through the dark and saw the bumper of some kind of regular old red car. Even though it wasn't anything spectacular, I couldn't help but feel a pang of jealousy. How had Rae, and even Grant, grown up so much, while I was still stuck inside myself, old and dusty and rotting with regret?

"Can't we pull into the driveway?" I asked, tucking my hand back into my lap to keep it warm.

Grant stared ahead, the expression on his face a mixture of guilt and sadness and something like misery. I knew that look, because that's what I always saw in my own face whenever I'd sent those fake-teeth pictures to Mom and Dad.

He turned toward me, then, and grabbed my hand from my lap. "I'm nervous," he said finally. "I don't know what to do."

"It's okay," I said, squeezing his hands. "She's your sister. We're going to go in there, ask her some questions, and leave. Okay?"

He leaned forward and looked at me, *really* looked at me, like no one had since the day I'd found Ella. And for that second, the world stopped spinning, and the stars quit orbiting around each other in their silly little dance, and everything was still. I was still, and I knew he could see it. Because the moment we'd started this road trip together, I knew that whatever had been churning in him about seeing Rae had gone still, too.

And maybe that was just what we were now: two people with broken sisters who needed to stitch each other back together with hand squeezes and stillness. And maybe that was okay. Maybe that was more than okay.

He cupped my fingers in his and breathed. "Okay."

# *twenty-one*

Grant's truck practically slid into the driveway behind Rae's red sedan. He shuffled up the icy steps, taking his sweet time like he always did, but I knew it wasn't because he was worried about slipping. I placed my hand between his shoulder blades and stood on my tiptoes to whisper in his ear: "We'll leave in less than an hour, promise."

Grant nodded once, took a breath, and pressed the doorbell.

A dog howled from behind the door and the blinds shook in the window. I grabbed Grant's arm and reminded myself that it was just a dog, just a dog, just a dog.

Someone's muffled voice swore from behind the door, just before it swung open. Rae stood in the entryway, two fingers hooked over her jeans.

Her eyes fluttered for a second as she looked at Grant. But I wasn't watching her; I kept my eyes on him, on the tight line of his lips and the way the skin on his neck was blotchy. Rae stole a glance at me, and then looked back at Grant. "Hey," she said, like he'd just come home from the grocery store. And then she turned to walk back into the house. "Come on in, if you want."

I watched the back of her neck as we followed her into the house. A small tattoo of some kind of lizard curled around the tip of her spine, poking out from under her shirt. Her hair was still short and spiky, and her skin still looked like caramel with a drop of milk splashed in, but everything else was different.

We stepped into a kitchen that had the same-colored walls as split-pea soup. The dog, which turned out to be a lumpy little pug, snorted at my feet. Rae plopped onto a stool and grabbed an apple from the basket next to her. "So what's up, little brother?"

Grant let out a short breath as he sank into the stool across from her. I stood, mostly because I felt almost invisible in Rae's presence.

Grant's head dipped between his shoulders as he cleared his throat. And he cleared his throat again. Rae rolled her eyes and took a bite of her apple. "Come on, Grant," she said, the clumps of peel rolling over her tongue. "Spit it out."

But Grant didn't spit it out. It was like he was frozen in one of those huge blocks of ice they try to preserve bodies in: eyes wide, staring off into space. Except that he kept making that grumbling sound in his throat.

Rae scoffed and tossed her half-eaten apple back into the

bowl. She jumped off the stool and said, "Okay, well, I have some things to do. So let me know when you want to talk."

I stepped in front of her. Rae's eyes flickered, and she was forced to look at me for the first time since she'd stolen my birthday party and made it part of her own personal escape plan. "We came to talk to you about the wolves."

There. I'd said it. I'd said it like they were real entities; I'd said it to someone other than Grant for the first time since they'd shipped me off to New York.

Rae took a step back, her eyes wide and her mouth hanging open. She looked like I'd just slapped her. The pug snorted at her feet and she scooped down to pick it up. She held it like a chubby, wriggling shield between us.

"You mean you came all the way up here"—she turned to look at Grant—"to talk about the *wolves*? Are you out of your freaking mind?"

Her eyes were filled with fire as she turned back around to me. "I always knew you took those stupid stories too far. I could see it on your face, even when you said you didn't believe it." She shook her head, and the pug wiggled with her. "Crazy. I always knew you were crazy."

It felt like my lungs collapsed in my chest when she said that word, that word that kept me staring at the ceiling every night. I gasped for air, clutching my stomach. If Ella were here—the one who used to say more words than she had breath for—she would step between us. She would tell Rae to shove off and that her sister wasn't crazy and that it didn't run in our family, or any of those other things people said about me. Then she'd say that she never liked Rae's stupid spiky hair anyway, so there. But Ella wasn't here. She hadn't been in a long time, and I was out of breath for words.

Rae dropped the pug to the floor and took a step forward. "I tried to be your friend, you know. Get you to lighten up, live a little. But all you cared about was drawing your dress pictures and hovering over Ella like some creepy stalker. Even your *parents* begged my mom to let you come over to hang out because they thought you needed to talk to someone!" Her lip curled into a snarl and my stomach lurched. She looked almost like the wolf I'd always seen in my mind: piercing eyes, quivering lips, ready for blood.

"And what did you freaking do?" Rae continued. "You tried to blame what you did to Ella on some wolf stories I'd told you years ago. You were always jealous of her." Rae slumped against the counter now, but this time she looked different. Before, when she'd answered the door, she seemed like she'd been pumped full of three-dimensional color: vibrant and bright and almost trembling with confidence. But it was as if the words she'd held inside of her had been powering her, kept her lit up like a Christmas tree, and now that she'd finally said them to me, she was starting to fade and become human again.

"They weren't just stories, Rae. Ella left me a note." I took a deep breath. "She told me they're always watching, that they're going to take her away. *That's* why we're here. This is where Ella told us to come."

Rae jerked her head up to look at me, and the expression on her face caught me off-guard. Her face wasn't furious; her mouth wasn't twisted in a sharp grin anymore.

She looked *scared*.

But in an instant, the fear drained from her face as she turned to scoop up the dog again. "I doubt it," she said, only this time it was softer, less convinced. "There's nothing up here to find."

Grant opened his mouth to say something, but Rae practically bolted from the kitchen, the pug tucked under her arm, before he had a chance to get words out. He turned to me instead. "Let's get out of here. We're not getting anywhere."

I glanced into the tiny dining room, where Rae was slumped over the table, absentmindedly twisting the stem of her half-eaten apple. "I think we need to stay a little longer," I whispered. "I think she knows something."

Grant nodded slowly, almost like he was afraid to admit he'd picked up on Rae's strange behavior too. He sighed. "Fine. But what excuse do we make up for having to stay the night?"

I looked out the window at the snow smothering the streets, the lamp posts, the hood of the truck. "I don't think we need to make anything up." I took his hand in mine.

"Snowstorm," he whispered.

————

Rae wasn't happy when Grant insisted we'd have to stay until the snow cleared in the morning. At first she tried to convince us that it wasn't even that icy out, and that the truck had four-wheel drive, so we should be fine. But when she went out onto the back porch to let the dog out and fell on her ass, she came back inside and grumbled, "Fine. You can stay in the craft room."

As it turns out, Rae and Grant's Aunt Deb—their mother's sister—owned several of the houses on this tiny block, and she rented them out for cheap. Rae had taken over this one last year when she started working at the Mobil down the street, and Aunt Deb shifted her things to the remodeled house next door. Her craft room, however, had stayed.

I snuggled into Grant out of necessity—it was freezing at this end of the house, and the pull-out sofa was only a double—but I couldn't say I minded. We both curled into lumpy, awkward sleeping bags that smelled like dust and beef jerky, and the space heater gave off a lukewarm blast of air from the corner. But somehow, as we peeked at each other through the sleeping bag zippers, it was enough to keep out the cold.

"Hey, do you still have the wolf journal I got you that time, for your birthday?" Grant whispered, tucking his nose into his sweatshirt.

I nodded. "Yeah, I have it."

"You ever write in it?"

I paused for a second and shifted my legs so that my socks weren't tangled on the bottom zipper. "No." I rolled onto my back and stared at a spiderweb crack in the ceiling. "I guess diary writing isn't my thing."

Grant wiggled in his sleeping bag so that he could prop his head up in his hand. "It could be your thing, if you wanted it to be."

I turned to look at him. "What do you mean?"

"It's just that you're one of those people that can do any-thing if you want to," he breathed. "You're kinda like magic, Claire." He quickly cleared his throat. "I just mean, you—you're one of those people who always makes me feel better when you're around."

My head felt fuzzy, and the walls wobbled around me. The only person who'd ever been magic in Amble was Ella. Maybe Grant had spent so much time thinking about the wolves and Ella with me that he'd started to confuse me with her. Because I wasn't magic; I couldn't make the stars bounce and everything look like it was drenched in pink sunlight and make people feel like they were flying just by listening to my laugh. Maybe I'd hugged Ella so hard that some of her light had rubbed off on me.

I looked up at him. "You really think that?"

"Yep," he said. And then he pulled his hand free from the sleeping bag and put it on top of mine.

"Then why didn't you come to my birthday party?" I pushed the sleeping bag down around me and sat up. "Why did you tell me to come alone, not bring Ella, if you weren't even going to show up?"

Grant scrunched his eyebrows and started that throat-clearing thing, and I thought he was going to give me some stupid excuse about how he had a runny nose or he had to wrap Christmas presents for his mom. But then he swallowed and said, "I don't know what you're talking about."

That wasn't what I'd been expecting. I said it again, slower this time: "You didn't come to my party. Even after that note." I felt a blush tingling on my cheeks when I said it, but I prayed it was too dark for Grant to tell.

Grant leaned forward so that his face was almost next to mine, and I swore he must have been able to feel the heat coming off my cheeks. "What are you talking about? I meant what I said in that note. I wanted to be there. But Rae told me that you didn't want me to come. She said you had a date coming or something."

"I was alone," I breathed into the dark. "I was alone that night." I suddenly had the urge to cry, and I started getting that prickly feeling in the corners of my eyes. I wished I'd known, I *so* wished I'd known. What would have changed if I'd known? Maybe I wouldn't have touched that cherry vodka because I'd have been too busy laughing and talking and maybe touching Grant. And maybe the wolves wouldn't have smelled it in the snow, and they wouldn't have ripped half of Ella's face off when they caught a whiff of her in the cornfield. It was too much; I couldn't think about it. I pressed my fingers to my eyes. "Why would she do that?" I whispered.

I waited, but he didn't answer. When I finally pulled my fingers from my eyelids, he was staring up at the ceiling with that look of misery and sadness swirled all over his face again. "Because those are the kinds of things Rae does." He sighed. "Those are the things she's always done."

We lay there, staring quietly into the night that peeked through the dingy window, inches away from each other but so far apart. After a long minute, Grant said, "Which is why it's so hard to believe you about the wolves, because Rae told those same stories too. Even though I really, really want to."

I felt something sharp poke a hole into my lungs. I really, really wanted him to believe me too, even though I knew he was still lingering on the border of staying put in black and white Amble, where even possibilities had to be made of concrete, rather than following me into the gray blur of wolves and shadows and almost-truths. I turned and looked at him. "You don't believe me because of Rae?"

He closed his eyes. "It's *hard* to believe you because of Rae. She...she made up so many stories about so many things, you know? I feel like she just spat lies—to me, our mom, everyone—until the day she left Amble." He turned and opened his eyes. They looked like glowing, green orbs under the moonlight. "That doesn't mean I don't want you to prove me wrong, or else I wouldn't be here with you. I want to believe you, like I believed her. Only I want you to actually be right."

I started to open my mouth to say something, but Grant just shook his head and said, "Sometimes you ignore the bad things about the people you love because you love them so much." He shrugged. "I did."

I looked at him just then, and he looked different and the same all over again. He was still Grant, out in the cornfield with a half-wrapped package in his hands and a half-crooked grin on his face. And he was still this Grant, too, with his star-freckled nose and eyes that changed shades of green depending on the time of day. But right then, there was this moment: that moment when all of a sudden you look at someone like you could maybe love them one day, and at the same time you realize that you've been looking at them that way all along without even knowing it. And how you realize you could have something better than what you've let yourself have.

That moment when you realize there is *more*.

I pushed my sleeping bag all the way down to my ankles and scooted closer to Grant.

"What are you—" he started, but this time I didn't wait. I pressed my nose to his, and then I kissed him.

I kissed him with enough force to power two years' worth of regret for leaving, and ninety-six hours' worth of understanding what I had missed. I didn't think about the cold outside, or the heat between us, or that there were supposed to be wolf howls tearing through the night. I just listened to my breath, and his breath, and how it tasted sweet and salty at the same time.

I didn't listen for howls or look for tracks. I didn't wonder if they were out there with Ella, waiting for me. Tonight, I let them wait. Because tonight was the kind of night I'd been waiting for, without even knowing that I had been all along.

# twenty-two

The rumble of a howl woke me from my sleep.

I jerked forward, dizzy, and fumbled for my phone on the end table. I squinted into the blue light: 6:37 a.m.

I blinked back the dreams that were starting to ebb away and took in my surroundings. An ancient, pearl-colored sewing machine loomed in the corner next to the space heater, which had kicked off sometime during the night. Plastic bins full of oblong buttons and tangled ribbons clustered together in every inch of free space in the room.

The craft room. Rae's house.

I remembered.

From somewhere outside, another howl pierced my ears, my heart, and I tried to breathe, breathe, breathe.

"Mmm," Grant murmured next to me. I looked down at him, at his hair poking out in a million directions and his lashes looking like tiny dandelion seedlings, delicate and ready to float into the wind.

"Do you hear them?" I whispered. I brushed my hand through his hair.

"Mmm," he said back. And then he curled into his sleeping bag.

There was no way I was going back to sleep now. My mind ticked through the possibilities: Were they in the wooded reserve we'd passed, a few miles from here? Were they slipping through the icy streets, searching for me?

Did they have Ella?

I slowly unzipped my sleeping bag and tiptoed into the hallway. I was almost to the front of the house when a patch of buttery light spilled into the mouth of the kitchen. Quickly, I shoved myself into the shadows lining the hall.

Someone banged open one cabinet, and then another. Then a grumble, followed by a string of curse words.

Rae.

I tipped my head out of the shadows and watched her. Her spiky hair was even more chaotic than usual, except for one side that lay limp above her ear. She must have been sleeping. Or at least trying to.

She practically stomped through the kitchen, swearing, unearthing a box of Cinnamon Toast Crunch and a fat, chipped bowl. After she poured her milk, she plopped into a chair and sighed so heavily that I swear the floorboards shook beneath me.

The kitchen lights illuminated the swollen, purple skin under her eyes as she pushed the cereal around with her spoon. After a minute, she dropped the spoon into her bowl with a *clang* and started to flick through her phone.

"I can't believe this," she groaned, staring at something on the screen. "Where the hell *are you*, Ella?"

I swallowed the sick feeling congealing at the back of my throat.

*Where the hell are you, Ella?*

So Rae had known something about Ella's disappearance all along. And still she hadn't said anything to me, to Grant. She'd lied.

Again.

I bit on my lip to keep myself from spewing out all the things I wanted to say. I balled my hands into fists and squeezed.

Something *click, click, clicked* through the kitchen and I drew myself back into the shadows.

"Harold, go back to bed," Rae said, but the pug snorted and wriggled at her feet. "Go," she repeated, nudging him with her slippered foot. Harold snorted, and started *click, click, clicking* again.

Toward me.

"Crap," I said under my breath as I watched the lumpy little dog waddle toward me. Now what?

"Harold, get over here," Rae hissed, her chair scraping the tile as she stood up. "Don't go back there. Come on, let's go outside." She patted her pajama pants, and Harold made a quick U-turn back toward the kitchen.

The back door slid open and shut and I let myself breath again.

If I was going to do this, I knew I only had a minute— two, tops.

I crept silently through into the kitchen, careful to duck as I passed the sliding glass door where Rae stood next to a knee-high snowdrift, holding Harold's leash. When I got to the table, I snatched the phone, hands shaking.

I slid my finger over the unlock button and the phone yawned to life.

I knew Rae was hiding something, but nothing could have prepared me for what I saw.

Rae's face smiled up at me from the screen, and she actually looked pretty. Her hair was smoothed down and the way the dusky sunlight soaked her face made her look younger, less worn.

And next to her stood Ella.

*My* Ella, with her arm wrapped tightly around Rae's shoulder. Her hair fell in straw-colored waves over her fleece jacket and a knitted cap created a halo around her head. Only this hat didn't have ears.

She was beautiful—all sunlight and strawberry-stained cheeks. And she was smiling, the real kind. With teeth. I could barely see her scars in this picture.

*Her scars.*

This picture was taken after I left Amble.

I pinched the screen to expand the background. Rows of scraggly beech trees jutted out from the snow. My head snapped up to look out the sliding door.

Beech trees. And snow.

This picture hadn't been taken that long ago. It could have been just weeks ago. Maybe even days.

My fingers fumbled over the screen as I hurried to type

in a phone number. My heartbeat slammed against my rib cage as I pushed *send*.

The sliding door flew open and Rae stumbled into the house, practically dragging Harold in behind her. She froze, her eyes darting from me to the phone in my hands and then back to me. There was a stretch of time where I thought she might not freak out, where she might just calmly ask for her phone back and then ask me what the hell was going on here.

But this was Rae. And, of course, I was wrong.

She let out a low, guttural sound and lunged for me. I screamed and shoved an elbow into her chest to keep her back, but she still managed to grab hold of my hair and pull.

*Hard.*

She dragged me to the floor and knocked the phone out of my hand. Ella's face skidded across the tile and bumped into the island with a thump.

"That's none of your business!" Rae screamed in my ear. "You think you own everything, that you can do whatever you want to anyone. You can't! You can't just take things from me!"

Just then, the spark of animosity I'd started to feel toward Rae when we were both back in Amble burst into a full-fledged inferno. I reached up and dug my nails into her wrist until she howled and let go of my hair. Then I scrambled to my feet, and as soon as I was vertical, Rae wound back to hit me.

"No," I said, snatching her wrist and squeezing. I stared into her eyes, all wild and feral and furious. "You aren't going to hurt me anymore."

"Claire?" Grant's voice, still heavy with sleep, wafted into the kitchen. His mouth dropped open as he glanced back and forth between me and Rae. "What's going on? And what the hell is *this*?" Grant held up his phone, where both Ella and Rae smiled back at me from the screen.

Rae jerked her wrist free, panting. She made a lame attempt to smooth her hair back. It didn't work. "It's a picture. Obviously."

Grant stepped forward, still holding the phone out in front of him. Dawn had just begun to spill over the horizon, and a patch of morning light stained his face as he moved toward us. For a flash of a second, I caught a glimpse of his expression.

And it was furious.

"Tell me what the hell is going on here. Right now," he said through gritted teeth. He clamped a hand on Rae's shoulder and practically shoved her into a chair. "No more stories. No more lies."

Rae sighed, rubbing her wrist. She wouldn't even look at me. *Good,* I thought.

"Fine," she said, glaring up at Grant. "I saw Ella about a week ago. But I didn't ask her to come here. I didn't even know she was coming. All of a sudden, she just showed up on my doorstep with a backpack."

My heart thudded to a stop. If the wolves had taken Ella, why would she have a backpack?

"She said she took the bus up here, that she was on her way to somewhere else, but she didn't tell me where." At this, Grant lifted an eyebrow, but Rae raised her palms and said,

"I'm telling the truth. I don't know where she was going. Anyway, she was only here for a half a day at most. And then she left."

"What did she want from you?" Grant asked. He still hadn't removed his hand from Rae's shoulder.

Rae shrugged. I could tell she didn't want to say anymore, but Grant wasn't about to give her a choice. "She just asked a lot of questions about ... escaping. That was her word, not mine. 'Escaping.' She wanted to know how I'd managed to get out of Amble—and *stay* out—without getting dragged back in." Rae swallowed. "She asked how to get away from something you don't want to be around anymore."

"What else?" Grant asked.

Rae shook her head, pressing her fingers into the corners of her eyes. She looked miserable, and I didn't care. She continued, "She said she was on her way to meet up with someone who could help her. I told her to call me whenever she got where she was going, but she never did." Rae's fingers began to shake. "She seemed really freaked out when she left. She—she kept saying she had to get away from 'him,' but she didn't tell me who that was."

"Why wouldn't you tell us?" I whispered. And then fury washed over me again, sharp and dangerous, and I yelled, "WHY WOULDN'T YOU TELL ME?"

Rae's head snapped up and in a flash she was back to normal. No more shaking, no more tears. "Because you don't deserve to know," she hissed. "You hurt her, didn't you, you psychopath? You left her out in that cornfield to die. And now you're pretending to actually give a shit about what

187

happens to her, and dragging my brother along with you? Fuck you, Claire. You don't deserve Ella. You never did."

"No, fuck *you*, Rae!" Grant roared. He snatched his hand away from her shoulder, as if her skin was laced with as much poison as her words. "I came with Claire because I wanted to. I have a mind of my own, you know. You'd know that if you'd stuck around, maybe called once in a while. Do you know what it feels like to watch someone you love run away, to disappear? DO YOU?"

Grant towered over her, panting, waiting, but Rae said nothing. She just stared up at him with empty eyes and without a hint of remorse. I watched his fists clench.

I gently touched Grant's back and said, "No, Rae, you don't know what it's like. You were always the one leaving, and you never once thought about anyone but yourself, about what you were leaving behind. I left Ella because I had to, not because I wanted to. And I came back for her." I balled up the edge of Grant's sweatshirt in my fist. "If anyone deserves Ella, it's *me*. You're just a lying, conniving bitch and you deserve *no one*."

Grant's chest rose and fell for what felt like the first time in a minute. I slid my hand into his. "Come on, Grant, let's go home," I told him.

I didn't look back.

# twenty-three

When we were about ten miles from Amble, Grant said, "Rae was never the same after that Robbie guy dumped her."

I rubbed my eyes and blinked at him. The sun cast geometric patterns across his skin: stars and squares played around his eyes. The worry lines in his forehead, the way he drove with one hand looped over the top of the steering wheel and the other looped around my wrist—he looked like one of the most beautiful things I'd ever seen.

The thing about Grant was, he was what I'd call super innocent. Not that he hasn't kissed a girl (obviously), or done whatever else, but that whatever he did, he meant it. He held words on his tongue as if they were razor blades that could cut and he needed to be careful. He only went to places when he needed to be there, and only smiled when he felt it. That was what made his smiles so much more special; like finding a twenty-dollar bill on the street three days in a row. You never thought it would happen to you, but when it did, you were dumbstruck with wonder. So when he held my hand and told me about Rae on the way home, I knew he meant what he said.

He told me that what he'd said in Alpena was true; he'd been devastated every time Rae threatened to leave. And that before she ran away for the last time, with Robbie, she used to feel bad about that. She used to make Grant banana pancakes and hug him and play Twister with him and their old basset hound, Murphy. But after she left and went to Chicago, she never called. She never came back home. Even after Robbie left her in Chicago only two weeks later, Rae refused to come home. She spent the next year doing odd jobs like waitressing and lawn cutting and living God knows where, until she ran out of money and boyfriends and decided to move up to Alpena to live with Aunt Deb. She never did come back to Amble, or to Grant.

"It's hard to feel like someone's going to leave you any second, any day, you know?" Grant swallowed. "Like they're just going to disappear into thin air."

I nodded. "Yeah. I know how that feels." I did know, unfortunately. I'd always known that Rae was going to leave. I'd felt her slipping away before she got into Robbie's beater and drove down the highway. That pain was supposed to be temporary, though, because I was going to leave too.

I was supposed to go make dresses in New York, even if Ella had sealed her fate with a bottle of orange nail polish and a bench that now said *Ella Graham lives here.*

I guess, when it came down to it, I always knew somehow

that Ella and I wouldn't be able to stay together forever. Even if neither of us left Amble, there would be jobs and boyfriends, and then husbands and probably kids, and then we'd see each other on Christmas and Easter. I guess even when you love someone with everything you have, there's still no way to guarantee that you can keep them with you.

My mind drifted back to the map, the visit to Rae, the diary. It was looking more and more likely that Ella had chosen to leave Amble, that she'd packed up her toothbrush and headed north on her own. But the questions of why and who—or *what*—she was running from still lingered like a pungent scent that clung to me and wouldn't let me go.

I had to find the other diary.

If *The Diaries of Ella Graham: Part Two* was from the past year, then *Part One* had to be from the year immediately following the accident. I'd only been gone two years, so it made sense that there were two diaries. And I knew that Ella hadn't kept a diary before, not when I was in Amble. And when I'd searched her room before I found her in the cornfield, I'd found that same purple notebook, and it had been empty then.

*Part Two* left me clues about Ella's planned escape, and that she was afraid. I hoped *Part One* would tell me what she was afraid of.

I sighed. Lacey Jordan's sharp words bit at the back of my brain: *Mmm. Rumors. Just like those rumors about how your dad screwed up the evidence when he was out looking for Sarah Dunnard and couldn't wrap up the case. Some people even said he hid*

*it on purpose, that he went all psycho out there. But those rumors
turned out to be true, didn't they? Runs in the family, I suppose.*

And then Rae's: *Crazy. I always knew you were crazy.*

*Crazy.*

Crazy or criminal?

Lies or the truth?

Was there anything that fell in between?

There was this sliver of light between what was real and
what was a lie that I couldn't quite reach on my own. The news
articles and missing police reports and endless rumors had clotted up my mind. But lingering beneath the headlines was the
whisper of something else—something closest to the truth—
that could explain the thread between what Dad had found at
the edge of the Dunnards' backyard and what had attacked Ella
in the cornfield.

Like always, there was a space between the wolves and the
print on the computer screen, between possibility and what
everyone in Amble preferred to believe.

I was starting to realize that this was somehow bigger than
finding Ella. This was about finding the truth.

"Grant." I chewed at the corner of my lip. He stole a quick
glance at me and kept driving without a word. Waiting. My
pulse quickened. I was losing it. "I need to know the truth.
About something. About everything." My voice cracked. It was
all I could get out.

I expected him to put on his cop face and scrunch his
nose as he pondered his question. He'd want to know the spe-
cifics: if I meant the truth about the wolves. Or Ella. Or Dad.

Or me.

How could I explain it was all those things, but most of all, I needed the truth behind what stitched them all together?

But Grant didn't ask any questions. He didn't furrow his eyebrows or pick at a hangnail or otherwise stall. He just reached for my hand, slipped his fingers between mine, and said, "Yeah, I could use a little more of that myself right about now."

The tires crunched on the ice as we pulled into my parents' driveway. As I hopped out of the truck, I noticed ribbons of tire tracks weaving across the driveway. Lots and lots of tire tracks.

"Hey," Grant said slowly, scrunching his nose. "I thought your parents didn't have their New Year's Eve party last night?"

My eyes scanned the tire markings. There had to have been at least six or seven cars here at one point. "Yeah," I said. "They didn't."

We both looked up at the windows, which were lit up like fireflies. Except for the broken weathervane in the front yard, everything seemed normal, quiet even.

But as soon as we stepped through the front door, the hairs on my arms pricked, and Grant held his breath next to me. Something was very, very wrong.

"Claire?" Mom called out from the kitchen. "Claire, come in here please."

I grabbed Grant's hand and pulled him forward. He didn't even try to talk me out of making him come with me.

Mom sat at the kitchen table, cradling a cup of tea and doing that kind of rocking thing she and Aunt Sharon do. Her eyes had this glazed-over look, and even though she said,

"Oh, hi Grant," when we came in the kitchen, her eyes never left the wall behind us.

I dropped Grant's hand and knelt down in front of her. "Mom, what's going on?"

She looked at me with watery eyes. "The reporters from Channel 6 have been here all night. The police think they might have found something that was Ella's."

I looked at Grant, who was digging furiously through his pocket. "No, Grant. The police wouldn't have called you," Mom said, sighing. "It's a holiday. Mike said trainees aren't supposed to work on holidays."

"I could help," he said softly, more to himself than to either of us.

Mom smiled. "I know, honey. You *are* helping, by being here with Claire." As soon as she said it, fat tears began to slide down her cheeks.

I closed my eyes. As angry as I was with my mother for letting Dad send me away when I needed them both, I still hated to see her cry. She was one of those criers who could be in movies, she was so good: a single tear trickled down to her chin, big eyes, quivering lips. I replaced her face in my mind with Ella's smiling, happy one and screwed up the courage to ask, "What did they find?"

"Claire, we shouldn't discuss—"

"Mom!" I yelled, standing over her now. "Stop treating me like I'm this glass window that's going to shatter if I get some bad news. Tell me what they found. *Please.*"

This time, she closed her eyes and set her full tea mug

on the table. "They found one of Ella's mittens. The orange ones she made. At a bus station in the Upper Peninsula."

"The Upper Peninsula...in *Michigan*?" Grant asked.

Mom nodded solemnly and pretended to sip her tea.

All of a sudden, I wasn't there anymore. I was back in the cornfield two years ago, looking at Ella's damaged, bloody body lying in the snow, her hands smothered in orange wool. "Did they have blood on them?" I breathed.

Mom burst into a choking sob and said something I couldn't understand. "Mom, stop, it's okay." I grabbed her hands and pulled them away from her face. "Those are the mittens she was wearing the night the wolves—the night of the accident." Grant handed me a paper napkin from the counter and I gave it to her. "It was probably just old blood."

Grant nodded. "Or it might have been someone else's orange mitten."

Mom and I both shook our heads at the same time. The odds that anyone else had a lumpy orange mitten with speckles of blood on the thumb were slim. But then Mom surprised me with something else. "The guy who works at the snack station at the bus stop in Marquette said he saw her there after they showed him her picture." She dabbed under her eyes. "Why was she there?" she asked, looking at me now. "Why would she be there?"

I looked at Grant, and read in his eyes that same thing that was going on in my head: *Was that where she headed after she left Rae's?*

"I don't know, Mom." I said, patting her hand.

"Claire and I are trying to find her, too." Grant stepped

forward and placed his hand on Mom's shoulder. "Do you think you can help us?"

I tried not to cringe. The last thing I'd wanted was to remind my parents that I was still searching. They already thought I was crazy enough, looking for wolves they didn't think existed, so what would they think about me scouring remote towns and diary entries to find Ella?

But Mom just nodded and put her hand on top of Grant's. "I'll do whatever I can to find her."

Grant nodded again. "We need you to tell us where all Ella's old stuff is, like stories and things she made when she was little."

I scrunched my nose at Grant, but he pretended to ignore me. He must have a reason for wanting to dig through Ella's old Barbies and sticker books.

I waited for Mom to make the same face that I did and to tell us both to get out. But she just nodded and said, "I'll show you where I keep all the girls' old things."

I looked at Grant, who just smiled his crooked grin back at me. It was funny, because I'd always thought that Ella was magic, and now Grant thought that I was magic. But maybe Grant was magic too, and his magic was that his sincerity in everything he did made people do crazy things, like open up a box of construction paper stories and trust that he'd be able to find the answers hidden there.

———————

"You can stop staring at me like that now," Grant said, not bothering to look up from the box he was digging through.

"Like what?" I asked. "Like I think you're a little unbalanced for wanting to search through a box of baby dolls for clues? No can do." I smiled, and Grant lifted his head just in time to catch it.

"You told me the diary you found said *Part Two*, right?" he asked, pulling free a stuffed hippo with a missing eye.

"Yes, but I wasn't anticipating searching through a box of moldy stuffed animals to find *Part One*."

"What better place to look for an old diary than in a box of old stuff? Besides, in my deputy training program, I learned that you're always supposed to go through the victim's possessions, every time, whether you think they matter or not. You never know what you might find there."

*Victim*. He said the word "victim." Not missing person, not runaway. Victim.

My heart sank with disappointment. If Grant considered Ella a victim instead of a runaway, which police case, exactly, was he thinking about? The case of the girl who slipped out from under Amble's heavy fist, or the case of the girl whose face got shredded open on a star-speckled night?

And if he was thinking of *that* case, then what was he thinking about me?

Crazy or criminal?

Or something else entirely?

"What are you thinking about?" Grant asked, his mouth hitched in a tentative smile.

I shook away the thoughts polluting my brain. Grant

knew me, trusted me. Just because the rest of Amble considered me crazy, it didn't mean he did. "I'm just thinking that I don't think we're going to find the first diary in that box."

"Why not?"

I tossed aside a sock monkey with a missing eye. What was with all the stuffed animals with gouged-out button eyes? "I think the first diary is from just over a year ago, and Ella hasn't looked at or played with this stuff in ages. I just don't know how it would've ended up in here."

Grant shrugged. "You never know. And at the very least, we could find something else important."

I guessed I couldn't argue with that.

For the next twenty minutes we sifted through Ella's past: her stories, her stick figure drawings, her first mangled attempts at knitting and sewing. I suddenly found a lump in my throat that I had to keep swallowing down.

"What about this one?" Grant asked, tossing a faded, green-construction-paper story at me. This one was tied together with starred ribbon.

I read the title: *Why Fairies Aren't as Good as Whales*. Only *Fairies* was spelled "Farees." I shook my head and laughed. "This, right here, is going to tell us where Ella is. I mean, at the very least, don't you want to know *why* fairies aren't as good as whales?" I winked and tossed the book back to Grant. "I do."

Grant flipped through the book, his eyebrows furrowing at the pages. "Hey Claire, did you know that fairies can zap you into dust but whales eat millions of pounds of stuff that looks like dust?"

I smiled, but the hole where Ella belonged hurt when I did. I pressed my hand to my chest. "Makes sense to me."

I started to dig through the box again when Grant flipped open a notebook and scribbled something on it. I leaned over. "What's that?"

Grant finished what he was writing and shut the cover. "Just taking some notes. It's a cop thing." He grinned when he said it, like he knew it was corny before it even came out of his mouth.

We both reached into the box at the same time. Grant pulled out some kind of fabric-covered book and I grabbed a yellowing paper from the bottom. The top of the paper was covered in scrawling pink letters that read, *Claire is so Good!* I smiled as I ran my fingers across the bumpy wax letters, imagining Ella's tongue sticking out as she wrote them. There was a picture of the two of us that she'd drawn: two wiggly little stick figures with bows. I guessed I was the bigger one. Under the drawing were the words *Dear Claire. Thanks for being the best in the world. Thanks for giving my unicorn a bath. Thanks for giving me extra cookies. Love, Ella.*

I let out a choking sound, but I wasn't sure if it was because I was about to laugh or cry. This was the Ella I knew, the one we all knew. Not the Ella who wrote strange poetry and half-eaten words in her diaries. Where was this Ella, the one who was a terrible artist and dressed up as a narwhal and ate too many cookies for breakfast?

"What's this?" Grant asked, more to himself than to me. He flipped through the pages of what looked like just another construction-paper story. But the jagged drawing on the cover made me freeze.

A wolf.

"What does it say?" I breathed, but Grant didn't reply. His eyes scanned the pages, and as he read, the skin between his eyebrows began to wrinkle up.

After a minute, he glanced up at me, shock stretched across his face. "I think you should read this." He handed me the book.

I flipped to the first page and saw two stick figures: one short with a mess of blond hair, the other tall with a thin smile and a bald head. Ella and Dad. The words on the page read:

*Once upon a time, Dad and I were walking through the cornfield when he got scared. He told me to go wait by the road.*

I flipped the page.

*He was gone for a long time. When he came back, he looked even scareder. That's when he told me about the wolves.*

*Dad says there's wolves all around and that he has to protect us. That's what he was doing in the cornfield. He was trying to find them.*

*But afterward, he said it's our secret. He said I can't tell anyone or it will scare them. So I wrote it in this story because it's a story and stories can be real or made up. You never know.*

I handed the story back to Grant, dumbfounded. "Why would she make that up?"

Grant cleared his throat as his hand swept across the page. I waited for him to tell me whatever was on his mind, but he just kept kind of growling, like he was on autopilot, as he wrote, forgetting that he'd wanted to say something. He scribbled furiously.

Finally I said, "Okay, seriously, what are you writing?"

He snapped the cover closed again and picked up the paper book. "I don't think she was making this up. Ella's other stories were all about creatures and magic and all that. This one is a little too … *real.*"

I picked up the book and tried to see what he saw, but I couldn't. "I mean, yeah, out of all the stories, this one *could* have happened. But I'm pretty sure it didn't. My dad thinks the wolves are total bullshit. No way he'd go 'hunting' for them one day."

Grant muttered something and raked his fingers through his hair. I blinked at him. "My dad thinks they're total bullshit. Right?"

"I overheard something one time, when I was working late at the station," he said slowly, his eyes still on Ella's story. "Seth was on the phone with someone—I don't know who—and he said something like, 'I'm going to catch that Mike Graham in a lie one day soon. I'm going to make him admit he thinks he saw wolves out there on the Dunnard case. This town deserves to know the truth about him.'"

"The truth about him? What's the truth about him?" I couldn't keep the panic from edging its way into my voice.

Grant shook his head. "I don't know. All I know is what the paper reported: that your dad screwed up some kind of evidence on the Dunnard case and resigned shortly after that. I have no idea if he did it on purpose, or if something made him go crazy out there, but Seth is hellbent on proving that's what happened."

Just then Grant's phone began to buzz in his pocket. "Hold on a sec," he murmured, touching the screen to read the text.

I thumbed through the pages of Ella's book. Had Dad ever given me any indication that he believed in the wolves, ever? I forced my brain to stretch back in time.

No, I didn't think so. Not that I could remember.

I shoved all of the stories and one-eyed stuffed animals back into the box and started to haul it to the basement, my mind still reeling.

"Hey Claire. Come here."

I set down the box and turned. Grant was bent over my TV, pressing buttons with one hand, his phone in the other. "How do I turn this on?"

I jabbed the power button. "What's going on?"

He pressed buttons until he got to the local news. Splashed across the screen were the flickering lights of a bus station. A reporter with bushy hair stood in front of it, her lips moving over the microphone:

"…Single mitten was found at this bus stop early in the morning. The attendant has positively identified the girl as fifteen-year-old Ella Graham, the missing person from Amble, Ohio. Although records show Ms. Graham seems to have bought a ticket head toward Iron River, Michigan, she never boarded the vehicle. Local and state police are still searching for her at this time."

Then they flashed a picture of Ella across the screen; what was left of her mouth was raw and pink. I had to look away.

The walls were churning and groaning, shifting against the floorboards and pressing in all around me.

*She never boarded the vehicle.*

I knew where Iron River was. A boy that went to my high school—Gabe, I think—used to live there before his parents moved to Amble when he was six. I remembered him telling me that Iron River was so cold, his snot used to freeze to the inside of his nose in May. It was in the Upper Peninsula, right at the Wisconsin border.

Was this the place Ella had told Rae about, the place she was going to meet someone that could help her?

And if it was, why didn't she get on that bus?

What got to her before she could escape?

I closed my eyes, trying to force away the thoughts eating at me. The police were looking for Ella. The media were looking for her. Grant and I were, too. But it seemed like the more people looked, the faster time ticked and the world crumbled around us and the further Ella slipped into the darkness.

# twenty-four

I was frozen. I didn't know where to go next. But luckily, Grant did.

He didn't say anything the entire way into town the next morning. When the reflection off the snow fell on his face a certain way, for a second I couldn't see his mouth. A ribbon of white light slithered across his skin like a scar. It made my stomach lurch and I had to look away.

I jumped out of the truck as soon as he parked it along the curb. It seemed like I was doing everything faster since the news story: brushing my teeth, eating, even sleeping. But time was moving quicker, and so was Ella, and if I wanted to find her I had to keep up.

"Come on," Grant said, guiding me toward a tiny cafe across from the diner. "We need to get something to eat, regroup. Strategize."

I had to admit, the thought of a massive latte and a sandwich was pretty appealing.

Grant's fingers grazed my back as he led me past the shops. When we walked by the bead shop, I couldn't help but glance inside. I'd never be able to pass it without thinking of Ella. I almost passed the stationery shop up completely, but something in the window caught my eye.

It was a wolf.

"Hold on a second." I pulled away from Grant to look in the window. Yes, that was it—the same wolf journal with glued-on eyes Grant had given me two years earlier. I squinted at a small sign under it that read, *More wolf items inside!*

I turned back to Grant. "Hey, can we stop in here for a sec?"

Grant shrugged, rubbing his eyes. "Sure. But seriously, I need a coffee. You can only stare at stuffed animals and stick figures for so many hours without caffeine."

I stood on my tiptoes to kiss his cheek. "Ten minutes. Promise."

The bells to the stationery shop jingled as we walked in. But they didn't really sound jingly; it was kind of like there was a sock stuffed in them so the sound came out muffled. In fact, everything in the shop looked kind of muffled in a way. The walls were muted gray, and the rugs were a hodgepodge of faded blues. Even the cards and stationery that lined the walls looked smothered in dusty light. While everything else outside seemed to be moving faster, it had come to a screeching halt in here.

I walked the perimeter of the shop, searching for wolf-related things. Candice Dunnard's had shop opened shortly before I'd left Amble, so I'd never been inside, but I'd heard about it. Mrs. Dunnard had always been known around town as a little bit of a "wolf freak"—she was always touting Amble's legendary wolves to the (few) tourists who came here, and when there were reports of a rabid wolf in Minnesota attacking an elementary school playground, she tried to capitalize on the news by selling little beaded *Wolf No More* talismans out of her house. Then she opened the shop and started stuffing it with journals and carvings and books, all about wolves.

Ironic that her own daughter had gotten snatched up by them.

There were rows and rows and dusty cards, and a table full of rose-colored stationery in the middle of the shop, but no other wolf things. Finally, after another loop around the store, I found a single, lopsided shelf near the back. But there was only one row of wolf journals on it, and that was it.

"I thought this place was supposed to sell a bunch of wolf stuff?" I said. "There's, like, nothing in here."

The skin between Grant's eyebrows puckered. "Yeah, I know. There used to be a ton of weird stuff in here—at least there was when I bought that diary a couple years ago. I don't know what happened."

I stepped toward the glass-case counter and reached to ring the service bell. Maybe I could at least talk to Mrs. Dunnard about the wolves. My fingertip had just grazed the surface of the bell when something on the corkboard behind the counter caught my eye.

*Graham.*

My last name, smattered across a news article headline. But another yellowed article covered up the rest of it. I stepped back and took a good look at the corkboard. Dozens of articles were splashed across it, some with pictures of winter cornfields and black-and-white houses that looked eerily similar to mine. And some with just the name Graham.

No, *all* with the name Graham.

I heard Grant breathing behind me, probably trying to process the same thing I was. I pulled away from the counter and stepped behind it.

"What are you doing?" Grant whispered. "You can't do that."

"Grant," I snapped. "My name is all over this lady's store. Like hell I can't go back here." He turned quiet then, and I immediately regretted the sharpness in my voice. I looked back at him. "I'm sorry, it's just... this is freaking me out, okay? Just give me sec."

He nodded, and I turned back to the board.

All of these articles, every single one of them, was about my family. I pulled off one that had a picture of the house that looked like mine—because it *was* mine—and started reading.

*Amble police chief Mike Graham faces local retaliation after stepping down from the Sarah Dunnard missing persons case. The home where he resides with his wife and daughter was vandalized late last night. The case is currently under investigation.*

I squinted at the grainy photo of our house. Everything looked the same except for the deep hole near the back, so dark and jagged it looked like something had tried to take a bite out of it. But I knew better; it was the damage caused by the arsonists. And just above it, two lines of sprawling, angry letters, but I couldn't make out the words.

I reached up to put the article back in its place when another headline caught my eye. The date on this one was from January 2nd. The same date as today. The same date as on my one-way ticket to New York, the same date stamped onto the sticker on my suitcase only two years ago.

*Victim's Sister Named a Suspect in Attempted Murder Case*

Carefully, I plucked the article from its pushpin.

There was a picture of the cornfield where I'd found Ella that morning, only now it was all wrapped up in police tape. I skimmed the faded letters. It was mostly about the incident, how Ella was found by her older sister, how she was in a medically induced coma for the week following her reconstructive surgery.

But there was one paragraph lingering at the end, kind of as an afterthought. Only to me it meant that the whole universe was crashing down on me and the stars snapped from their strings and got tangled in my hair.

> *A paring knife with the victim's blood on the blade was found in the older sister's possession the following day, automatically making her a suspect. Following an investigations by the police, Claire Graham was*

*released without further questioning due to the evidence being circumstantial.*

I didn't realize I was holding my breath until Grant was behind me, patting me on the back and whispering "Breathe, Claire" into my ear.

I spun around to face him, my cheeks hot and everything else inside me numb. A flicker of an image, white-hot and dangerous, sliced across my memory. "Ella's blood was on a knife. In the cornfield."

Grant's head dipped below his shoulders. He didn't say anything.

"How many more, Grant?"

He took a step back, palms raised. "How many more what?"

"How many more articles are like this?" I took a step forward and rubbed my hands against my eyes to blot out the tears. "How many more are out there? And what *else* is in the police records that we can't seem to find?"

Grant's whole body slumped and he closed his eyes, like just looking at me was too much for him to bear. "I don't know. But I swear to God, Claire, I don't know why the records aren't in the database."

I felt like I'd been punched in the stomach. I stood there, in front of Grant, gasping for breath. "That's why the whole town's furious I didn't get charged—there was a freaking *knife* on me."

Suddenly, the floor started to tilt beneath my feet and my

head got all fuzzy. I leaned over and pressed my forehead to the cool glass of the counter, forcing air into my lungs.

When I blinked open my eyes, a smear of silver and brown swallowed up my vision. I blinked again, and a knife tucked into the glass case took shape.

I pulled my face from the counter, still blinking away the black spots dancing before my eyes. The knife was nestled in an old wooden box. At first, it looked just like any other knife, but when I got past the blade, I saw that the handle was wooden, carved into the jagged image of a wolf.

"I've seen this knife somewhere before," I said to Grant.

"Of course you have," answered a warbling voice that was definitely not Grant's. I spun around to find Candice Dunnard leaning up against the entryway to the shop's back room. She tilted her pointy chin up and looked down at me. "Your father bought one from me years ago. Why don't you ask him to borrow it the next time you're out hunting wolves?"

In my mind, the same wooden box tumbled out of the hall closet while Ella dug through the mittens and hats. "*Ew,*" she'd said, slamming the box shut. "*Dad has the weirdest stuff.*"

I must have looked like my brain wasn't working for a second as I stood in front of her, open-mouthed and stunned into silence. She didn't wait for me to respond. "Your family ruined my life. Now get the hell out of my store. You're not welcome here."

I shook my head. "But I don't understand—"

"Your father hid evidence in my daughter's case. I'm *sure* of it. Something that might have led to a conviction, to closure for me and my family. And then all the drama of the resignation," she said, throwing her hands in the air, "and the rumors about how there were wolves out there that took Sarah. And then your sister's various cases, which have completely overtaken any investigative powers the police mustered for my daughter these past two years. Your family is nothing but a bunch of liars." She gritted her teeth, disgust practically radiating off her skin. "There are no wolves, unless you count the ones with the last name Graham."

Just then I felt heat and light and safety. Grant's arm looped around me, gently guiding me away from Candice Dunnard. I let him pull me away from her vile words, from her twisted Graham-collage splattered throughout her rundown store.

"Get the hell out!" she screamed, one last time for effect. We were already on our way out the door. The words sounded muffled, like my ears were stuffed with cotton balls, and I knew I needed to sit down—and fast—before I passed out.

I took a shaky step onto the sidewalk and slammed directly into Lacey Jordan.

"Watch it!" she yelped as she pushed me away from her. I gasped, my lungs choking on the icy air. Lacey brushed back her hair and glanced at her friend, who had a face I kind of remembered. History class, I think. Third period. A million years ago.

It was right about then that I noticed that Lacey and her friend weren't the only ones staring at me.

A group of kids about my age was clustered around the door to the diner where I'd found Grant. A dozen pairs of eyes watched me, their mouths zipped into tight lines. Two people I didn't recognize stared shamelessly at me from the shop across the street.

It felt like the entire town had been put on pause, and all of its residents were trapped in place by the concrete that filled up their heads. And every last one of them was watching me.

Hunting me.

Like I was the wolf.

*There are no wolves, unless you count the ones with the last name Graham.*

My back tingled as Grant's fingers brushed between my shoulder blades. An alarm pinged in my chest; I needed to tell him not to touch me, not now. It was too dangerous. I was too dangerous.

But it was too late, anyway. Their eyes bounced between us, pausing for a fraction of a section over Grant's hand making contact with my jacket. He wasn't even touching my skin, but the fact that he was within a centimeter of my clothing seemed to be enough to classify him as crazy and criminal, too.

"You missed my New Year's Eve party the other night. Don't worry, though, I'm having another little get-together tonight. You're coming, *right*, Grant?" Lacey asked, her eyes narrowing. It was a loaded question, thick with a meaning that she tried to keep smothered but failed: *You're still one of us, right, Grant?*

Grant gave a quick shrug of his shoulders. "Depends on when I get off work, I guess." He stared at the crack in the cement between us when he said it.

Lacey watched him for a long second before saying, "It'd

probably be a good idea if you came. Alone." She didn't even bother to pretend to be nice to me this time, and now I knew why—it had less to do with my dad and everything to do with Amble. I was everything this town didn't want to believe in. And I'd sucked one of its best assets into my little orbit of crazy. Just a little too close for any of them to bear.

Grant nodded and pressed his fingers into my back. "Come on, Claire, let's go." I let him guide me to the truck, even though his fingertips felt like knives. Well, I assumed it was his fingertips I felt poking through the fabric of my jacket. But even after we were in the truck, my skin still stung.

And I realized it wasn't Grant at all.

It was the bitter warnings from everyone else in Amble— watching me, threatening me with tight-lipped mouths and angry eyes. Their warnings nipped at my skin all the way down the street.

"*Get out*," they whispered. And I knew they meant it.

Just how long I had until they threw me out, I didn't know.

# twenty-five

It wasn't hard to convince Grant to take me back to the station to search through the database. Even though I knew he was worried about getting caught again by Seth, he was more worried about me. At this point, there was no place safe for me in Amble.

There were still no case files in the database, just like before. There were articles, though, and they were mostly about Ella. But every once in a while one would mention me. After almost an hour, the words began to melt away until all I could see were the facts beneath the surface of the story.

I was Ella's older sister.

I was fifteen years old.

I was wanted for attempted murder.

Despite the evidence, there was some kind of conclusion the police had come to that kept me from rotting in jail for the rest of my life. But without any official police records, it was impossible to tell why.

*Why?*

I rubbed the skin between my eyes and stared at what seemed like the hundredth article on the screen. Grant sighed, his back turned toward me as he stared out the window at the dying sunlight.

I clicked off the screen. "I'm done looking."

He turned around and plopped into the chair next to me. "Good."

I sighed, burying my face in my hands. "All of this doesn't even matter anyway, not without records or a file."

Grant looked at me for a long second. I could almost see the gears churning behind his eyes. "But the thing is, you *did* have a file. At least, you did a couple years ago, when I first started my training."

I blinked. "I did?"

Grant tapped his lip. "Yeah. I remember an actual, physical file labeled with your name. Like, one on paper. I remember seeing it in a pile on your dad's desk when he was entering stuff in the database. See, we used to keep physical files, but then when Seth took over he wanted to put everything in the same place so it couldn't get lost. So he had your dad input records digitally. I think we still have some of the old files, though, the important ones that Seth wanted to keep copies of." He shook his head. "I didn't even think of that file. There's a chance we still have it."

My heartbeat quickened. "Did you ever look in it? In my file?"

His face changed then, like the light dimmed in his eyes and the creases above his cheeks gave away that he remembered something he'd long since pushed away. He cocked his head to the side, observing me like he wasn't quite sure if I would bite his hand off if he got too close. It was the first time he'd ever looked at me like that. It made my heart drop into my stomach.

Then he reached out and placed his hand on my knee. "I'll be honest. I tried to look in it, but I couldn't get ahold of it for long enough. I only saw a couple of pages." He cleared his throat. "Can you remember anything else about those few days after the incident?"

Could I? There were only flashes of that week, starting with the night of the party, like someone had taken a fat eraser and rubbed away all the parts I wouldn't be able to stand. I remembered the way the Robbie and his friends smelled like sweat and cigarettes. I remembered the icy feeling in my chest when Rae said that Grant wasn't coming. And I remember the way the stalks smelled like Cherry Blast body spray, and that was how I found her. And bloody orange mittens. And snow.

The next week was even foggier. There was the wet smell of the police station. The therapist making scratching noises with the pencil when she wrote. There was the smudged glass outside Ella's ICU room. And there was a cameraman for Channel 6 standing on the front steps of the hospital with snowflakes in his dyed hair. There were Dad and Mom's hurried whispers wafting in from the kitchen before they thought I was awake. And pills. I remember pills. Little pink pills that Mom and Dad and the therapist said were for anxiety. Pills I stopped taking when I met Danny because you're not supposed to mix those with vodka.

I turned to Grant. "I don't remember a lot. I drank a lot that night. But I loved my sister, Grant, and I would never try to kill her."

Grant nodded slowly. "I know you wouldn't. And that's what you said in your statement."

"Oh yeah? What else did I say, since you seem to know me better than I do, *Grant*?" My voice was sharp and the words were bitter on my tongue, and I didn't know why. I didn't know why I was panicking over the fact that Grant had seen the inside of my real file. The inside of the real me.

Grant scrunched his nose and the Big Dipper folded in on itself. "I *do* know you better than you know yourself." He took a tentative step toward me. "I always have."

When I didn't answer, he kept going without even stopping to clear his throat. "I thought it was strange, too, how you never got charged, even with all that evidence piling up. But that thing about the knife in your possession ... they didn't find it in the field near Ella."

My heart fluttered with hope. No knife next to Ella meant that my memory was faulty, webbed with cracks caused by trauma. It was a lot better than being a suspected murderer.

"Your mom found it," Grant said. "In your jeans pocket, the next day."

Every ounce of hope I'd built up rushed out of me, a flood of heartbreak, as he continued. "She gave it to your dad, and the department sent it in for a DNA scan," he said. "It was Ella's blood on the tip." He started to pick at a hangnail, but thought better of it and kept going. "But your Dad testified for you, said that Ella had cut her finger with it earlier in the day cutting an orange."

"And did she?" I asked, my cheeks growing hot. It was a strange thing, hearing about myself from someone else.

Grant shook his head. "I don't know. But that wasn't the only thing that saved you." He took a deep breath. "Ella saved you, too. She told the police she didn't even remember you being there, in the field, until the very end when she heard you singing."

I closed my eyes, and for a second I saw Ella, her face in stitches and her eyelids purple, her hair in matted ringlets around her head in the hospital bed. "She probably didn't remember anything after leaving the party. She didn't remember a lot after the surgery, I know that."

"Maybe," Grant said, pushing in the chair.

Panic swelled in me again and I inched toward him. "*Maybe*? You don't believe me, do you? You know, for someone who knows so much about everything, you could have told me."

Grant stepped back, watching me like I was a wolf, snarling and snapping, but I couldn't stop. "You already made up your mind about me a long time ago, didn't you? You've thought I was crazy this whole time, and you didn't even have the guts to tell me."

"I swear, I—"

"So what do you believe, Grant?" I took another step toward him. I was close enough to him now that I could bump his chin with the tip of my nose. "You read my file while I was in New York, and they all said I'm a murderer.

I'm crazy. But then I come back here and you *help* me try to find Ella." I clenched my hands to keep them from shaking. "You've been helping me try to find the wolves, even though you didn't tell me what was in my own file. Even though you don't know if they exist. What is *that*?"

Grant rubbed the skin on the bridge of his nose and shook his head. I held my breath, and everything in the moldy little office waited with me. I swore even the clock stopped ticking. Whatever Grant said right now, in this stretched-out second, mattered more than anything he'd said in the past week. The past seventeen years, really.

He let out of a puff of air. "I don't know."

My heart deflated and sank into my stomach. I couldn't look at him, so I stared at the watery brown stain on the carpet instead. "How do you not know?" I whispered.

"Claire, listen." He lifted the tip of my chin. "What I mean is, I don't know what really happened out there that night. But I only needed to read a few pages of your file to know that I believed you. I've never thought you were guilty. Not for a second. Whatever else that file says, it doesn't even matter."

"What about the wolves?" I whispered.

Grant sighed. "I don't know. I'm not saying they don't exist, but there are some things I can't explain."

I pulled my chin away from his fingers. Same as Grant, some things with the wolves I couldn't explain. But that didn't mean they didn't exist. It was just so hard to grab hold of the truth through the secrets and lies. If I could just find the truth—the whole truth—about one thing, maybe I could figure out the rest by deduction.

"We have to find my file. The real one," I said.

"Claire, I'm not even sure—"

"I have to look," I said, more forcefully this time. "Please. I need to know everything."

Grant hooked his hand into mine. "Come on, I've got the keys to the file cabinets. Let's see if your old file is still in there." And without another word, he led me down the hallway and into a small alcove outfitted with three steel cabinets and a shoddy-looking desk. I winced when I saw the nameplate: *Mike Graham.*

He shoved a key into the center cabinet, the tallest one, and pulled the top drawer free.

I held my breath as his fingers darted over the files, one after another, until he reached the end of the row. "Weird," he said finally.

"What is it?"

"Your file's not in here, either." He glanced up at me. "Look. Even though some of these files are empty now, at least the names are still on the labels. But there's nothing at all in here with Graham on it."

That settled over my brain like a layer of dust. "But why wouldn't it be there, with all the other old files?"

Grant just shook his head, and reached down to pull open another drawer, even though it was labeled "LAST NAMES H-M."

I poked around the makeshift office, but all I found was

a stack of blank manila folders and a string of empty coffee mugs in desperate need of a wash.

Finally, I came to Seth's office door. I twisted the knob, but the lock clicked in place.

I chewed my lip, thinking. There was no logical reason why my file would in Seth's office.

Was there?

His bulging eyes and puffy belly popped into my mind. *You look just like your father when he's trying to lie. All twitchy.*

Seth's reaction to my presence at the station had seemed extreme, especially since Dad didn't pose much of a threat to his position as chief anymore. Was it possible he'd been reading my file, too?

"I think we should check in here." I tapped a knuckle against the door.

Grant's face clouded over. "I don't think it'd be in there. What would Seth need with your old paperwork?"

I shrugged. "I don't know. But it's the only place we haven't looked." I glanced back at him. He was fiddling with his keys, running his finger over the teeth of a particularly thick one. I moved toward him and wrapped my hand around his wrist. "Don't worry. I'll be in and out. There can't be that many places to look, right?"

Grant nodded slowly. "Okay, but you have to move quick. I don't know when Seth's coming in today." He slipped the key into the lock and pulled open the door.

The chief's office was even smaller than the alcove and the database room in back. My stomach hitched when I saw a dusty gray square staining the wall next to the desk. I traced my finger along the perimeter. Which picture had been in this frame again? I think it was one of me and Ella at the Christmas concert, Ella still decked in her outrageous angel wings. I pulled my hand away.

There was only one beat-up file cabinet in the corner, and it wasn't even locked. I pulled the first drawer open and pawed through the folders: procedural manuals, payroll, and a bunch of other yellowing documents that didn't look important.

Nothing with my name.

I opened the second drawer. This one was mostly empty, except for an old radio with a hole in the speaker and two hanging files. I looked at the first one.

Bingo.

*Graham, Claire.*

I opened it.

The first few pages were official reports on the incident, how they found me at the scene rocking and unresponsive to questioning, how Mom turned in the paring knife for DNA testing. These must have been the same reports Grant had read.

I flipped the page and a name I didn't recognize stared up at me.

*Fourteen-year-old Patrick Gillet made the 911 call when he discovered the victim and suspect in the cornfield at 8:56 a.m.*

Patrick Gillet.

His name bumped against something in my brain, forcing me to remember. I did remember; I knew he went to school me. He must have been in a grade between me and Ella.

A pair of eyes the color of a cloudy morning popped into my mind.

I gasped. Patrick Gillet was the same boy Ella wrote about in her diary, the same boy who'd found us in the cornfield.

My mind raced. Patrick had been at the scene that morning too—he'd seen the gory aftermath of Ella's attack. The last page in Ella's diary flickered in my head.

*He's going to kill me.*

"Claire, hurry," Grant called from the other side of the door. "You've been in there forever."

I blinked until the words melted away and I suddenly felt sick. I flipped through the rest of the pages, searching for anything else I could find about Patrick. But there was nothing.

I was about to close the file and tell Grant to lock up the office when the edge of a crisp, stationery-thick sheet of paper caught my eye. It was the last page in my file. I slipped it free and stared at a seal of some sort, an image of a twisted oak tree with budding leaves.

*Havenwood Mental Institution: Private Records*

I stared at the paper in my hands, unable to comprehend. What was this doing in my file? I scanned the page, and when I saw my name, my fingers started to tingle and the breath clotted in my throat and everything got very, very stuffy.

*Fifteen-year-old Claire E. Graham has been referred for an evaluation for residence in our inpatient treatment facility. Diagnostic tests reveal that there are no physical ailments contributing to mental health; however, there is a family history of psychosis. Because Ms. Graham is currently a minor, and, subsequently, her legal case has been temporarily cleared, our team, including Ms. Graham's parents, has decided a weekly outpatient treatment program with our satellite psychiatrist, Dr. Samuel M. Barges, in Manhattan is the best course of treatment at this time. It is recommended that the patient be treated for mental illness instead of facing prosecution.*

I sank onto the wobbly desk chair and tried to breathe, breathe, breathe.

My parents hadn't shipped me off to New York because I was scared, because I was in so much pain from watching Ella suffer. They sent me away because they *had* to.

It was either that or send me directly to Havenwood, which was the kind of place they sent deranged women who murdered their babies for spilling grape juice on the carpet.

It wasn't the lack of evidence, or Ella's inability to remember, that got me off without any charges. It was because they thought I was legitimately crazy. Certifiable, even.

Had Grant seen this letter?

I pressed my palms to my face and tried to snuff out the images, the thoughts, flashing behind my eyelids.

"Claire!" Grant barked, and I jumped. "Seth's car just pulled up—you're got to get out of there *now.*" He poked his head into the doorway, his face polluted with panic. He glanced at me and then the file. "Hurry, hurry, hurry. Put it back and get out. Let's go!"

Something in me snapped back to life and I spun around to cram my file back into the hanging folder. I started to shut the door when I noticed two hasty letters, scribbled in pencil, on the second file tab.

*M.G.*

"Let's go, he's walking toward the door!" Grant yelled behind me.

I bit my lip. There was a chance this was nothing, that this file didn't have anything to do with Dad. But there was an even bigger chance that it did.

Quickly, I grabbed it out of the hanging folder and shoved it under my jacket. Then I slammed the cabinet shut and raced out the door.

Grant's fingers shook as he tried to jam the key into the lock. Just behind him, the knob to the front door began to rattle. I wrapped my hand around Grant's and squeezed until it stopped shaking. The key slid into the lock with a click.

I didn't let go of his hand as we ran down the hallway, our footsteps muffled by the faded carpet. I heard the hinges of the front door yawn open just as I pulled the back door shut behind us.

# twenty-six

When we pulled into my driveway, I breathed a sigh of relief. The Explorer was gone, and the house sat dark and empty. No parents to face. At least for now.

"Stay," I breathed, pulling the file from my under my coat. "I want you to look at this with me."

I thought Grant's eyes were going to pop out of his head when he saw the manila file in my hands. "Did you—did you take that from Seth's office?"

I chewed on the corner of my lip. The last thing I wanted was to get Grant in trouble—or worse, *fired*—but I had to know the truth. I nodded and tipped the file into a patch of sunlight so he could see the initials. "I think Seth's keeping a secret file on my dad, and I want to know why."

Grant blinked at the file and then looked back up at me. The way the sunlight hit his face made his lashes look like tiny matchsticks. He squeezed my hand. "Well then, open it."

I took a deep breath and turned to the first page inside.

It was a picture. Not of my dad, but of a cornfield. I recognized it from the newspaper articles I'd seen. It was the makeshift backyard behind Sarah Dunnard's house, part of the clearing near Lark Lake. This was where the police had reported finding the pinpricks of her blood, staining the base of the cornstalks.

It wasn't news. I flipped to the next page.

Another picture, and for a second I thought it was a duplicate. But then I saw the blood.

A cluster of stalks just beyond the back porch, splattered in angry slashes of blood. It pooled into the snow like a liquid halo.

Grant saw it too; he reached over me to turn back to the first picture, and then laid them side-by-side. In the newspaper picture, the blood-stained stalks were gone, and so was the clump of snow in front of them. It was almost like they'd never existed.

"But how—" I started, wrinkling my eyebrows.

"There's only one explanation," Grant said slowly. "Someone must have tampered with the evidence before the reporters came."

So the rumors were true—someone had tampered with the evidence in the Dunnard case. "But why?" I asked. "And why would Seth think it was my dad that did it?"

Grant shook his head. "The only thing I can guess is that because your dad was the first on the scene, Seth thought it was most likely him."

I flipped over the pictures and kept going. There were

three more images: one of a mutilated print in the snow, something oval-shaped with blurry edges, and another of a small depression in a snowdrift.

I squinted at the photo of the print. "Animal?"

"Maybe," Grant said, taking the picture from me. "It does kind of have that triangle shape to it, like a paw print. But it's too messed up to tell for sure."

"What's this one?" I asked, holding up the second photo. There was definitely some kind of shape in the snow, like something had been nestled in it, but I had no idea what. It almost looked like two shapes: a perfectly round depression, and a larger, lumpier one beneath it.

"No clue," Grant said. "But Seth must have thought it was important."

I moved on to the third photo: another depression, but this one long and thin and stained with blood at the very tip. My heart stopped and suddenly the air in the truck's cab became very, very still. Grant swallowed and cleared his throat. He didn't have to say anything; I knew what he was thinking.

"A knife," I said slowly. "This looked like it was made by a knife. And it's the same shape and size of my dad's hunting knife." Never mind the blood in the snow where the tip must have fallen.

Grant breathed. "So that's why Seth's hellbent on proving your dad did this."

I snapped my head up to look at him. "He could have just been carrying the knife that day. It could have fallen out of his pocket. It doesn't mean anything. And the cornstalks and paw prints—who knows what that was." I took a breath. "And anyway, if Seth had all this evidence against him, why didn't he just take it to the crime unit in Toledo and have Dad thrown in jail? Why hide it?"

Grant didn't say anything; I could tell he was thinking. Frantic, I flipped through the remaining pages. There had to be something else here, something that screamed "wolf" instead of "murderer."

There were only two pages left. The first was a small slip of paper the size of an index card. It read, *Abbreviated Medical History of M. Graham* across the top.

This was the kind of card you find stapled to the file in your doctor's office, the kind they update every year when you go in for a check-up. Seth had been digging deep to find something, *anything*, to prove Dad's guilt.

I scanned over it. It looked pretty standard, from what I could tell. There was a list of recent check-ups and cholesterol tests; one visit listed for a sprained wrist over five years ago. Nothing out of the ordinary. I looked at the bottom of the card, where the word *Prescriptions* was neatly printed. Under it, there were two words—one I'd heard of and the other I hadn't.

The first was Paxil, an anti-anxiety medication. I remembered the tiny pills from when they'd been prescribed to me in the days following Ella's attack.

The second was something called Clozapine.

"Do you know what Clozapine is?" I asked Grant, but he just shook his head. I bit my lip. "Maybe it works with that anxiety medication, like a mood booster or something."

I slipped the card back into the folder and pulled out the last page, an enlarged photo of the house currently looming in front of me.

But in this photo, the side of the house near Dad's shed was still charred and hollow, and the angry black words still screamed across the siding. This time, they were blown up enough so I could read one of them.

*Watching.*

I threw the image back into the folder and slammed it shut.

"What is it?" Grant asked, worry etched in the lines around his eyes.

I shook my head. How could I explain the way that word curdled in my throat like sour milk; how whenever I read it, I read it in Ella's hurried print.

*They're watching you, Claire.*

I looked up at the house, at the off-color patch of paint along the side. A web of snowflakes stretched across the windshield; the snow was coming down faster now, smothering everything in tufts of white.

"Can you help me with something?" I unbuckled my seat belt. "I need to see what's on the side of the house. Can you help me do that?" I looked steadily at him. "Can you help me figure out the truth?"

Grant leaned over then and kissed me, warm and determined, and pulled the key from the ignition. I led him through the snow, even though it soaked our jeans up to the knee. When we reached the back of the house, I grabbed his hand

and pressed it to the fresh coat of paint. "Feel that? This is where the new paint starts. I scraped off a little of it the other day."

"I remember when this happened," he said as he ran his fingers along a ridge in the siding. "It was big news for Amble. Practically everyone in town came here as soon as they heard about it, but your dad had already painted over it. He was in the middle of painting when the reporters showed up." He scratched at the paint. "This should come off pretty easy. He didn't have time to prime it."

I touched the edge of the letter left behind, the one that looked like it could have a curve. "What do we need to do?"

"I have some paint thinner and a wire brush in the back of my truck. I suppose it wouldn't hurt to give it a shot." Grant wedged his thumb under a crack in the paint and a chip fluttered to the ground. "Yeah, see? It might work."

I laughed, an awkward sound I wasn't used to. "Who drives around with paint thinner and a wire brush in the back of their truck?"

Grant smirked. "The deputy trainee program has many perks, Claire. Besides my paper-filing and coffee-making duties, I also get to scrub graffiti off of Amble's important landmarks in the summer. Such as the elementary school. And the dumpster in the back of the diner."

Then he kissed my cheek so gently that it felt like the memory of a kiss instead of the real thing. "Be right back," he said, his lips lingering on my skin. And then he was gone, while I waited with my hand cupping my face, like if I held it there long enough I could keep his kiss forever.

We started to smooth the paint thinner over the spot with

a couple of massive sponges that Grant also apparently needed to complete his deputy duties. It made the layer of paint watery, and soon it began to drip into the snow. I cringed as I watched the flecks of red turn to pools. It almost looked like blood. I hadn't really thought about what I was going to do *after* I stripped the house down to its secrets.

Grant barely needed to use the wire brush; the paint practically melted away, as if it had wanted us to know what was hidden beneath it all along. I wiped off the last of the paint that hid the curved letter. It turned out to be a *U*. My eyes ran over the rest of the word it belonged to: *you*. I started to feel sick all over again.

Grant stepped back from the wall, pulling me with him. He squeezed my hand as he strung the crooked words together.

*We're watching you, Graham.*

A wave of nausea washed over me. I clenched my stomach as I bent into the snow. I didn't even feel the cold seeping through my jeans.

*They're watching you, Claire.*

Another warning. Another threat of something deadly lingering ahead, waiting. Watching. Another set of eyes— human or animal—waiting to hurt us.

*Breathe.* Grant's voice was in my head and suddenly I was out of the snow and in his arms and wrapped in a blanket on the couch.

I closed my eyes as I listened to his heart beating in his chest. Real. Solid.

Safe.

After a few minutes, the rhythmic thumps began to warp into a low-pitched groan. And then they slowly stretched into something like a howl.

"Grant," I whispered.

He pressed his finger to my lips. "Shhh."

I gently pulled my ear from his T-shirt, but his heart kept howling.

No. The wolves kept howling.

"*Grant.*" I threw off the blanket and ran to the kitchen window. Another howl ripped through the cornfield.

I felt his breath on the back of my neck as I stared out the window.

The stalks at the edge of our yard began to shiver, and I thought for sure I was seeing things. I rubbed my eyes until they burned and looked again. Now I could hear them snapping, even through the window. Grant's hand clasped my shoulder and squeezed.

Nothing in the entire universe could have prepared me for what I saw come staggering out of that cornfield.

Dad stumbled through the snow, wiping the snow off the sleeves of his jacket. He started to make his way toward the back door, and for or a second I thought he saw the graffiti. But I quickly realized he wasn't even looking at the house.

Dad hesitated in front of his shed, staring at the door. He circled it—once, twice—like a wolf analyzing its prey. Then he bent down to inspect the lock, turning it over in his hand.

My pulse raced.

Could he tell I'd tried to open the door, that I'd tugged at the lock? No, he would have said something before.

Right?

Slowly, Dad stood up, still staring at the door. And then he turned and stared straight at me through the window.

# twenty-seven

"Claire, are you here?" Mom's voice wafted in, along with a flurry of snow and a stuffed grocery bag.

*Mom.* Thank God.

"I'm here," I called back, watching Dad wipe off his boots on the back porch.

"Can I help you with that, Mrs. Graham?" Grant asked, and before she could answer, he had already lifted the paper bag out of her arms. Mom smiled, and then winked at me when he wasn't looking.

"Got any tea in there? My throat's a little scratchy," Dad said. He smiled at me. "How 'bout you, Claire-bear? Want some tea?"

I stepped away from him. "No thanks."

He cocked his head to the side, watching me, trying to analyze me with his investigative training.

I turned away. "Maybe you're getting sick because you're

spending so much time outside. In the snow," I challenged, watching as the snowflakes made webs across the window-panes.

Behind me, Grant sucked in a breath.

Dad cleared his throat and said, "Well, that could be the case. Seth's been sending me out to look for those graffiti vandals. You know, the ones that messed up the school." He shuffled to the kettle and lit the burner.

I caught Grant's eye. He shook his head once, just slightly, so that only I would see. And then he went back to unpacking the groceries.

Dad was lying. I remembered that first day in the station, when Grant and I searched the database. I'd overheard Seth telling Grant he'd been working on the vandalism case himself.

The tea kettle screamed, and Mom hummed to herself as she poured the steaming water into two polka-dot mugs. She hooked her fingers around the handles and carried them to the table, Dad trailing behind her.

"What do we do?" Grant murmured, handing me a bag of lettuce.

"I think we need to get some answers," I whispered back, "before we assume anything."

Grant nodded. He scooped up two loaves of bread and shoved them in the bread box on the counter. I smiled to myself. Even two years later, Grant still knew how to locate everything in my kitchen.

I squeezed his hand. And then I turned to face my parents.

They sat at the tiny, bow-legged table by the back window, each drinking from their mugs. Dad's socked feet touched Mom's bare leg as it bounced beneath the table. They looked normal, like someone else's parents sitting in a regular kitchen, on a regular day, reading depressing news stories about things that didn't happen to people like them. I felt a sharp pang in my chest, and I realized that I missed them like this. I missed them the way they were before I knew better. Before I knew about all the secrets they kept.

"Claire? Grant? You guys want something to eat?" Dad asked, setting down the paper. "There's some pie in the fridge."

I stepped into the dying afternoon light and slowly sank into an empty seat across from them. Grant lowered himself into the seat next to me. "Dad. I need something from you."

They both stared back at me blankly, and I froze. There was so much I didn't know, so much I wanted to know—about Ella, about Sarah, about *me*—that I didn't know where to start.

Mom set her mug on the table and folded her hands, waiting. I stole a glance at Dad. His eyes roamed over me, analyzing me, checking for evidence of guilt or deception. I decided then to start with the subject that would bring up the least resistance. They both knew I'd come here to find Ella, so asking questions about her might not cause Dad to harden.

I took a deep breath. "There are a lot of things about Ella's case that aren't adding up for me. Grant's been helping me do a little research And I know you guys think I'm this fragile thing or whatever, like I can't handle any kind of news about Ella. But I'm not, I swear. I'm not going to freak out and bust through the window and run screaming through the cornfield." I choked back a smile, but they didn't seem to get the joke. Dad just nodded and Mom continued to blink at me. "Dad, I need you to tell me what happened the day you found Ella. Really." I set my hand on top of his. "The truth this time. All of it would be nice."

Mom pressed her lips together, over and over again like she was trying to smear on her lipstick. Dad looked at Mom. Mom looked at her mug. And I waited until I thought the silence and the wind rattling the back doorknob would shatter my eardrums. "Please," I said. "I really need you to."

Dad leaned forward and pinched the bridge of his nose. "The day we found Ella—"

"Mike, don't." Mom squeezed Dad's wrist, and I couldn't help but think about Grant's long fingers around my skin. And just like that, his fingers were there, warm and soft and safe.

Dad carefully peeled Mom's fingers away, one by one, looking at her like he was afraid and confident in his decision at the same time. She slid her hand away.

"The day we found Ella, she'd been out there for at least five hours. We weren't ever sure how much time there was between when you arrived back at the scene and when the Gillet boy showed up."

I stared at him, images clicking through my brain like a rusty Rolodex. The last thing I remembered was the singing, or at least I thought. But as Dad's words melted into my brain, more ribbons of memories, snipped into bite-sized pieces, flickered to life. There I was, my bike stopped outside of Grant's house. But by that time the police were there, the house all lit up in blue and red watery light. I couldn't go in, I couldn't ask them. Then they'd find Rae, and I wouldn't be able to keep my promise. Then there was just my breath, and snow, and a mile of broken cornstalks. Running, running, running to the split-level house on the other side of the Buchanans', the one that looked like it was made out of matchsticks. A boy younger than me in between the stalks near the house: blond hair that curled at the tips and heavy-lidded eyes. The one Ella had that picture of, pinned to her corkboard up in her room. Patrick Gillet.

Patrick Gillet had been in the cornfield the same time Ella was attacked.

Something cold prickled up inside me, but I forced it down, for now. I wasn't ready to entertain the idea that someone Ella trusted and loved so much had hurt her so deeply.

I cleared my throat. "Yeah. I remember that."

Dad continued. "Patrick went with you back to the field and waited until we came." He rubbed his fingertips along the edge of the table, back and forth, back and forth. "You were sitting next to her, kind of rocking. And singing. It was ... it was hard to see."

Mom shifted so that she could pull Dad's fingers into hers. He patted her hand. "There was a paring knife from our kitchen there, at the scene. It was a few feet from where Ella was lying."

Grant's knitted eyebrows and wobbly words popped in my head: *They didn't find it in the field near Ella. Your mom found it in your jeans pocket the next day. She gave it to your dad, and the department sent it in for a DNA scan. It was Ella's blood on the tip."*

"I thought they found it in my pocket the next day?" I said to Mom, tapping my finger to my lip. How could my file at the police department say something that was so critically different from what the person who wrote it was telling me now?

Dad looked at me—really looked at me—for the first time since he'd started talking. I thought he might be trying out his cop voodoo mind magic on me, but there was a softness lingering in the corner of his eyes that was usually impossible to find. "I was the first one at the scene. I found it there, and I knew where it came from. And I saw the blood on your hands, and I just... I just couldn't leave it there. I couldn't leave you there."

He let go of Mom's hand and pressed his palm to his forehead. "It was wrong, and I got busted for it like I should have, anyway. Seth was on my ass after the Dunnard investigation started, and I don't think he trusted me to scan the scene alone. He came up while I was trying to clear the evidence." Dad sighed heavily and continued. "He found the imprint of the knife in the snow, with the blood, and he knew something had been there. I had to play stupid while we searched the field, looking for it, knowing it was in my pocket the whole time."

A thought bloomed in my mind and I blurted, "You wrote my reports, and you cleared all the evidence in my case out of the police database, didn't you? So they wouldn't ever find out you took the knife?"

Dad shot Grant a look from across the table. "Yes, I cleared it. But not only to keep me out of trouble with Seth. To keep you out of trouble, too."

I felt my forehead wrinkle. Something still wasn't adding up. "But why was Seth so suspicious of you during the Sarah Dunnard investigation? You guys had worked together for years. He'd always trusted you."

Dad shifted in his seat and took a swig from his now lukewarm tea. "It's no secret that I screwed up that investigation. She just reminded me so much of you girls." His voice cracked over the words, and Mom slid her arm over his shoulders. His face went splotchy, and for a second I was sure he was going to cry. I glanced up at Grant, who looked at me with eyes as round as moons. "She was so young—she looked like a miniature version of you, Claire—and when I found that doll in the cornfield, I just—I just couldn't keep searching for her. It was going to kill me. I had to resign." He looked up at me, eyes shiny with remorse.

But I just stared back at him. I could almost feel the color draining from my cheeks, the heat dripping into my stomach and starting to burn.

*When I found that doll in the cornfield.*

I remembered the images in Seth's secret folder, the ones he'd taken the first day of the search for Sarah. Cornstalks. Blood. Prints.

No doll.

I glanced over at Grant, who looked so ashen under the

kitchen lights that I started to worry if he was actually breathing. After a second, his chest rose and fell, and I cut my eyes back over to Dad.

He was still watching me, faking his crocodile tears. What kind of response did he expect from me?

Something told me to be very, very careful.

I blinked quickly and patted his hand. "It's okay, Dad. It's over now." The words sounded limp coming out of my mouth.

But it seemed to be enough for Dad, because he continued on. "Seth never got over that. Called my mistakes 'irresponsible' and 'inconceivable.' And then when it happened to Ella, and I saw how they got her the same way, I couldn't let them think it was you, Claire."

I narrowed my eyes at him. There was something still hidden under this snippet of truth, and it had everything to do with the word "they."

How *they* got her.

Grant must have noticed it too, because he blurted out, "Why?" He pulled his hand from my wrist and slapped it to the table. "Why would you do that with evidence? You always taught me that an officer's first duty is to protect the people, and tampering with evidence leaves them vulnerable, *not* protected."

Dad let out a low breath that came out like a whistle. "Claire is not the threat here. She's just a girl, my little girl. I couldn't—I didn't want to see anything bad happen to you, Claire. But I couldn't hide it forever. Seth suggested we search my house for the missing knife after the doctor looked at all those cuts on Ella. And I knew I had to tell them I found something. I washed it clean and gave it to him, but they still found a tiny speck of Ella's blood on it when they sent it in." Dad sighed and shook his head. "I've felt like a criminal ever since."

"We did it because we love you, Claire," Mom chimed in, suddenly reanimated. "We were trying to protect you."

No. There was more. I wanted him to say it—to *admit* to me—that he'd believed in the wolves all this time. And then I wanted him to apologize a million times for trying convince me of my own insanity.

"There's another reason you did it," I said, my voice even. "What about the wolves, Dad?"

I stood, and the sound of the chair screeching against the floor echoed through the kitchen. "Ella's attack was almost identical to Sarah's, only you never found Sarah. There are rumors that you saw something in the cornfield when you were still looking for her a few months later, something that made you go all psycho and quit the case. And you just said yourself that I'm not the threat. So then, what is?" I didn't wait for him to answer. "You sent me away because you were afraid the wolves would find me and kill me, like they almost did Ella, like they probably did to Sarah, only you used that whole insanity plea thing to help me escape. Admit it to me. You at least owe me that."

"Claire." Mom stood now, her eyes equal with mine. It was a weird moment to realize it, but I guess that's when I noticed that we were actually the same height, me and Mom.

I don't know why I noticed it right then, but it must have had something to do with that shock thing where you think of pointless things and sing Christmas songs you hate because you're not sure what else to do anymore.

She took a step forward, and all of a sudden she looked like she'd grown three inches. "We sent you away because you needed help, honey. You needed to get away from here, from what had happened with Ella. You were still talking about the wolves, and not eating and not sleeping and not *living*. You needed space. You needed Dr. Barges' help. We never tried to conceal anything from you." Mom placed a tentative hand on my shoulder. "Honey, the only secrets you kept were your own. You just saw what you wanted to see that day."

"Does Mom know?" I whispered, staring at Dad. I was shaking and sweating and starting to feel like they'd made a mistake when they didn't send me to Havenwood. I didn't wait for him to answer. Instead, I ran to the hall closet and started pulling the tangle of scarves from the shelf.

It wasn't there.

The other knife, the one Dad had bought from Mrs. Dunnard's shop a few years back. The knife Ella and I had found in the closet the night of my birthday party. The one that had left an imprint in the snow in the clearing behind Sarah Dunnard's house. The one with the blood on the tip.

I ran back into the kitchen. Mom still stood there, and now Grant was standing next to her. They both didn't look surprised in the least by my antics; in fact, they almost looked sad.

Dad still sat at the table, his shoulders slumped like I had beaten him with my words. I wasn't done yet. "What did you see out there, Dad? When you were looking for Sarah?" I was pleading now, desperate for the truth. "If you can tell anyone, it's me."

He looked at me for a long minute, his eyes ringed with bags that looked more like bruises. This was it. This was the moment that would make this whole thing right or break my heart.

Dad pressed his hands to his face and said, "It's not real. I don't believe it."

"I believe it." Grant sat back down at the table, his eyes locked on Dad's. "I believe Claire. And excuse me for being a little brash, but I think you do too, Mr. Graham."

Dad's head snapped up and his bottom lip hung out. The only sound was the clock ticking in the corner, the one that turned seconds into minutes and made time crawl. I held my breath in my lungs.

But Grant didn't stop to clear his throat or rub the skin between his eyebrows. He kept going: "You're the one that taught me about motive, my second day in training. Remember? You said everyone has a reason for doing what they do. It doesn't make sense, you withholding evidence from either case. Not unless you had more convincing reasons to believe that Claire's innocent, or you found something that proves what happened to Sarah Dunnard. You wouldn't have hidden that knife in your pocket if you believed these attacks were caused by a rabid raccoon or a crazy girl or whatever."

Dad rubbed his eyes, and in that second he looked more

exhausted than I had ever seen him before. Than I had ever seen anyone before, really. "I never found Sarah," he said, his voice cracking around her name. "I'm not sure what happened to her. And that's all of it. That's the truth. Conversation closed." He grabbed his mug off the table and lumbered toward the sink.

Mom gave me a withering look and followed him.

I bit back all of the vile words I wanted to scream as I washed him rinse his mug. Seth was right; Mike Graham never told the truth, at least not all of it. The difference was that this time he wasn't going to get away with it.

I turned toward the window and look out at the sherbet-colored sunlight staining Dad's shed. He was hiding something in there, something he was extremely careful to keep hidden.

But I was going to find it.

# *twenty-eight*

I stormed out of the kitchen and into the foyer and threw open the closet. This time, instead of looking for the wolf knife, I was searching for one of Ella's scarves. Dad tried to get all authoritative with me. He tried to tell me that I wasn't allowed to go out with Grant, that I needed to stay home for once. But I didn't listen; I didn't even respond.

This wasn't my home anymore.

I hopped into Grant's truck, which was already warm and waiting—he'd quietly slipped outside when Dad started yelling. And then we drove through the iced-over roads of Amble, just biding our time until Mom and Dad fell asleep.

Given how twitchy Dad had been near the shed, Grant suggested that we should take a look inside. He didn't say it, but I could tell by the way his eyes had that empty look, and how he couldn't stop chewing at nonexistent hangnails, that Dad's erratic behavior had really freaked him out.

And then there was the doll.

The moment I got in the truck, I'd flipped through Dad's file again. According to the report, there was never a doll at scene. I tried to remember the articles I'd read, and was pretty sure there'd never been any mention of a doll there, either.

He'd been the first at the scene, just like he was at Ella's attack. He'd found evidence at both scenes that he wanted to keep hidden, so he took it. If what he'd said to me was true, he'd taken the paring knife to keep me safe. But why the doll?

Who was he trying to protect?

And what had he found while I was in New York that made him quit Sarah's case and resign as chief?

I glanced at the watery green lights of the dashboard. Midnight. "I'm sure they're asleep now," I said to Grant.

"Let's move." The truck rumbled as he stepped on the gas and made a sharp turn down Main. We were only a couple of miles from my house, but we'd spent the last few hours driving aimlessly around town. There wasn't anywhere in Amble where I was welcome, and unfortunately my status as town pariah had also crippled Grant's social life.

Grant cut the headlights when we turned down my street, and slowed the truck to a stop a few yards from my house. He nodded. "Looks like everyone's asleep."

The house loomed over us, all of its light snuffed out. In the darkness, its red siding looked almost black. And everything was eerily quiet.

We crept out of the truck and through the cornstalks, Grant's flashlight leading the way. I tried not to think about what else was hiding in there.

When Dad's shed came into sight, the flashlight clicked off and Grant threaded his fingers through mine. He squeezed my hand and pulled me forward.

"Where's the key?" he whispered. I could just barely see the outline of his other hand wrapped around the padlock. I winced as I stuck my hands into the snow, fumbling around until I made contact with a smooth surface. I grabbed the garden gnome by his oversized hat and tipped him over. Grant pull the key out from under its feet and inserted it into the lock.

*Click.*

The sound was so loud in the midst of all this quiet that it sounded more like a gun firing than a lock. Grant went rigid next to me. But nothing happened. No one came.

Carefully, he unthreaded the lock from the handle and pushed open the door.

The darkness was so thick and dusty, I felt like I could drink it in. I coughed, and Grant stumbled into something that sounded heavy and painful. "Shit," he mumbled. "That hurt."

"It's too dark in here—we need more light. Turn on your flashlight."

"Can't," Grant answered from somewhere to the left of me. "It's too bright. I'm afraid your dad will see it from the house."

"Fine, give me a sec then." I fumbled through my coat pockets for my cell phone. When I found it, I touched the screen and a soft blue glow stained the floor in front of me. "Let's look for something a little more practical."

Grant flicked on his cell phone too, and in a matter of minutes he found an old, oil-based lantern and some matches. With a snap and a quick burst of flame, the inside of the shed was doused in light. "Let's put this on the floor," he said, tucking the lantern under a wood bench. "We only need a little light."

And it was true. I'd forgotten how small the shed really was, especially on the inside. It'd been years since I'd been in there.

It looked like it had been about that long since Dad had been in there, too.

Everything was coated in so much dust, it gave all the objects inside a fuzzy, out-of-focus look. I wiped my finger over a sawhorse, and the dust clumped on my skin. I glanced around. It seemed like nothing had been used or touched in years, and there was no trace of anything strange that I could start with.

Grant's voice cut through the silence. "Look," he said, pointing at the floor. I tilted my head around the sawhorse to see what he was talking about.

A perfectly preserved set of footprints, standing in the center of the room. And they looked fresh. Well, fresher than anything else in this space.

I looked under my feet and saw my own footprints settling in the dust, all chaotic and scattered. Grant's, too, were slapped haphazardly throughout the shed. But these footprints, the new ones, were smaller.

"Someone was in here," I said, inspecting the prints. "These don't belong to Dad."

Grant squinted through the shadows stretched across the floor. "No, they don't."

We started to search the area encircling the prints, pulling out old pots and moldy garden gloves. Grant started sifting through cardboard boxes, but it turned out they were filled with a tangle of fishing lures.

I closed my eyes and tipped my head up, attempting to stretch out my neck. Exhaustion fell over me like a warm blanket, and all at once I remembered how tired I was. I opened my eyes.

My mouth dropped open when I realized what I was looking at.

A little knitted bird with a fat, beaded eyes hung from the ceiling above me. It was blood red.

"Grant," I said slowly. "I found something." I pointed.

Grant's head tipped up next to me. "Oh shit," he said. "Shit."

"Ella," I said.

The footprints, the knitted bird dangling from the cross-beams—it was all Ella. And it was recent; she must have left these things behind right before she disappeared. The bird wasn't dusty at all.

"Look, there's some kind of box above it," Grant said, pointing to a small shoebox balancing on the crossbeams, just above the bird. "We have to get it down." Without hesitating, he hoisted himself onto the wooden workbench and stood. His silhouette made shadows dance around the shed.

Outside, I heard a howl.

I shook it away. I had to focus.

Grant easily reached the shoebox, tapping it until it tumbled into his hand. He jumped down with a thud, then took a deep breath before he pulled off the lid.

The doll.

It was a homemade doll, something Mrs. Dunnard probably stitched together while waiting for customers at her shop. Its hair was made of yellow yarn, and its dress of gingham. Two button eyes stared blankly at me.

It was covered in blood.

Almost every inch of the fabric was soaked, except for the hem of its dress.

I closed my eyes and swallowed. "Grant, put it away."

*Breathe, breathe, breathe.*

A howl came again, this time quick and furious and full of wanting.

*My dad had murdered Sarah Dunnard.*

*Why else would he have hidden her doll in his shed?*

Another howl. Closer.

"There's a note," Grant said. "And … this." His voice sounded far away.

I opened my eyes. "This" was a smear of tarnished metal and jagged wood and glittering, gem-colored eyes. Dad's missing knife.

"Give me that," I said, holding out my hand. "He can't hurt anyone else. I won't let him."

Grant stared at the knife for a second and said, "Maybe I should hold on to it. This is evidence." But eventually, he put it into the palm of my hand. I shoved it in my pocket, trying not to think of the blood congealed on the tip.

"Here's the note." Grant handed me a sheet of paper with torn edges. It was Ella's handwriting, so rushed that this time she even forgot to dot her letters with hearts.

*He was going to hurt me like he hurt her, so I told them to take me away. I had to go.*

All of a sudden, everything got wobbly and the lantern light started to flicker. I clutched the workbench. I'd been searching for Ella, certain something feral had carried her away from Amble as she screamed for someone to find her. But the "he" Ella was afraid of wasn't a snarling, snapping wolf or the boy with the heavy-lidded eyes. It was her own father. The entire time I'd been holed up in New York, Ella was being hunted from all sides.

*He's going to kill me.*

A white light flooded my vision and I was sure I was going to pass out. I squeezed the workbench harder, but my fingers felt numb.

"Claire, we've got to get out of here. Hurry!" Grant's voice, warped and muffled. Then there were arms around my back and under my legs and I felt like I was floating.

Another beam of light soaked the contents of the shed, and then there was yelling. Loud. Furious.

Dangerous.

"Go, go, go," Grant whispered from somewhere above me. Dry leaves clawed at my skin as he carried me into the cornfield. The lights from the house splashed across the stalks, illuminating their brittle gold in short bursts of color.

One after another, the howls tore through the sky.

As Grant carried me away from the frantic floodlights, I wondered which was more lethal:

What was inside the cornfield, or out.

And did it even matter anymore?

# twenty-nine

"Breathe, Claire, breathe." Grant's eyes floated in front of my face, soft and full of moonlight. A cluster of cornstalks bent over us, shielding us from the falling snow with their twisted leaves. The scent of a bonfire flooded my nose.

"It's okay. We're safe."

Something snapped a few feet away and I jumped to my feet. Grant grabbed my shoulders to keep me steady. "We're not safe. We're not safe at all," I choked. "My dad's a murderer, my sister thought he was going to kill her. She let them take her away, Grant." My chest constricted with panic and I gasped for breath. "She let the wolves take her to get away from him, and now I don't know how to find her." Thick sobs began to clot up my throat.

Grant pressed his body flush with mine and tucked my head into the space beneath his collarbone. His heartbeat thumped against my skin.

But it didn't drown out the howling.

I pulled my head from his neck and listened.

More howls, long and melancholic, spanned the cornfield. Things snapped and popped all around us, and Grant clutched me tighter.

A flash of gray.

And the blink of a yellow eye.

"Grant," I whispered, "they're close."

He rubbed the back of my neck. "They're right over there."

I spun around. Smoke billowed toward the star-speckled sky, and a bonfire snapped and crackled from a few feet away. Laughter bubbled over into the space between us and the party.

"Come on," he said, pulling me forward. "We can ask them for help."

I jerked my hand back. "How can they possibly help with this?" What did he expect? That we'd ask them to help us catch the wolves and they'd say, "Sure, no problem. Let me get my net"?

"We could ask someone for a ride back to my house. Then we could think about our next move from there."

I sucked in a breath. Okay. Okay, that could be good. Some time to collect ourselves before we went out hunting for wolves. I took a step forward.

A wet pile of snow gave way beneath me and I stumbled right into the middle of Lacey Jordan's party.

"Claire?" Lacey said from the other side of the stalks. I could see through the bonfire smoke that she still had the fat caterpillars crawling along her eyelashes. "What are you doing here?"

The fire snapped in the center of Lacey's oval-shaped backyard, casting shadows in the spaces between all of the people huddled there. They were a blur of yellow Amble High letterman jackets and snow boots, of cigarette smoke and freedom. And every last one of them was staring at me.

Grant's fingers touched my back and I let out a breath. "I brought her with me," he said. "We need a ride back to my house."

Lacey stepped around the fire, trailed by two girls who also had caterpillars for eyelashes. Must be an Amble thing I'd missed out on. She narrowed her eyes at Grant. "Leaving so soon, Grant? Now that's rude."

Something rustled in the shadowed space behind Lacey, and I felt Grant's body go rigid next to me. "Look, Lacey, we're not looking for trouble. We just need a ride."

The space around us had grown tighter, and all their shadows fell in watery patterns across my boots. If it wasn't so cold, I would have been sweating. They were trapping us, hunting us. They all thought *I* was the threat, while the whole time wolves and murderers encircled them, watched them.

Hunted them.

"What are you doing, hanging around with *that*?" a boy about my age said. He had crept up next to me and I hadn't even noticed. I could smelled the beer on his breath. He reached over me and shoved Grant's shoulder. "You really shouldn't hang out with crazies, Grant. Might rub off on you."

Grant's fingers left my back. He stepped in front of me and pushed the guy back. "Cole, why don't you go back over to that cooler, get yourself another beer, and leave her the hell alone."

A howl bounced in the space around us and I swear my heart stopped beating. But it was only Cole, whose laugh sounded more like an injured dog than a human. "Oh yeah? Why don't you go find us some wolves, Claire?" He leaned in so that his salty breath plugged up my nostrils. He whispered, "Why don't you use them as an excuse to tear my face off?"

The next thing I saw was snow.

I sank into the drift as Grant gently pushed me out of the way. He let out a low, growling sound—like something I'd heard in the corners of Manhattan when I was being hunted there—and lunged at Cole.

The two boys kicked up snow around them, and it sparkled in the air around the fire for a second before dusting the rest of the party. Lacey turned to me and screamed, "You ruined my party!"

Everything around me ticked in slow seconds. My brain went foggy, like the smoky air, and all I could see were the corners of the stars trying to peek out from beyond the fire.

I stood up, bracing myself against a bent-up stalk. Grant and Cole were still rolling through the snow. Lacey was coming toward me. The wolves were waiting, still deciding which of us would get new scars tonight.

Grant slammed Cole into a card table positioned at the foot of the yard. It seemed like it wobbled for ten seconds before it tipped over, crashing into the snow and taking down a riot of liquor bottles with it. A vodka bottle cracked open down the middle as it crashed into the metal legs of the table. Liquor splashed everywhere: on the tips of my boots, on Cole's jacket, in Grant's hair.

And the scent of cherry filled the air.

"No," I whispered.

Lacey stood in front of me now, her eyes blazing from under her clumped lashes.

I didn't know which would come first: the wolf's teeth in the back of my neck or Lacey's hand across my face. Either way, it was going to hurt.

But the only thing that happened was the snap of a stalk and a howl close enough to make the entire clearing shudder to a stop. And next came the screams.

The flash of gray wove itself through the boundary of the clearing, its eyes gleaming like orbs in the light of the fire. Bottles clinked together as they were dropped, forgotten, in the snow. Snapshots of boots and arms, varsity jackets and too much makeup clicked through my brain, but I didn't move. I wouldn't move until I saw messy brown hair and pale green eyes and freckles.

"You've gotta get out of here." Fingers clamped around my wrist, and I let myself be pulled toward the edge of the yard. It took another three seconds before I realized it wasn't Grant.

I pulled my wrist free. "Where's Grant?"

"Come on, Claire, we've gotta go. My house is right over

there. He'll be fine." Half-lidded eyes. Hair that curled over his right ear.

Patrick Gillet was leading me away from the party, away from the wolves.

# *thirty*

"In here," Patrick breathed, holding the front door to his matchstick house open for me. I stepped over the hole in the front porch that lingered at the doorway like an uninvited guest.

Why Patrick Gillet was inviting me into his house, even though the howling had finally stopped, I didn't know.

Something about the way he leaned against the house made my stomach flip-flop. Of all the people I'd seen in Amble, he looked exactly the same as he did in the picture on Ella's corkboard. I couldn't help but imagine him leaning over Ella the same way he leaned in the doorway, his fingers tangled up in her hair.

I must have forgotten I was staring at Patrick himself instead of his picture because he waved a hand in front of my face and said, "Hello? You coming in?"

I took a step away from the door. "You know who I am, right?" I asked.

"I know who you are," Patrick said dully. "Ella said you'd find me eventually."

My heart jolted in my chest, and I swore Patrick could hear it fluttering against my ribs like tiny bird wings. "She said I'd come looking for you?"

He nodded. "Yeah. I've got something I'm supposed to give you. Why don't you just come inside for a sec?"

I followed him into the house and wove through a living room dotted with flannel furniture and smelling like boiled cabbage. Patrick headed toward a tiny room with bunk beds that looked like they might break if he jumped on them too fast.

He sat on his bed and I flinched as the frame wobbled around him. And then he lifted the edge of his mattress and pulled out a pink canvas notebook.

A diary.

There was the missing piece of her, the one I'd been searching for, wrapped in this boy's fingertips. And I couldn't help but feel a tinge of jealousy poison my excitement, when I should have been feeling so many other things. How could Ella have left her secrets with him and not with me?

Patrick leaned over warily and tossed the notebook into my lap, like if he got too close I would bite him. "Here. She gave this to me a few days before she left." His heavy-lidded eyes flickered as he looked me up and down, and I couldn't decide if he was just inspecting me or if he was genuinely freaked out by me. Maybe even a little of both.

I flipped open to the first page. *The Diaries of Ella Graham: Part One*, it read, in wiggly purple letters.

I felt Patrick's eyes still on me, still watching. I lifted my head. "Have you read this?"

He gave a stiff nod. "She told me I could." And the way he looked at me just then sent a shiver down between my shoulder blades.

Something about the way Patrick shrugged and stared so sadly at the book made me think of the picture, the one with Patrick's lips grazing Ella's temple as the sunlight poured between them.

I looked up at him. "Did you love her?"

"Still do," he replied, without missing a beat.

I flipped through the pages, watching the words blur together. "Why didn't you just give this to me when you heard I was back in town?"

Patrick stood up and went to the tiny window. Just past his head I could make out the bonfire still raging, smoke churning into the empty night. "She told me to give it to you when you were ready. I don't know what 'ready' is to Ella, but you sure as hell made a mess of everything." He turned around to look at me. "Seems like it's time to know the truth."

I felt my heart beating in my neck. *Time to know the truth.*

Did I want to?

I didn't know how much more truth I could take tonight.

"I don't believe it all, you know," he added.

I glanced up at Patrick. "Why wouldn't you? You don't even know me."

Patrick pulled his bottom lip between his teeth and sat still for a second, staring at the stained carpet under his feet. "I think Ella was still angry when she wrote this. She didn't understand yet." He looked at me. "I think she'd look at that year after the incident a little differently now."

Of all the things Patrick was telling me, he stunned me the most with the word "angry." I couldn't comprehend how Ella could have been upset with me—of all people—after the attack. I knew I should never have let her walk home alone that night, but I was the one who searched for her, who found her. I stayed with her and sang to her until the police came. I visited her every day in the hospital until they shipped me away.

I didn't expect angry.

The walls felt like they had fingers, they were all so close to me. They were touching me from every corner, tousling my hair and licking my skin clean. Trapped. I felt trapped. The air was being sucked out and I was going to be stuck here with this awkward boy, destined to rot on his mud-stained carpet.

I stood. I had to get out of here; I was suffocating. I loosened Ella's scarf around my neck and headed for the door. I would read the diary and go to Grant's. He had to be back home by now. And then we'd figure out what to do next.

I couldn't go back home to read, I realized; I couldn't ever go back.

I trudged through the snow, into the cornfield halfway between Patrick and Grant's houses just as the stars began to fade and sky began to bleed into that charcoal color that comes before dawn. I plopped next to a thicket of broken stalks, and I couldn't help but think of that day with Rae, when she told me she was leaving and I told her she was crazy. And now Rae was the one telling me I was crazy. Funny how things change.

Sucking in a lungful of the bitter air, I started to read.

---------

## The Diaries of Ella Graham: Part One

*January 2nd*

*I overheard some of the nurses talking about Claire yesterday. I didn't catch it all, but they said something about how they were told to watch her because she's being investigated for my attack right now. There's a rumor going around town that she's crazy, that she's going to plead crazy in court or something. And you know what? That whole rocking and crying while she watches them clean my stitches isn't going to help her case. I gave her a note to warn her they were watching her.*

*And today, she's gone.*

*She left for New York today. Mom and Dad said she's going to stay with Aunt Sharon for a little while. They said she needs to rest for a while because the accident made her scared.*

*I say it made her crazy pants for real.*

*She wouldn't leave my hospital room. She even sat there while they stapled my mouth shut. Mom told me it's because she feels guilty about what happened. Well, she should.*

*I told her I was scared. She didn't listen.*

*This is her fault.*

*January 15th*

*A boy came to see me today. He was waiting for me when I got out of speech therapy. It was THE boy, actually. He brought me sunflowers. Where he got sunflowers in the middle of winter, I don't know, but I don't care. It was perfect.*

*It was even more perfect when he asked me to meet him downtown.*

*So I was looking through the closet for that big purple scarf I made a few weeks ago to cover my mouth up, when I found that weird knife box. Only this time it was empty. I never did find the scarf either. Claire must have taken it with her to New York. She always gets everything.*

*February 8th*

*Well, Dad officially resigned as chief today. Which means he's going to be hanging over me even more than he and Mom do now. I can't stand it anymore. Something is always keeping me trapped here.*

*March 9th*

*It's not fair that Claire gets to be in New York and I'm stuck here forever. Mom and Dad won't let me do anything. They won't let me see the boy. They won't let me skip therapy. They won't even let me take driver's ed, like every single other person in my class. They hover over me like vultures. I have to get out.*

*April 19th*

*Four months since my face got ripped off, and they're still always watching me. Every day, I feel them watching me, waiting for me to snap. I don't know if they're ever going to stop. I need to talk to the boy about his plans.*

*Maybe they can come take me away, too.*

*June 18th*

*I found something today. Something very, very bad.*

*I don't know what to do about it.*

*I can't tell the police. My dad is still the police.*

*I think he's hurt someone. Maybe even killed them.*

*Her attack was just like mine, only they can't find her now.*

*I'm afraid he's going to kill me too.*

*August 1st*

*My counselor says I need to forgive Claire. I'm trying, I really am. But it's hard.*

*Sometimes I think about what my life would be like if she hadn't left me. I probably would have gotten that babysitting job for the Wallace boys, and I'd be saving money for a car or jewelry or Cedar Point tickets, but the littlest one was freaked out by my scars. Instead I'm figuring out how to say my R's with my new lips, like a toddler.*

*Sometimes I hope I never see her again.*

The rest of the diary was just a tangle of entries about secret plans and escaping and nothing else about me. She'd been so upset that once she burned off all her anger toward me there was nothing left to write about.

I closed the diary and clutched it to my chest.

I wished I'd known.

Ella's resentment toward me cut deeper than any of the scars I'd left behind. If I had known, maybe I would have tried to come back sooner. Maybe I wouldn't have let Mom and Dad shove me out of Amble in the first place. I could have stayed with her.

I could have taught her how to drive (after learning how to myself). I would have told Dad to let her grow up, to stop trying to snuff out all the things that made Ella *Ella*. I would have snuck her to picnic dates with Patrick and made her lemongrass soup while her stitches healed. I would have held her, helped her, loved her.

My whole body ached with regret. It was funny, because I'd always wanted nothing more than to leave my sleepy town behind, but now I wished nothing more than that I'd stayed.

I wished I'd never left.

Ella's words rang in my ears: *Four months since my face got ripped off, and they're still always watching me. Every day, I feel them watching me, waiting for me to snap. I don't know if they're ever going to stop. Maybe they can take me away.*

The wolves. Ella was so afraid of our own father that she chose the wolves over him. She let the wolves take her from Amble instead of staying here.

Would she have let them take her if I was still around?

No. *I* wouldn't have let them take her.

And Dad. I could barely think about him without getting sick. While I'd been in New York skipping class, Ella was trapped here, scared out of her mind that Dad was going to try to take her life.

Tears pricked the corners of my eyes.

How could I have made such a mistake?

It's true what they say—one night, one moment can change everything.

I wiped my eyes with Ella's old scarf and pulled myself to my feet. I had to go to Grant's. And as much as it hurt, I had to tell him what I'd found. I started in the direction of his house.

Something snapped behind me. I froze.

A shadow flitted between the stalks.

I slid my hand into my pocket and wrapped it around the handle of Dad's wolf knife.

*Claire*, something whispered.

I whipped out the knife. The wolves may have taken Ella, but they weren't going to take me.

*Claire. Claire.*

Another snap, and the stalks parted. I raised the knife, and my hands shook so hard I was almost afraid I'd accidentally stab myself.

Just then, something bulky but quick jutted out of the dark and twisted my wrist behind my back. A heavy hand clamped over my mouth.

Dad stared into my face, his eyes wild, more animal than human. And I knew all the guilt and regret and sheer heartbreak didn't matter anymore. It would never matter that I didn't stay in Amble with Ella.

Because I was going to die tonight.

# *thirty-one*

I tried to scream, but Dad's hand was so tight over my mouth that no sound came out. He dragged me to a small, oblong clearing about fifty yards from Grant's house. I could see the gabled roof poking out over the cornstalks.

If I could just get to him.

"Claire," Dad whispered into my ear, his breath hot and sour. "I'm going to release my hand as soon as you promise me you're not going to scream."

I nodded.

I was totally going to scream.

"I'm not going to hurt you, I promise. I'll even let you keep the knife on you in case you're worried about that. I just need to talk to you. I need you to let me talk to you."

I froze. If he was going to let me keep the knife, then he must have some other weapon in his pocket. I wasn't about to fall for that.

"I couldn't talk about what happened with Sarah in front of your mother and Grant," he continued. "They'd think I was crazy. Have me committed. I'm not crazy."

A shiver crawled up my spine. *I'm not crazy.* Those were the same words I always used to say.

Which one of us was right?

"I know the wolves exist," he said, loosening his grip on my mouth ever so slightly. "I've seen them too."

I reached up and ripped his fingers from my mouth, and he let me. I twisted my other arm free and stumbled back, holding his knife out in front of me. Dad just stood there, palms out, watching me.

"You've seen them?" I said, panting. "You've seen them, and this whole time you tried to tell me I was crazy?" I took a step toward him. "You sat there, in front of Mom, and told me that I was delusional, that the wolves weren't real. That there had to be some other explanation for why Ella disappeared. *You let everyone in Amble think I was crazy.* And *now* you're telling me the truth?" I clenched my fist around the knife. "You have no idea how tempting it is to use this right now."

Dad lifted his hands above his head—a cop move—and said, "You have every right to be angry with me."

My anger softened just a little. Just enough to lower the knife. "Why would you do that to me?'

"It's more complicated than that, Claire," he said.

"Why don't you try explaining it to me. All of it, this time."

Dad cleared his throat. "I was your age the first time I

saw them. Or one, I should say. A female. She was watching me from the cornfield as I was getting into my old truck. Gray fur. Yellow eyes. I tried to tell people about it, but they never believed me. They said I'd been listening to too many Amble wolf stories. So I learned to keep my mouth shut. I saw them periodically after that, but not often.

"Then, a few years back, they started following me again. I heard them everywhere. The stalks would rustle, and I heard their howls almost every night. They were driving me crazy. So I went into Candice Dunnard's new little shop on Main and looked at the wolf things she had in there. I didn't really know what I was looking for, just something to keep them away. I bought the knife," he said, nodding toward my hand.

"Two years ago, I was out in the stalks, looking for some kid's stolen bike. That's always where I used to look for things like that first—in the little clearing by the lake, not far from the Dunnards' place. Lots of kids went up there, and I almost always found something."

I nodded slowly. It was true. Everyone hung out at that clearing, and almost always something was left behind. The last time I'd been there, I'd left Ella behind.

Dad rubbed his hand over his bald head and continued. "I was near that clearing when I hear something. A growl. And then I saw the eyes and the teeth and everything. I thought it was going to attack me, but it had a different target."

"Sarah," I breathed.

Dad nodded. "I watched it stalk her, snap at her. So I got out the knife and I, uh, used it."

I looked at the knife in my hand. At the crimson staining

its tip. "Then why didn't you bring the body back to town, so people could see they're real?"

Dad suddenly got quiet. He smeared a clump of snow with his boot. "Because the wolf was too quick," he said slowly. "And I stabbed Sarah."

My stomach lurched and I tried to blink away the images of the blood-splattered cornstalks near the Dunnard house. "You killed her," I whispered.

"I didn't mean to," Dad said, and the sadness in his voice made his words sound heavy. "It was an accident. I was trying to protect her from the wolves."

"What'd you do with her?"

"Buried her. Far away from here."

I sucked in a breath, trying to collect my thoughts. "So you tried to cover it up by taking the doll and cutting down the cornstalks. You tried to call it a missing persons case," I said slowly, "but someone took pictures of the scene before you could clean it all up."

"Seth," Dad said.

"But why?"

"I—I couldn't remember what had happened for a while after that. I kind of just 'woke up' and I was back at the house, reading the paper. Then I got the call about Sarah being missing, and I went to the scene to check it out. That's when I found her. I guess I panicked then. I kept telling Seth not to come up there, that I could handle it myself. He must have thought that was fishy. He came up there while I was—while I was taking care of her body and snapped the photos for evidence. But that's not the information I shared with reporters."

"He has a file," I said. "Seth's keeping all those pictures in a file with your name on it. I don't know why—"

"Blackmail," Dad said grimly. "He told me he had proof I'd killed Sarah. Said he'd shout it from the rooftops if I didn't step down as chief and let him take my place."

My mouth dropped open. I always knew I hated something about Seth. It turned out it was because he was a sneaky, conniving creep. "Why didn't you just tell the truth? Why did you just tell him there was a wolf, that you were trying to protect her?"

Dad laughed, and the sound bounced in the space between us. "Claire, you know people don't really believe in the wolves. If I'd tried to pawn off Sarah's death on some legend after my knife was found at the scene, I'd be in jail right now. Or worse—Havenwood."

The wind lashed at my cheeks and chapped my hands. It was suddenly very, very cold. I shoved the wolf knife back in my pocket and tucked my hands into my jacket. "You should have at least told Ella," I said. "Then I don't think she would've left."

Dad's forehead wrinkled. "What are you talking about?"

"She knew, Dad. Ella knew about what happened to Sarah, what you did to her. She thought—she thought you might do it to her, too. She was afraid of you." I took a breath. "I found her diaries. She wanted the wolves to come get her, to take her somewhere. She didn't want to be in Amble anymore."

Dad groaned, his eyes shiny. He paced the perimeter of the clearing, thinking. Finally he said, "I'm stuck here. I'm one wrong move away from Seth leaking everything to the papers or to the Dunnards' lawyer. I've got to lie low for a while."

"I can do it," I said.

Dad stopped pacing and stood in front of me. Gently, he touched my cheek. "Claire, I need you to find her. I need you to tell her the truth—tell her that I'd never hurt her. Steal her from the wolves and bring her home to us."

I nodded, and leaned my cheek into his hand. "Grant will help me. We'll find her."

Dad smiled, a tentative little thing, and kissed my forehead. "I know you will."

# *thirty-two*

Dad and I came up with a plan.

I'd go to Grant's, tell him everything about Dad, and ask him to help me find Ella. Dad would tell Mom that I'd gone back to New York in the middle of the night, and that Grant had decided to go with me. He'd say that I realized I'd never be able to stay in Amble again, not with my history. Then he'd spread this message like a stain all over town.

The walk to Grant's house was quick and painless. The sky was stained with pink, the snowfall had slowed, and I took it all as a good sign. But when I stepped onto the Buchanans' sagging front porch, all of that hope drained out of me.

Angry black words crawled across the porch, the windows, the front door. Words that had been written in the hours nestled between dark and dawn. The hours when wolves came out to hunt, according to Rae, and when their howls broke apart high school bonfires.

I touched the word "psycho" on the front door. Black smudged my fingertips. Still wet.

I followed the trail of paint that had run down the door and pooled at the welcome mat.

A box of matches lay scattered across the porch like forgotten strings of seedlings, plucked from the ground and left to die. I picked up a match and examined its tip: blackened, but not charred. An almost-spark that never caught fire.

My hand shook as I reached for the doorbell. Grant's living room was thick with shadows, so much so that it was like they'd put up a curtain of fog in front of the bay window.

The door creaked open and a puffy eye peeked out at me from the other side of the doorframe.

"Oh. Claire." Grant's mom opened the door and stared back at me, the skin under her eyes purple and blotchy.

"Hi, Mrs. Buchanan. Um, is Grant here?" I asked softly, because it felt like if I spoke too loudly she would shatter in half.

That must have been the wrong question, because her head drooped as she pressed her fingers over her eyes. "He's not here." She pulled in a breath between her teeth. "I can't find him anywhere."

"Didn't he come home last night? When did you see him last?" I asked. But the words sounded stale and foreign, like they weren't coming from my mouth. Like they were disconnected from me, like they came from the wind and the trees and the cornfield that was swallowing everything and everyone up around me.

Laura Buchanan looked out past me and into the rolling gray underbellies of the clouds. "Yesterday. Before he went to your house." She bent down and picked up a single matchstick, rolling it between her fingertips. "And then I woke up to this. At least I shooed them away before they lit the matches."

I couldn't find words, not a single one. They were clotted together in the back of my throat. I blinked for an extra second to temporarily erase the site of Grant's mom surrounded by words I wish Amble had never found. They were the same words they'd used to torture my family, and now they were punishing Grant for being with me.

*Remember, Grant, Amble doesn't like crazy.*

Laura sighed and flicked the match to the porch. "I guess I better call the police."

"*No.*" It was the first word that snapped into my mind. "I mean, I think I know where Grant is. He said he'd meet me for breakfast this morning, at that diner downtown."

Dad couldn't come here. He couldn't see the graffiti that bit at the sides of the house, at the almost-fire littered across the porch. I didn't want him to see the disaster I'd created. The same disaster he'd tried to keep hidden under a layer of paint and handful of lies.

I could find Grant.

Laura's eyes narrowed. "Are you sure, Claire?"

I smiled my best no-teeth smile. "Positive. I know where he is." I turned and stepped over the rotting part of the staircase and headed back toward my house, and I felt Laura's eyes burning through the back of my head. It was almost like I could hear snippets of her thoughts. They whispered, "*What did you do with my son?*"

I stepped off the porch and clutched my chest. I couldn't freak out, not now. I couldn't give Laura a reason to think I wouldn't find him.

I called his cell phone. The ringer hummed in my ear, and after six, seven times, Grant's voice clicked on: "Hey, this is Grant. Leave a message after the beep."

*Beep.*

I hung up the phone.

"Okay, Claire, think." I paced the patch of dirt road in front of Grant's house. Images from Lacey's party flicked through my head. Grant and Cole wrestling in the snow. Knocking over the card table. Spilling the cherry vodka.

All over themselves.

And then the wolves came.

"Oh God," I whispered. They couldn't have taken him. They wouldn't have.

They might have.

I stopped pacing and tried to breathe, to clear my head. Okay, what had Grant said about investigation before, when I saw him at the diner my first day back in Amble? Something about always starting at the beginning.

I thought about going back to Lacey's house. That would make the most logical sense, I mean, that *was* where the wolves first struck tonight. But the wolves weren't logical creatures.

For me, there was only ever one beginning with Grant. It was the beginning I'd longed for, for years. The one I thought of when Grant scratched the back of his head with his pencil in Algebra. When he showed up at my house after Thanksgiving dinner, cheeks rosy and eyes glowing, stealing Mom's pecan pie right out of the tin. It was the beginning that almost began in the cornfield two years ago, when he slipped me that note and told me to come to my birthday party alone. It's where Ella's beginning happened, the turning point where the whole course of who she thought she was going to be changed. It was Dad's beginning, too—that's where he found the wolves hunting Sarah Dunnard and his life tipped on its axis. That clearing nestled between Lark Lake and Route 24 was a constellation of beginnings and endings, of life and almost death.

It was exactly the kind of place to go looking for wolves.

# *thirty-three*

I didn't know if the wolves would be there waiting for me. I didn't know if they'd be hovering over Grant, snarling and snapping at his face, threatening to turn him into a stitched-up version of himself like they did to Ella. Or maybe he wouldn't be there at all.

I stopped just outside the clearing. I was still lugging around Ella's diary, and I knew I couldn't keep it with me.

I had to let it go.

I kicked over a lump of snow near the base of a cornstalk and tucked the diary into the cold. I didn't want Ella's past anymore. I wanted her future.

I shoved my chapped hands into my pockets and started to trudge forward. In one pocket, my fingers brushed against the blade of Dad's knife. In the other was something soft and knitted. I pulled out one of the two things I'd brought back to Amble with me: Ella's periwinkle bird.

I'd never taken it out of my pocket since I'd come back into town.

I shoved the bird back into my jeans and glanced into the cornfield, its stalks groaning under the weight of the weather that was surely on its way.

As soon as I stepped into the field, I thought that panic would consume me, swallow me up and make me shiver with regret. But it never came. I looked at the swaying field around me, the one that kept better secrets than even I did. I wasn't scared anymore.

I was determined.

I grabbed the knife out of my pocket and crept forward.

I knew they were watching me with their yellow eyes. I could feel them.

But I kept going.

The wind blew and something brushed against the back of my neck, something sharp and bitter sliding against my spine. I yelped, whipping around to stab whatever was there. I jammed my knife through a bent stalk, which groaned in defeat before it fell.

I let the air out of my lungs. No wolf. Not yet.

I was almost to the clearing, just to the right of it. Almost to the spot where I'd found Ella like a broken bird. I wondered if I'd know the exact spot when I got there, if it would still smell like a hint of Cherry Blast body spray or there'd be speckles of old blood tattooing the base of the cornstalks. I pushed my body through the snow. One foot in front of the other, the edge of the knife's blade gnawing through my palm.

Then I saw it, nestled in the snow like a precious jewel.

One drop of crimson.

I bent over it, shadowing it like a sinewy tree bending under the weight of the weather. The wind blew my hair into a tangle around my eyes, but as hard as the world tried to keep it from me, I saw right through the web of gold across my eyelashes.

Blood.

I leaned closer.

It smelled like metal and earth; a tiny, glistening star blowing up the universe right in front of my face.

It was fresh.

My veins froze, my heart stopped beating, the clouds lumbered across the sky, the world still tipped so heavily that I was about to roll off in a jumble of oceans and continents. The wind blew snow into the neck of my jacket.

One more drop, and then another.

A trail of bread crumbs to the big, bad wolf.

My boots crunched quietly through the drifts, the soles of them pressing next to the droplets, which were now becoming quarter-sized pools and beginning to run into each other.

Bloody little hearts, beating in the snow.

My bloody, broken little heart beating in my ribs.

And then I heard something in the stalks rustle.

And I looked up.

And it was there—he was there, just like I somehow knew he would be. Because everything I'd ever let myself love withered here, in this cornfield, under the weight of the stars and the sky and the wolf's snapping, yellowed teeth.

There are moments in life when everything in the whole

world really does stop: the water in the ocean stills, the wind drops off, your lungs stop begging you to breathe. Even your brain quits, and everything you ever thought about history finals and fashion school and sloppy first kisses with someone you already knew wasn't the right person disappears like melting snow. And all that's left is this:

*Why?*

And then this: *How?*

Until that melts away, too, and there's only this: *I need you to be okay. I need you to be okay. I* need *you to be okay.*

This was that moment. Finding Ella was that moment, too—only this was worse. Way worse. Because when I'd found Ella, everyone still thought I was just another Amble girl that snuck sips of fruit-flavored liquor and dreamed of running away.

But Grant, he was light and warmth and a breath of *I love you* and *I need you too.* He'd reeled me back in on my string, invited me to join him and the rest of the world in actually living. Breathing. Smiling real smiles, with teeth and everything.

*I need you to be okay.*

I stepped closer, and the wolf with the watery eyes I saw in my dreams stared back at me. Its lip pulled back around its teeth in a warning.

Grant lay in the snow, his hair matted against his forehead with clumps of sweat and blood. His eyelids were purple, his lips white, his breath shallow.

His heart still beating.

A low rumble escaped from behind the wolf's teeth, and I snapped up to look it in the eye.

"I'm not afraid of you," I told it.

It blinked slowly, opening its mouth to reveal a line of congealed blood looping around its teeth. And I swore it said back, *Why not?*

I squeezed the handle of the knife still in my palm. *Because there's nothing left to lose anymore.*

And then I howled, louder than the wolves, louder than the rush of blood in my ears, louder than the street traffic in Manhattan. I stabbed, stabbed, stabbed until the air was sliced into ribbons around me, and the sun was poked full of holes, and the whole world turned bloody.

# *thirty-four*

"Claire? Did you say something?"

A gigantic light swayed above me, making the face in front of me flicker in and out of darkness. I rubbed the skin around my eyes; it felt lumpy and puffed up like it was full of tears that hadn't been let out yet. Had I been *crying*?

I clutched the table in front of me, grasping for something solid. The face shifted into focus again as the light drenched us both. He squinted at the ceiling that held the cord until it shuddered to a stop. "There," he said with finality, like now that the puzzle of the swinging light was solved, he could figure out the mystery of me.

I stared at the ridges slithering across his forehead, the way his nose was a little too bulky for his face. I knew this guy; I'd met him before.

The last time I was in here for questioning.

He touched his nose and looked at me, like he could read

my mind or something. What was his name? Rob, Rich? Why couldn't I remember? It didn't matter; it was disturbing.

But at the same time, kind of comforting.

Because maybe Rob/Rich really could tell me what had happened to me and why my eyes were almost swollen shut and why there were stitches gnawing at the center of my palm.

"Do you remember how you got here?" He watched me as I rubbed my fingers over the stitches. I looked up at him.

"Not really."

"Do you remember how you got those stitches?"

I shook my head.

He leaned back in his chair and let out a long breath. "Do you remember who I am?"

I bit my lip and stared at the purplish skin under his eyes. Somehow I couldn't get over the itchy feeling that this was a trick question, or that he was trying to make it one. But it didn't matter anyway; I really didn't know any of the answers. I puffed out my lip and whispered, "Yes."

Something in his eyes flickered and his shoulders sagged, like he was melting from the top down like an ice cream cone under the sun. He scribbled something on his notepad and asked, "How do you remember me, Claire?"

"The last time," I said. "The last time I was here." But I knew it was a lie as soon as I said it. Because all I could think of was *Grant, Grant, Grant* and the way he'd looked at me in this very office while were searching for my criminal history: like the earth had cracked open and sucked in all the light. *That* was what had happened the last time I was here.

"The last time you were here," he started, swiveling

his chair to grab a fat file on the corner of the desk, "was because you were a suspect in your sister's death."

"My sister didn't die." I dug my fingernails into my jeans until I could feel them through the denim. "She didn't die."

Rob/Rich flipped through the file before pausing to squint at a piece of paper. He cleared his throat and said, "Sorry about that. When I first saw the pictures of the scene, I thought she was gone. Guess I never could get it into my head that she made it somehow."

Then he did something I never thought was possible. He did something almost like magic—almost as magical as Ella and Grant—but a lot less pleasant. He pulled out a glossy photo from the file and set it in front of me.

This ripped open my brain, and he plucked out sharp little memories that I thought I'd forgotten. He pulled them out like fragments of broken glass caught in between folds of soft skin: deadly intruders that were never meant to find a home there.

Ella's eyes stared at me, half-lidded and drained of all their color. Blood pooled in the creases of her nose, screamed across her sallow skin, braided its way through her hair.

Blood pounded in my wrists.

My throat.

Beating, beating, beating in my shattered little heart.

I was somehow still alive right now. Barely.

He was watching me; his eyes smothered my skin, pressed the breath back into my lungs. I couldn't look at him. I couldn't look at her. I chewed on my lip until it tasted like metal.

Rob/Rich slid another photo across the table. The skin between his fingers was shiny with sweat. Why was *he* sweating?

I shouldn't have—every spark in my brain told me not to. But I saw the paleness of his eyes and the muscles in my neck made me lean over so that I could see him again.

Grant's picture, next to Ella in the snow. Dead eyes, blood-speckled nose that used to be lined with stars. Two bloody angels lying side by side. It was a horrifying thing to see both of their bodies mangled between the cornstalks.

My head snapped up. "Where's Grant?"

He cocked his head to the side as he ran a finger over Grant's picture. "Hospital."

I let out a puff of breath. "He's alive?"

Rob/Rich's eyes snapped to mine before he reached for the file again. I was a feral animal, a wolf with yellow eyes and yellow teeth, and I couldn't be trusted.

Two more photos slid across the desk. One next to Ella, one next to Grant.

One of an imprint. One of a knife.

Both in the snow.

The one by Ella was the imprint of the paring knife, the one I'd shoved into my back pocket the night of my birthday party and Dad had taken from the scene.

The other was the carved wolf knife with jeweled eyes.

Both were just inches from their bodies.

Both were smothered in blood.

"There was a weapon that could be traced back to you, both times," Rob/Rich said, still staring at the photos. Still afraid to look at me. "Both times you were found at the scene. The crimes were the same." He looked up at me now, cupped my eyes with his. "We can't ignore the evidence this time, Claire. Not even for your father."

"You need evidence? Ask Lacey!" I yelled, slapping my hands against the table. "And Patrick. Lacey Jordan and Patrick Gillet. They saw the wolves, you need to talk to them. They'll tell you about the wolf attack at Lacey's bonfire. It was right by where they—where they found Grant." I tried to swallowed up the image of Grant's bloody face, but it had burned itself into my brain. Permanently.

He shook his head. "No one has been able to locate Mr. Gillet at this time. It seems as though he's skipped town. And we've already questioned Ms. Jordan. She denied the existence of any sort of party."

I closed my eyes and tipped my head back against the chair. *Damn it.* Of course Lacey would deny having a party, let alone seeing any wolves. Hating me would be a good enough reason itself, but her mother would murder her if she found out about Lacey's binger bonfires. Plus I was sure she was trying to avoid the whole "crazy" label. Smart girl.

"Ryan." The voice came through the door first, and soaked through to my bones. And then Dad followed, his eyes heavy, shoulders slumped.

"I'm sorry," Ryan said as he stood to meet Dad. Their faces were so close I thought their noses were going to smash into each other. "We can't let her go—"

"I know," is all Dad said. His head dipped between his shoulders. "I know."

Ryan started toward me and my heart beat, beat, beat against my ribs. Should I run? I should run. But where would I go? Where could I go where they couldn't find me, where the wolves couldn't either?

How could I go where Ella went?

"No. Please." Dad choked back a scratchy sound in his throat. "Let me do it." Dad stepped toward me and pulled a pair of handcuffs from his back pocket.

I didn't run. I couldn't hide. There was nowhere to go where the wolves wouldn't gnaw apart every piece of my life until all that was left was cracked and brittle bone. I held out my wrists and stared him in the eye.

"You know I didn't do it," I said.

Dad carefully snapped the cuffs around my wrists. "You're under arrest for the attempted murder of Grant Buchanan."

# *thirty-five*

The cuffs made the skin on my wrists sting. They made me think about birds and wings and angels.

I thought about Ella in the Christmas play as the angel Gabriel. The way her dimples looked like deep little sockets under the lights, how the tips of her wings were stained orange in typical Ella flare. She looked so beautiful, just like an angel on fire.

There was one part in the middle of the play, right after the angel Gabriel came to tell the shepherds about baby Jesus. Ella was standing off to the side of the stage, and someone had tried to follow her with the church's crazy excuse for a spotlight. The light around her quivered and trapped her in bars made of shadows. It was only for a second, and no one else probably noticed, but I never stopped watching her. She looked like a dimpled bird whose wings poked through the bars of its cage. And then it was gone and she was free.

I shifted my hands so that the cuffs slid down my arm. A ring of shiny pink already crawled around my wrists, and I'd only been wearing them for three hours.

I might be wearing them the rest of my life.

If I had wings like Ella's, I would let them poke through the bars of this cage so they could catch the breeze from the station door that kept opening and closing. I'd let the breeze ruffle their tips until they caught a big enough gust of wind to help me slip through the bars. And it wouldn't even matter if I had handcuffs, so, so heavy or not; I would still fly away, away from the cement and earth and into the place where Ella was now. Wherever that was. If I had wings, I could find her.

I could find the wolves.

I'd fly so close to the cornfield that the stalks would tickle my stomach as I flew by. And I'd find them there, howling and snapping and waiting to steal someone else's soul. I'd kill them, all of them. Or maybe just the one with the yellow eyes. And everyone would see that I'm not crazy, that I would never hurt Ella or Grant, that they were all so wrong.

Why couldn't I remember?

That's what they were all thinking out there in their moldy-smelling office. *Why can't Claire remember?*

*Is she lying?*

Was I?

No. I could only remember in snapshots. A flash of a knife here. Constellations of blood there. Eyes, all gray, everything gray, staring up at the sky. Howling and paw prints that were smudged to look like nothing at all.

The feeling of metal sinking into skin.

Into wolf skin. It was definitely wolf skin. Wasn't it?

Seth's voice floated by my cell before he did. He stood outside my cage and wrapped his paws around the bars, smirking. "Just checking on you," he said, but there wasn't a drop of concern in his voice.

I didn't bother to say anything to him.

He tipped his head forward so that the fat of his chin dribbled through the bars. "I always knew you were batshit like your father. It was only a matter of time." He pulled away and two red stripes raced down his forehead. "One Graham down, one to go."

And then he was gone, just like a bad dream.

Minutes ticked by, but I don't know how many.

The phone rang in the alcove, just down the hall from my little cell.

Footsteps on floorboards and a sigh so heavy that I swore the whole room dimmed around me.

"Hello?" Dad answered, and I heard his body sink into a creaking desk chair. He sighed again. I could almost see him rubbing his forehead, elbows planted to the desktop. "Dr. Barges, thanks for calling me back."

I held my breath. *Thanks for calling me back?* Why had he even bothered to call my ridiculously useless doctor? So that he could answer Dad's rhetorical questions about the state of my mental health? *So, Dr. Barges, do* you *think Claire is insane?*

"Right," Dad said into the phone. "Listen, doctor, I'm at a loss here. You're the best in the country for this kind of thing." He choked back a breath. "I need you to give it to me straight. Did Claire do this because of... of her... what did you call it? Anxiety over the accident? Or mental illness? Or what is it?"

If I could have burned a hole in his head with my eyes, I would have. If I was crazy, then he was just as big of a lunatic as I was. He would never admit that, though. Not with Amble breathing down his neck. So this had to be some kind of act; he had to be doing this for the sake of looking like the normal, concerned father instead of the crazed wolf hunter.

There was a long pause on the other end. The floorboards creaked; the coffee machine gurgled somewhere down the hall. I held my breath. I needed this answer just as much as he did.

Time ticked away, ate at my skin, poked a hole in my heart.

Tick.

Tick.

Something like a palm slapping the desk echoed around me and made me jump out of my skin. "But we sent her all the way to you in New York," Dad said. "Do you know what I had to do to keep her out of the system here? I would lose everything—my *life*—if anyone ever found out the measures I took to keep her safe."

A pause. "Will she hurt anyone else? Herself?"

Another pause. Then a sigh.

"You really think Havenwood is our best shot?"

*Havenwood.* I pressed my palm to my mouth and choked back a sob that bubbled up from my throat. I hadn't realize I'd been holding it in for so long—years even.

"Okay, we'll just have to do that then. Thank you, Dr. Barges. We'll be in touch." *Click*.

I shoved both of my fists against my lips and stuffed the sobs back down until they sank into my stomach.

Dad's shadow spilled into the hallway. In a second, he was standing on the other side of the bars, hands in his pocket, his forehead lined with stripes of sweat. He blinked at me, watched me. I'd never felt more like an animal in my life.

"I just got off the phone with Dr. Barges," he said, shoving his hands deeper into his pockets.

I pulled my fists from my mouth and licked away the tears that had pooled in the creases of my lips. "I know."

"He thinks your only shot of getting out of this is pleading insanity. He'll testify on your behalf." Something jangled in his pocket, and a second later he pulled out a fat set of keys. "He thinks Havenwood is the best place for you, Claire."

"I know," I whispered. The sob threatened to crawl its way back out of my throat.

Seth's booming laughter echoed from his office. Dad glanced down the hall, and then starting flipping through a ring of keys. "We don't have much time," he whispered.

I blinked at him, my brain slow to shudder to life. "What?"

He stopped at a fat silver one and shoved it into the lock. "You have about thirty minutes tops before Seth comes back here to check on you again. He's still suspicious of me, wants to make sure you don't go disappearing on him before he has a chance to drive you over to the county prison." The lock clicked and my cell door creaked open.

I jumped to my feet and rushed to the door. "But you'll

get fired! You'll lose everything." I bit my lip. "Amble's going to retaliate against you for this."

Dad just looked at me, his eyes soft and watery, and brushed my sweaty cheek with the back of his hand. "It's going to be okay," he said, but he didn't sound convinced. "You'll go and find the wolves, find Ella. And then you'll come back and clear my name." And then another key, another click, and my handcuffs were off.

"Clear *our* name," I said, planting a kiss on his cheek. He held the door open, probably to prevent it from creaking again, and I slipped out. I turned to look him one last time. "I'll be back before you know it," I whispered. And then, like a little bird, I flew out of my cage and into the night.

# *thirty-six*

The wind cut into my skin as soon as I stepped out the back door of the station and into the night. I tucked my hair into the collar of my shirt to block out the chill creeping down my neck. Snow littered the tiny parking lot. Nothing moved, nothing breathed. At least not anything I could see.

Dad had given me the gift of time. How much, I didn't know, and I had no idea where to start.

For a split second, I thought about just running, about climbing on the next bus to Michigan, to the Upper Peninsula, and escaping before they even had a chance to catch me. But everything about that felt wrong.

I had to see Grant. That's what I had to do first.

The one good thing about Amble is that you can see just about anything you might need from wherever you're standing. I could see the roof of the hospital—if you could even call it a hospital—poking up over the town like a cement-colored stalk peeking out from the snow. I started running.

The cold gnawed at the raw skin on my wrists, and my lungs ached. But my legs kept moving forward, one boot print after another. I wanted to stop, to lean over and grab at the stitch in my side until it quit hurting. But I felt the weight of the invisible time bomb strapped to my chest, tick tick ticking away the last slivers of any future I had a chance at.

*Grant.*

*Ella.*

I said their names over and over in my head, watched in my mind flashes of their dimples and eyes and tutus and half-grins. And I kept running.

Sometimes I caught a flash of something shifting through the cornfields. I knew it was them, waiting for me, growling at me.

I kept running.

There was nothing the wolves could do to pull me back into their universe. There was no message they could send me that would make me want to cut through the field and tear them apart. There was only this:

*Grant.*

*Ella.*

A howl pierced through the night, and then another and another. Ice dripped down my spine, and it wasn't from the cold. I whipped around the corner and was blinded by the lights lining the hospital parking lot. I stopped just long enough to clutch my stomach and forced the air back into my lungs. And then I stepped inside.

"Can I help you?" asked a chubby woman behind the front desk.

I stepped up to the desk. "I'm here to see Grant Buchanan."

She tipped her head forward and stared at me over her thick glasses. I bit my lip and looked away. Did she know who I was? It wouldn't surprise me, since gossip hung in the air around Amble like smog in Manhattan. My only shot was if enough time had ticked away and she didn't recognize me as Mike Graham's pariah daughter.

My head snapped up. "I'm Rae Buchanan, Grant's sister. Can I see him?" It was a long shot, for sure, but it was all I had.

The woman looked at me for a long time before scribbling something down on a sticky note. "Visiting hours end in twenty minutes."

"I'll be done in fifteen."

She kept writing for a second, then nodded. "Better hurry then," she said without looking up. "Second floor, room sixteen."

I headed for the elevator. Everything ticked around me: the buttons on the wall, the blood in my veins. It was all moving too slow, but way too fast at the same time. My time was running out, but I wasn't moving fast enough to catch up to it.

The doors creaked open and I bolted.

14.

15.

16.

Room 16. My stomach lurched when I saw his name scrawled on the whiteboard outside the door. Under it, someone had written *Cranial contusion, multiple facial wounds, abdominal injury.*

If only they knew.

I opened the door so that a sliver of the room came into focus. There was a machine that churned in the corner, whirring and beeping on repeat. There was just the tip of Grant's ear, poking out of his pillow. I stared through the crack in the door, waiting for that ear to move, his head to shift, his voice to croak out an awkward sound. He didn't move.

If I stared at his perfect, pink ear long enough, then maybe it would be okay. Maybe his face would be the same, and there would be no angry claw marks striping his lips. Maybe he'd still have his soft voice and sweet words still stuck in his throat and maybe they wouldn't have been taken away like Ella's.

His head twitched and the tiniest corner of a bandage slid into the sliver of the room I could see.

"Hello?" he said, just above a whisper.

The sound of his voice punctured my lungs, and all the breath I'd been bottling up seeped out. His words; he still had them. He could still use them.

I stepped into the room and shut the door behind me with a quiet click.

Grant blinked at me from behind a cluster of bandages. They looped around his head and shadowed his face like tufts of gauzy clouds. Another set completely smothered his nose.

But his mouth, his lips, they were still there.

The way he stared at me, his eyes glassy and empty, punctured my lungs and my heart and everything else inside all over again.

"Grant," I whispered as I sank into the chair next to his bed. "It's Claire. You remember me, right?"

He blinked at me slowly and then closed his eyes. His head tipped back on the pillow and I thought for a second he'd fallen asleep. My heart clawed its way into my throat as I watched him lie there, his mouth open and the reflection of the florescent lights pooled into the creases of his lips. My brain grabbed at an image that I'd just seen, one that looked something like this. *When* had I seen this? I pressed my hands over my eyes.

Grant's picture skidded across the desk at the station, his eyes closed and his head surrounded in a halo of blood-speckled snow. His mouth was open then too, and the Big Dipper on his nose was soaked in congealed blood.

I watched him. He could have been dead, if it weren't for beeping machines telling us both he wasn't. I got up and sat at the edge of his bed.

"Can I see?" I asked, even though I wasn't sure he wouldn't answer me. Or if it mattered if he did. I touched the edge of the bandage on his nose.

Grant's eyes snapped open, but he didn't say anything. He just watched me, and as much as I wanted him to look at me like he had just a day ago, there was nothing. But he didn't stop me, either.

Gently, I pulled at the edge of the bandage until it slid off. A line of angry stitches zigzagged through Grant's star-freckles and sliced off the handle of the Big Dipper. I felt the tears climb up my throat before I felt them on my cheeks. Something in Grant's eyes flickered, but he still just watched.

I touched the tip of his nose. "Did you know I used to think your freckles looked like the Big Dipper?" My finger trailed down to the bandage at his throat that was held in place by a spot of blood. "And that the handle pointed to your eyebrows? That's one of my favorite things about you." A smile crept onto my face as I thought about how much I'd wanted to touch the tip of that handle on Grant's nose two years ago, when he gave me my birthday cupcake in the cornfield. How I'd finally gotten to, that night in Alpena.

Grant's eyebrows knitted together as he watched me. He swallowed and said, "You have one too."

My heart thumped so hard in my chest that I almost didn't hear his words. I dropped my fingers from his bandages and forced his voice back into my head. I didn't want to lose his words; I couldn't lose them. "What do you mean?" I asked.

He propped himself up in bed and flinched as the IV tube wiggled in his hand. He slowly, carefully, reached for my wrist and flipped it over, like I was the one cut up and fragile. His finger traced over a rectangle of tiny freckles that spilled onto my palm from my wrist. "Here's the dipper part of the Big Dipper," he said as he touched each freckle. Then he slid his finger across the pink scar left behind from my blood oath with Rae. "And this is the handle."

I touched the scar. "A long time ago, Rae made me promise her that I would never tell anyone where she was going. We made a blood oath." I watched him carefully as I said it. "I still don't know why she did it with a knife and not a needle or something less ... violent."

"Rae always did have a flare for the dramatic." Grant

sighed as he touched the scar again. He glanced up at me. "Did you keep your promise?"

I thought about the days after, the way Dad used to scare me just by looking at me. How he probably knew I could have told him where Rae was, but I wouldn't. How I finally told that Ryan guy, when I was being interrogated about Ella, because I couldn't stand it anymore.

"No," I said. "Only for a few days." All of a sudden, I felt the weight of the time bomb ticking on my chest. The second hand was ticking louder, echoing in the space between us, warning me. I had to go if I wanted a future outside of Havenwood, outside of Amble. With Grant.

But did Grant want a future with me?

I sucked in a breath. "Grant, I have to go. And I don't think I'm coming back." I forced the next part out of my mouth: "I don't know if we'll see each other again."

Something behind Grant's eyes flickered, a tiny spark of recognition. Or maybe it was fear. Whatever it was, it was quickly dimmed by the pain medication dripping through his IV. He blinked for so long that I wasn't sure whether he'd fallen asleep.

"Grant?" I touched the tips of his fingers.

He started back to life and shook his head. And then he wove his fingers through mine. "Can you keep a promise to me?"

I bit my lip as I watched the way his fingers bent around mine. It seemed like it would be such a weird mix: my toothpick fingers all tied up in his long, rough ones. But somehow they looked okay together, like his hands were meant to be big enough to swallow mine up and cover them from the cold. And I thought about the one other promise I'd ever made, the most important one: to keep Ella safe.

I hadn't kept that one.

"Can you at least try, Claire?" Grant asked as he squeezed my fingers. "Sometimes promises don't work out the way you want them to. But the most important thing is that you at least gave it your best shot."

The fact that he was even talking to me right now, even though his words were kind of slurred from whatever was dripping through his IV, was a miracle to me. The fact that he even *wanted* to talk to me was another miracle.

"I can try," I told him.

Grant swallowed and tipped his head toward the ceiling. He took a deep breath. "How did I even get here?"

His torn-up face in the photographs flashed through my brain again. I closed my eyes. "I found you in the cornfield," I whispered. It was the truth, as much of it as I could keep from slipping between my fingers anyway. I'd found Grant in the cornfield, injured before I got there. And then the wolf.

And then the knife.

His voice cut through the images in my head. "Can you promise me that if I leave with you right now, we'll make it out of Amble before anything … happens to us?"

I looked at him—all of him—for the first time since I'd stepped in this room. Dozens of stitches screamed at me from under his bandages, every last one of them possibly my fault.

"I don't know." I pulled myself from the edge of his bed. "I don't remember how everything happened. I just found you in the field and your head was bleeding and I don't even know—"

"Claire, are you capable of hurting me right now?"

I looked at him and what used to be left of his Big Dipper nose, and everything in me melted. "No," I whispered.

He nodded once. And then he tugged the IV needle out of his hand without flinching.

I tried to breath. "Are you sure you want to leave with me? What about your job, your mom, your friends. Your future?"

Grant shook his head as if he were trying to shake out the remnants of the pain medication from his brain. "I don't have a future here anymore. You know how Amble is. They never forget when you betray them." He touched my cheek. "And there's not really a future without you in it, anyway."

My chest exploded with something like happiness, or maybe just utter fear. Everything about Grant looked unstable, from the slur between his lips to the cloudiness behind his eyes. I wasn't sure if he meant what he said or if he just wanted out of that hospital bed, but there had to be some part of him that still trusted me under all those narcotics if he was willing to go with me.

Right?

I didn't give him a chance to change his mind. "We've gotta hurry," I said as I grabbed his arm.

Grant ripped the heart monitor off his finger and pulled himself up. As soon as he stood, his knees buckled and I almost tumbled down with him. "Sorry," he murmured, and he sounded way more messed up than I'd thought. "They put something strong in that IV."

I pulled him up and opened the door. My heart sank when I saw the cluster of hospital employees puttering around the nurses' station. "How are we going to get out of here?" I whispered.

"Ella," Grant said, like it was the most obvious thing in the word.

Warmth flooded over me like an exploding sun and I gasped. *Ella.* Of course. Her diary entries. The secret escape route in the hospital when she came here for speech therapy.

I nodded. "Come on, I know where to go."

# *thirty-seven*

We slipped through the door and straight into a stairwell across the hall. Ella's speech therapy used to be down the hall adjacent to Grant's room, so if I had to guess, this was the stairwell she'd written about in her diary. At least, it had to be, because this was our only option.

"Do you remember what Ella wrote?" Grant said as soon as the heavy metal door shut behind us. "Because there's a security station at the bottom of these stairs."

"I remember. There was something in there about how they do rounds every twenty minutes."

Grant nodded. "Then let's hope and pray for the best."

I started down the stairs, two at a time, and felt Grant just behind me until I reached the last step. When I turned around, he was still halfway up the stairs with his palm pressed to his side.

"What's wrong?" I said as I started back up the stairs.

"I'm … fine." He sucked in a breath. "I just … this one hurts." He tugged at his hospital gown until I could the outline of a bandage wrapped around his rib cage. Speckles of blood had started to seep through the layers of fabric.

I touched his side. "We don't have to—"

"No." He shook his head. "No. Let's go."

I pulled his hand into mine and led him the rest of the way down the stairs. When we got to the bottom, I pulled open the door and poked my head out.

The security station was empty.

I couldn't even begin to believe my luck, especially since I was never lucky. I grabbed Grant's hand. "We're going to have to run for the side door, past the receptionists' desk."

He squeezed my fingers. "I can do it."

"Okay," I breathed. "Let's go."

I heard nothing but Grant's hitched breathing behind me. I felt nothing but his sweaty palm on my scarred one. Even when a voice rained down on us from the ceiling speakers, I only heard Grant's words, saying: "Go, go, go!"

I shoved my shoulder into the door and flew into the parking lot, my hand still tucked in Grant's. The light, which had looked like a beacon less than an hour ago, leered down at us now and threatened to tell everyone our secret.

"Where do we go?" Grant huffed from behind me. His fingers slipped from mine as he bent over to clutch at his side.

I glanced up at the cornfield stretched between here and Grant's house. "We need to get your truck. And then we go north."

Grant lifted his head and I had to look away. I couldn't

look at the pain that had snaked its way into every line on his face and every fleck of green in his eyes. He coughed once and then pulled himself up. "Okay. Let's go." And he started jogging.

I followed him as the lights strobed over us. And when we hit the edge of the parking lot and made our way toward the road that cut through the cornfield, I followed the sound of his heavy breathing.

I followed. But this time, I followed because I made the choice to. Because I knew that being with Grant was the path to a future that made sense. Because I loved him.

I love him.

For a long time, we didn't speak. Nothing twitched in the sinking stalks, only the stars hovering over us breathed in their own little universe, while we breathed in ours.

I didn't even think about the wolves, or finding Ella, or how Dad was most definitely going to lose his job and his reputation over this. I just listened to my own heart thumping under my ribs, Grant's breath pulsing in and out of his lungs in quick bursts, and the crunch of the pavement under my feet; Grant's feet were still wrapped in hospital socks.

Porch lights began to pop up on the other side of the cornfield like lightning bugs flickering to life. We turned down the dirt road that led to Grant's truck and our only shot of getting out of here together.

Then he jerked to a stop in front of me and I slammed into him—hard. His knees buckled and we both fell to the frozen road.

"Grant." Panic rose in my throat. "What happened? Can you get up?"

He rolled onto his back. Both of his hands were pressed to his side, and they were both covered in blood. "I think my stitches broke," he groaned.

There was so much more blood than I thought could be possible from a quick graze of wolf's teeth or a swipe of a claw. My head was fuzzy; everything smelled like metal.

I breathed into my sweater. "Let me see."

Carefully, I pulled up the side of Grant's hospital gown and pulled back the soaked bandage.

A wound that looked like a gaping mouth sliced across Grant's rib cage. It was so deep that its center was purplish and puffy with blood.

It was the exact width of a small knife.

My brain felt itchy, like there was a sharp piece of memory still stuck there: the weight of the knife in my hand, the way my muscles felt when I tore through the wolf's skin.

Maybe it wasn't the wolf's skin.

I pressed my scarred palm against Grant's open cut. "It should've been you," I breathed.

I listened to his shallow breaths for a while before he finally said, "What?" His words were so soft that if the night wasn't so still they would have been swallowed up by the wind.

"I should have made a blood oath with you, not Rae." The tears came, hot and fast, and they felt more like goodbye tears than sad tears. Not because I thought Grant was going to die here due to broken stitches, but because I somehow knew that my time was up.

"What would you have promised?" he asked softly. The tips of his fingers touched the edge of my palm.

Just then, the cluster of stalks behind Grant twitched to life. I gasped.

They twitched again, and at the same time something snapped from the other side of the road. A shadow slipped through the stalks until its pricked ears and yellow eyes materialized next to Grant. He let a strangled little cry and clutched his side. "Oh my God. Oh my God."

There was the rustling sound again, and when I turned around there were more wolves: some scrawny and wiry, some so solid I wondered how they'd hidden in a half-rotted cornfield for so long. A low growl vibrated in the throat of the yellow-eyed wolf.

I turned back to it, lifted both of my palms still slick with Grant's blood. "Please, don't," I begged.

The wolf's nostrils flared as its eyes bounced between the blood on my hands and Grant's pained face. And then it snapped before I had time to even think.

Bone to bone, teeth on skin.

Warmth that bubbled and dripped from my shattered scar.

It was a solid three seconds before I realized I was screaming.

That Grant was screaming too.

I dropped my face to his chest and pressed my broken hand to his rib cage.

And I waited. And sobbed out the words to "Hark the

Herald Angels Sing." Because there was nothing left to try for, nothing left to do but wait.

Their breath curdled around us, hot and urgent and wanting. From behind my eyelids, I could see the flash of lights, probably the reflection of the stars in their eyes. There was the howling that sounded like sirens.

There were claws that felt like fingers around my arms, and teeth that felt like handcuffs. And there was Grant's voice, muffled and far away as my body was ripped from his.

And then there was darkness.

# *thirty-eight*

It's strange, but sometimes I miss the cold.

I miss the bite of winter wind against my neck, the delicate spiderwebs of ice stretched across the windowpanes. But mostly I just miss the open, empty sky and the whir of bike tires as I ride through the cornfields.

But there are plenty of things to like about spring, too.

I stretch out on my blanket so the grass tickles the soles of my bare feet. People are watching me as they pass by—so many people, more people in this park than in all of Amble combined. Every once in a while, one of them will give me a strange look as they walk by, or mumble a string of syllables under their breath. But then someone in a white coat sweeps them away, toward a cluster of buildings at the back of the park and I'm alone again. I know these people think it's weird that I'm already barefoot in April, when the air still nips at their skin. But they haven't been to a place as cold as Amble.

I flip onto my stomach and check my cell phone: 11:31 a.m. I have an appointment with Dr. Barges in a half hour.

Now that I'm back in Manhattan, I see him three times a week instead of one. That was part of my plea agreement back in Ohio: regular, intensive therapy sessions, a structured program, and the right medication.

Even then, sometimes I still see them.

I'll be on my way to Dr. Barges' office and I'll see a flash of gray tucked between the skyscrapers. Every once in a while, I'll hear a howl.

But just as quickly as they try to take over my brain, the Clozapine washes them away and they disappear. Dr. Barges explained to me that Clozapine has a ridiculously high success rate in treating hallucinations. So far, it works.

Dad wasn't as lucky.

Because his psychotic episodes started so many years ago, his body eventually became immune to the effects of Clozapine. He started to see their gem-colored eyes and smell their hot, sour breath again. He started to hear them howl.

But he didn't tell anyone, not until he told me, and not until he was too late. So an innocent snow angel lost her life to wolves and Dad lost his to a guilty verdict and a lifetime of inpatient treatment at Havenwood.

I dip my toes in the grass and pull a notebook from my messenger bag. I open the cover and a slip of paper falls out. A note.

From Ella.

I unfold it, careful not to smear the colored ink inside.

Her loopy handwriting sprawls across the paper, heart-dotted letters and all.

*I'm coming.*

My face breaks into the grin as I clutch the note to my chest. Ella sent this one to me, along with a copy of her train schedule, two weeks ago. My heart still throbs with happiness when I imagine greeting her at Grand Central Station, throwing my arms around her and breathing in her magic. I play it over and over in my mind, every day.

Three more days.

When Ella heard that Dad had been placed under psychiatric care in Havenwood after pulling the insanity card, and that I'd started treatment in New York, she took the first train back to Ohio to be with Mom. As it turns out, I'd missed the biggest clue of all in my search for Ella.

That postcard, pinned to the center of her corkboard: *Welcome to Madison, Wisconsin!*

Patrick's cousins lived in Madison. Ella had met them at the bus stop in Marquette, and they took her the rest of the way to Wisconsin. Safe from wolves with knife teeth and free from a small town clotted with broken dreams.

The first time we talked on the phone, she told me she knew I'd find the diaries, that she left them behind to explain why she couldn't stay. Then she apologized a million and a half times for the entries, especially the ones that bit at me with her anger. But I don't even care about that anymore—I have her back.

Sometimes I think about asking her about the night of the attack, about the minutes before and the hours after.

About what she really remembers. I tried to bring it up once, but Ella just quickly switched to the subject of Patrick's new basset hound.

So we don't talk about those kinds of things.

It's probably for the best.

I turn to a fresh page in my notebook. A journal, actually. Dr. Barges gave it to me when I first arrived back in New York. It's just a flimsy little thing, nothing special like the gold-eyed wolf journal that Grant gave me. There's gold on this one too, but it's in the form of a pressed-in seal with a tree in the center and the words *Central Park Sanatorium* wrapped around the branches. Dr. Barges suggested I start using it to keep track of any relapses. Sometimes I do that, but mostly I just write letters to Grant.

I like to imagine what it would be like if he were here with me, living in New York instead of back in Amble. I tap my pencil to my lip. Today, Grant would be reading the paper and shoveling wobbly eggs into his mouth at the diner next to my apartment. I'd be watching him from across the table, wondering when was the next time I could kiss him like I wanted to without getting weird looks from strangers.

I smile and write it down.

Of course, he'll never read this.

The no-contact order that the Buchanans put on my family is in effect for at least another year. One phone call to Grant and I pretty much buy myself a one-way ticket to prison.

But last week, his name lit up on my phone, just for a millisecond before the screen went dark. He'd called me and hung up.

It happened again two days later, and another time just yesterday afternoon. I was leaving therapy when my phone rang, and I saw his name on the screen. I hurried to answer, and when I said hello, there was nothing on the line.

At least, I *thought* there was nothing. At first.

I stepped into a space between buildings and listened.

Breathing—shallow, hopeful—on the other end. "Grant, are you there?" I whispered. And then: "I miss you."

There was no response other than a *click*.

I shove my journal back into my bag and stand up, brushing the grass off my jeans. It's rain-washed and spongy, and it clings to my clothes like the grass in Amble never did. It's impossible to get rid of.

I bend down to grab my blanket and bag, and when I look up, I see a head with dark, cropped hair across the park. I blink and it disappears.

I shake my head. Impossible.

I start to move toward the street when I see it again—a flash of dark hair. I stop and turn.

"Claire, where are you going? It's time for your medicine." A squat, caramel-skinned woman in a white coat stands behind me, shaking a paper cup. My pills rattle around inside it.

I wave her off. "Just a second, okay?"

Grant leans against an oak tree. His arms are crossed over his chest and he tips his head to look at me in the space between the crowds. Our eyes meet.

And everything in me cracks open and my heart thrums in my chest and I'm running, running, running.

The white-coat woman is yelling my name, but I don't care. I don't listen. I don't need a paper cup full of pills right now. I just need Grant.

I drop my bag when I reach him. He looks down at me with his spring-colored eyes and smiles. The kind with teeth. Even though most of his star freckles have been replaced by a shiny, pink scar, he's still Grant and I still love him.

"You came to see me," I say, breathless.

His fingers brush my face and it feels just like a breeze. "Of course I did," he says.

I close my eyes and breathe in the scent of him: peppermint Chapstick and earth and home. I stand on my tiptoes and touch my forehead to his.

He kisses me.

His lips are so gentle against mine that I can barely feel them, taste them. I want more of him. I reach up to wrap my hand around the nape of his neck, to thread my fingers through his hair, to pull him closer to me.

But my fingers brush against something that doesn't feel anything like star-freckled skin or cropped hair, but feels everything like tree bark.

I open my eyes.

And he's gone.

*The End*

# Acknowledgments

I imagine that when you found this book, it was propped up on a "Young Adult Fiction" shelf, or arbitrarily ranked on a website under "Mystery, Thriller, and Suspense." In fact, there's a good chance you found it somewhere else entirely, since this seems to be one of those books that doesn't quite fit anywhere.

In truth, it's a love story. It started with a spark of an idea, a flash of an image: two sisters clinging to each other through the biting wind and insurmountable odds. My very first critique partner, Michelle Levy, asked all the right questions in order to bring Claire and Ella Graham to life. Michelle, you are wonderful.

I cannot even begin to express my gratitude to my agent, Victoria Marini, for loving Claire Graham as fiercely as I do. Your patience, guidance, and devotion to this book and my career have been my anchor, and your encouragement and willingness to push me are what continue to propel me forward. To my editor, Brian Farrey-Latz: thank you for understanding exactly what I envisioned for this story, and for plucking that image straight out of my heart and mind onto the cover of this book. To my team at Flux: Mallory Hayes, Sandy Sullivan, and everyone else who worked tirelessly behind the scenes to bring the best version of this book into the world: thank you, thank you.

I am continually humbled by the love and support I've received from my critique partners and beta readers. Thank you to Leigh Ann Kopans, Jamie Grey, Megan Orsini, Dahlia

Adler, Kelsey Macke, Amanda Olivieri, and a million others for reading and championing the early version of this book. Thank you to my sisters at The Secret Life of Writers—Heather, Stefanie, Leah, Kelsey, Farrah, and Alex—for the endless cheerleading. And thank you to my street team and the writing community in general, for your constant glitter cannons and goodwill.

To my advanced composition teacher, Mrs. Thomas: You probably never realized the effect you had when you told me you were going to use my essay as an example in class. Now you do. I also could not have done this without the beautiful people in my life: Kristen Jett, you are my guiding star; Hay Farris, you are my sun; Megan Whitmer, you are my breath of fresh air. Marilyn, Kristie, Matt C., Sarah G., Tracy: you are everything in between.

To my dad, for giving me a love of literature, and to my mom, for giving me a sense of adventure and the courage to follow it. To my brother, Zack, for loving me through all the late-night revisions and making your own dinner with only a little bit of complaining. I love you. To my soul sisters and very best friends, Keri Grieve and Sarah Slayton. I don't have a biological sister, but if I did, I would hope she would be exactly like you both.

And to Matt, my husband. Being a writer's spouse is not a glamorous job. There are numerous nights of cereal for dinner, piles of laundry that will never get folded, and too many hours of caring for small children to give me creative space. You've done all this brilliantly, but I'm most thankful for that first conversation we had several years ago, the one where I said, "I'm going to write a book." And you said, "Of course you are." I love you.

© Matt Hannah

## About the Author

Andrea Hannah lives in the Midwest, where there are plenty of dark nights and creepy cornfields to use as fodder for her next thriller. She graduated from Michigan State University with a B.A. in special education. When she's not teaching or writing, she spends her time chasing her sweet children and ornery pug, running, and dreaming up her next adventure. You can find her at www.andreahannah.com.